"I'M STUCK HERE NOW. In this time. I have to find a way to destroy the mirror, and that's the last thing Venn wants. How can I go back to Wintercombe . . ."

"Did you think Venn wouldn't move heaven and earth to find you? You told him you were . . . would be . . . his *granddaughter*. Even though his wife is dead and he has no children. You tell him that not only is it possible for him to change the past, but that in your time *he's already done it!* And then you disappear!" He shrugged, and sipped his coffee. "Come on, Sarah. Even for a normal man that would be unbearable. For Oberon Venn, it was like the descent into madness."

She nodded. He realized he didn't have to tell her that Venn had had his strange servant, Piers, virtually chained to the computer, spending every waking second combing every missing persons database, every police record he could hack into, phoning every hospital for miles around for news of her. Because there was no way they could let her destroy the mirror.

Not now.

"You have to come back with me," he said.

"I have work to do here! All Venn thinks about is getting Leah back from the dead. I can't help him with that. That's his problem. I suppose he's been working at the mirror . . ."

"Nonstop. And Jake . . ."

"Yes, well, Jake needs to find his father. They both want opposite things to me. Selfish things! I have to destroy the mirror, and that means destroying their hopes. Destroying my own existence."

OTHER BOOKS YOU MAY ENJOY

THE
SLANTED
WORLDS

CATHERINE FISHER

THE
SLANTED
WORLDS

OBSIDIAN MIRROR BOOK 2

speak

An Imprint of Penguin Group (USA)

SPEAK
Published by the Penguin Group
Penguin Group (USA) LLC
375 Hudson Street
New York, New York 10014

USA * Canada * UK * Ireland * Australia
New Zealand * India * South Africa * China

penguin.com
A Penguin Random House Company

First published in the United States of America by Dial Books,
an imprint of Penguin Young Readers Group, 2014
Published by Speak, an imprint of Penguin Group (USA) LLC, 2015

THE LIBRARY OF CONGRESS HAS CATALOGED THE DIAL BOOKS EDITION AS FOLLOWS:
Fisher, Catherine, date.
Obsidian mirror : the slanted worlds / Catherine Fisher.
pages   cm
Summary: While Jake continues searching for his father and is sent by the obsidian mirror to
multiple times in the past, Sarah and Venn battle with Summer for control of a powerful coin.
ISBN: 978-0-8037-3970-3 (hardcover : alk. paper)
[1. Time travel—Fiction. 2. Fathers—Fiction. 3. Missing persons—Fiction. 4. Coins—Fiction.]
I. Title. II. Title: Slanted worlds.
PZ7.F4995Oc 2014   [Fic]—dc23   2013018259

Speak ISBN 978-0-14-242678-4

Printed in the United States of America

1 3 5 7 9 10 8 6 4 2

THE
SLANTED WORLDS

When shall we three meet again?

1

If the past becomes a land to voyage unto, how
carefulle the journeyman must be. Will he not tread
in a nightmare of uncertaynties? Be enmeshed in
histories of which he knows nothing?

Like a man coming suddenly to a foreign land,
and speking not the language . . .

From The Scrutiny of Secrets *by Mortimer Dee*

THE BOMB FELL in a split second of silence.

Racing down the street, Jake felt the unbearable
pressure in his teeth and nerves; he grabbed at the unlit lamppost and threw himself to the ground.

The explosion was terrifying, a white starburst on
his retina. It blew out every window. Bricks and dust
roared down, glass shattered on his back and head and
arms. Lumps of rubble thudded on him.

For a moment he was blind and deaf in a fog of ash
and pulverized brick, afraid of broken legs and arms.
Then he coughed, dragged himself up onto hands and
knees, and turned his head.

The street was gone.

What had just been a square of Georgian houses
was now a vast crater spouting flames, lurid in clouds

of smoke. Fires erupted like volcanoes; as he staggered to his feet he felt sudden heat scorch his face.

It was hard to breathe. His eyes were gritty with dust, his hands black with soot that fell like rain.

A hand grabbed him. Noise buzzed in his ear.

"What?" he mumbled.

The blur became a man in a dark uniform, the letters *ARP* painted in white on his helmet.

With a crack Jake's hearing came back.

". . . said get to the shelter! Bloody bloody stupid kid!"

He shoved Jake fiercely away from the twisted lamp-post.

Searchlights stabbed the sky. Jake glimpsed his own hand, bleeding.

Dazed, he said, "Where is it?"

"The Underground! God in heaven, where did you come from? I had this street cleared!"

Jake managed a short bitter laugh. "This isn't the 1960s, is it."

The air-raid warden stared at him, taking in his carefully anonymous dark clothes, the narrow band of worked silver clasped around his wrist. Suspicion came down on his face like a shutter.

"What's your name? Where are your papers?"

"Jake Wilde." He stared at the ruined houses in sudden despair. The black mirror must have been in one of those houses, the glass Chronoptika that had transported him here from his own time. It had to be nearby, and it couldn't be destroyed by any German bomb, so was it there, under all that rubble? Before the dread of not getting back could grip him he said, "What's that noise?"

A faint, screeching sound. For a moment of sheer terror he thought it was another bomb, then the warden turned quickly. "Someone's trapped."

He ran into the smoke.

Jake wiped dirt from his face. Quickly he took out a small elegant square box from his pocket and touched its tiny screen.

"Piers? *Piers!* Can you hear me? Listen! It's all gone wrong. *I'm in the Second World War, Piers!*"

Nothing.

He had left them just seconds ago, gathered around the control desk. Now Piers would be fiddling and muttering over the controls, Venn—Jake's godfather—probably storming up and down the lab and lashing over furniture in his frustration. And Gideon, the changeling, would be watching with his sharp green eyes.

What a team. The blind leading the blind.

"Piers! It's Jake! Get me back. NOW!"

Already he knew they couldn't even hear him. Of course they couldn't. They were eighty years in the future, because this had to be the London Blitz of what? . . . 1939?

1940? His knowledge of World War II was sketchy, but obviously the mirror was at least twenty years out. The cell phone, even fitted with Piers's hopeful refinements, was useless.

"Hey you! Boy! Come and help! There's a woman still alive down here. Quickly!"

Jake thrust the phone in his pocket and scrambled over the debris. Roving searchlights made triple shadows of himself flit and stretch and vanish over the stacks of rubble. The ruined house slid and clattered under him, a mess of tiles and curtains and furniture and ragged bedding and the fluttering pages of books, hundreds of white fragments, a snowstorm of paper.

How could anyone be alive under this?

The man was crouched by a slab of roof tilted at a crazy angle. He was saying: "I can't dig you out . . . I'll have to get help. The second wave will be over any minute."

"Don't worry, dear. I'll be fine." The whisper was muffled through layers of debris.

The warden stood, blew three sharp blasts on a whistle, but no one came, so he threw himself on the bricks, hurling them away, feverishly working. Jake scrambled up next to him. They toiled together under the eerie lights, tearing at the stacked layers of the collapsed house, but it was useless, Jake already knew—there was too much rubble, the buildings smashed to chaotic twists of metal.

And he could smell gas.

The ARP man glanced at the sky, his eyes white in a face black with dust. "They're coming back. We have to go."

"And leave her?" Jake stared, appalled.

"No choice."

Far in the distance, a wave of planes droned.

"It's very dark down here," the woman whispered. "Can we go now?"

Jake grabbed a floorboard, hauled it away. "Here," he said.

A small hole. The stench of gas rose from it, choking in his throat. He stopped. Fear was a slippery sweat in his chest. The whole thing could explode.

He should run. Find the mirror. Go home and try again. This wasn't his problem. This wasn't his time. How could he find his father, lost in the wastelands of the past, if he was blown to bits here, and the silver bracelet with him? It would be over, for him, Venn, all of them. He took a step backward.

The ARP man lay full length. "This gap might be enough."

Debris fell inward. The woman down there made a moan of terror. "Hurry!"

It held Jake in mid-step. As if in that landscape of smoke and flames and the hiss of escaping gas, it was the loudest sound.

He knew that terror.

He had been six. Maybe seven.

A beach of wide sand, great dunes against the hot sky. His mother in sunglasses and a blue bikini, on a striped lounger.

The heat. The obsession of digging.

He remembered the growing dampness of the sand. The spade slicing into its deep neatness. The tangled roots of dune grass above him.

"Help me!" the ARP man gasped.

Sudden abrupt weight. Sand falling in on him. The utter complete darkness of the world lying on him, on his chest, in his eyes, in his mouth and nose.

The terrible, stifled, silent scream.

"I can see her!" The man glanced around. "Not far down, but I can't reach. You're thinner. You could get down there."

He couldn't. He'd had nightmares for years about those moments of death, before his father's huge hand, his face in the sudden hole, his "Jake! Jake are you all right!"

They had told him it was only seconds, but it had been years.

And now Dad was trapped too, and he couldn't even find him.

He turned. He saw the black hole.

"I'll hold your legs." The man's face glistened with sweat. "For God's sake, hurry!"

Jake swore in despair, flung himself down, wriggled

to the edge, over. He squirmed down into vacancy, a blackness that hissed and spurted, so thick with dust he couldn't see his own hands.

Reaching out.

Groping.

His fingers stubbed on softness; he yelled, "I've got something."

He could breathe only gas. And then . . .

Warmth.

Her fingers were knobbly and arthritic. Foolishly soft, they clasped his, the bones beneath the skin bird-thin and brittle.

Her breath wheezed in the darkness.

"It's okay," he gasped. "I can get you up."

But he knew it was impossible.

"What's your name?"

His whisper was warped in the womb of wreckage. There was a rattle and the darkness shifted.

The hand held him tight.

"Alicia, dear. You don't have to worry. We're both fine."

An old woman. Her voice was frail but obstinate.

He said, "But we can . . ."

"Like I said, we'll be right behind you."

The drone of planes. He said, "Are you scared?"

"Not now. Not now you're safely here, Jake."

Astonishment almost made him let her go; he grabbed again, her fingers already colder.

"How do you know my name?"

Did she laugh? Could someone in that darkness laugh?

"They said I was a fraud. A charlatan. But we showed them, Jake, didn't we? We showed them all that Madam Alicia really spoke to the spirits. David says—"

"David!"

"He says 'See you soon.'"

She was delirious. She had to be. He said, "Listen! After the planes I'll come back and . . ."

"Too late. Only waited for you." Her fingers pushed something small into his. It crackled like paper.

"Take it," she whispered. "Time's up. Time's run out . . ."

Streets away, faint as a gnat's whine, he heard the bombs begin to fall.

"Find it, Jake. Promise me."

"Did you say David? My father, David?"

"I'm going now. *Promise me!*"

"All right. *Yes!*"

He was upside down, dizzy. Lost. No dad with huge hands was there to dig him out. With a crash, he felt the sand come down on him. He slid forward; yelled.

Then there was a tight grip on his belt; he was hauled back, earth in his nose and mouth; he spat it out and gasped, "Wait . . . No . . . Listen!" Blood in his veins thudded like explosions. "We can't leave her."

"Run!" the man yelled. *"Now!"*

For a second, on his back below the air raid, Jake felt time stop. As if her death happened then, and he felt it. He lost belief in where he was. He looked up and saw the bombers overhead and they were beautiful, a deadly chevron of diamonds; saw a plane picked out by a sweeping searchlight, the whirl of its propellers flashing segments of light.

Then he was on his feet and running, past the heaped houses, the rubble-strewn road.

It stretched like a dark runway. As he fled, his shadow elongated; the chasing planes came low and he saw London lit to the horizon by a flash of red, a nightmare of tilted buildings caught in stillness.

The entrance to the Underground gaped ahead like the mouth of a cavern among flames. As he reached it and leaped the sandbags, the explosions arrived, one after another on his heels in regular formation, the last a great roar that crashed him face-down into the filthy entrance hall.

He picked himself up, sore and numb.

The ARP man was already racing down the stairs.

Jake limped after him.

This was crazy. He felt as if he were in some inverted world, a speeded-up film where nothing was real. He'd been on the London Underground. In his time it was a bright, graffitied, glossy place. Not this endless descent into the dark and damp, his breath smoking, between walls of shattered dusty tiles, filthy with plastered posters.

He slowed, breathless, a stitch in his side.

A soft sound rustled below him; the murmur of darkness. As he descended, it grew to a hum, a rumble, then became the voices of people, hundreds of them, and as he reached a passageway and emerged under the arch, he found himself on a long platform crowded with refugees.

The railway line led into circles of drafty blackness. The platform was a dormitory. A music hall. An anteroom to hell.

Thousands of people were crammed there. They lay sleeping, eating, singing, talking in huddles. Campsites of makeshift beds divided the space. Dogs roamed the crowd. The air was warm with the stink of humanity, its sweat, its ordure, its cooking filling the circular echoing tunnels.

Jake leaned one hand against the clammy wall and bent over. He was breathless and so sore it made him feel sick, and his back ached from hanging in the hole.

He could still feel her bony fingers in his.

She was dead now. He felt sickened and empty and angry for an old woman he had never even seen.

Had known only for seconds.

But she had known his name.

His father's name.

Something crinkled in his filthy fingers; he un-clenched them and saw the scrap of paper she had given him, smudged and torn. Suddenly overwhelmed, he slid down to a crouch.

This was a disaster. The mirror could be anywhere under the ruins of London.

He was in the wrong time, and he might never see his father again. Or Venn. And for a moment his god-father's arctic blue stare turned him cold, the despair on that haggard face. All their plans, ruined forever.

The paper was a small cardboard ticket. It was pale blue, had one corner torn off. It said:

St. Pancras Station
Left Luggage Office
No. 615

For a moment he just stared at it. Then three pairs of sandaled feet came out of the crowd and waited in a line in front of him.

He looked up.

Among the crowded sleepers of the Blitz, three chil-dren were standing.

They looked about ten, maybe younger. Boys. They wore school uniforms—gray blazers, red-and-gray striped ties, grubby shorts, socks about their ankles.

"Get lost!" Jake snapped.

They were identical. Triplets. Their faces were podgily pale, their small arms folded. They each wore cheap round spectacles, and stared at him, calm in the chaos.

The first one said, "The Black Fox will release you, Jake."

The second nodded. "Speak to the Man with the Eyes of a Crow."

"And the Broken Emperor lies," the third one said, "in the Box of Red Brocade."

He stared at them in astonishment.

"What the hell are you talking about?" he snarled.

2

I will seek both high and low
both near and far and farther
In summer sunshine and in snow
in wood and field and water.
I will search and I will ride
all the wide world over.
I will scour both time and tide
until I find my lover.

Ballad of Lord Winter and Lady Summer

"ARE YOU SURE this is all the ID you've got?" The young man at the desk looked at her research student card doubtfully.

Sarah gave him her most winning smile. "Your receptionist said that would be enough. My tutor at Oxford made the appointment by phone. Professor Merton?"

"Ah. Right."

He glanced at the computer screen, typed something. She held her bag tight and watched his doubt dissolve.

"It's here. Can you sign in, please."

She wrote *Sarah Venn* in round letters and put the pen down. He tore the label off and fixed it in a plastic clip. "You have to wear this. And the white gloves. Please remember it's strictly forbidden to take photographs of delicate materials and manuscripts, or to remove anything from the museum."

She nodded as she fixed on the label. The words *Oxford* and *Professor* were certainly enormously effective. The fact that she had made the appointment herself, faked the ID, and invented the professor, even more so.

She crossed the room and sat in a chair by the window.

It looked down into the vast interior courtyard of the British Museum, the transparent latticed roof high above pure blue in the cold spring sunlight. She had never been here in her own time—the time she was starting to think of as the End Time, the days at the end of the world. Back then, London was—would be—Janus's territory, and this place part of his vast, forbidden Halls of Lore.

She took off her coat and unwound her scarf. Below, tourists browsed the bookstalls, munched on sandwiches at the tea stalls. Their children ran and screeched in the echoing space.

She couldn't get used to it.

The freedom.

The way they lived as if nothing would ever happen to them.

And yet within a generation or two, all this would be totally . . .

"Here we are."

She looked up, startled.

The young man was back, with a gray cardboard box file. He laid it carefully on the desk; she gazed at it in intense satisfaction. A peeling label on its surface, obviously years old, read:

11145/6/09 DEE, MORTIMER.

"Who was he?" The curator sounded curious.

She licked her dry lips, suddenly nervous. "A medieval scholar."

"Is it for a thesis?"

For a moment she had no idea what he meant. Then she said, "Oh . . . yes. Yes. My thesis."

He nodded and moved off, but not very far; he spread a sheaf of papers at a nearby table and began to work on them, giving her a quick, watchful look.

Nothing she could do about that.

Eagerly she pulled on the white gloves.

She took out a notebook and pencil. Then, her fingers trembling, she opened the file.

It contained a yellowing manuscript.

She was almost afraid to start. It had taken so long to get here. Weeks of research in stuffy libraries, hours of lying awake in her damp room in the hostel, worrying, thinking, planning.

It had become an obsession, more important than eating, sleeping, even surviving in this busy, dangerous city; the obsession of finding out everything possible about the obsidian mirror.

She was thin and worn out with it.

But she was a Venn, and they were an obsessive family.

She took out the manuscript; it was a single page, light and crisp at the edges, some sort of thin skin, terribly fragile, smelling faintly of mildew. On top was a more recent note on blue paper. She already knew what that was, and smiled at the familiar handwriting of John Harcourt Symmes, the stout, rather pompous Victorian seeker after magic whom Jake and Venn had met in the past, whom she had once seen burst through time into Wintercombe Abbey.

On the covering page he had written:

This Page is the only surviving fragment of the work of the legendary Mortimer Dee. His book, The Scrutiny of Secrets, *is of course, lost, known only in brief quotations by other writers. But this small scrap seems to be in his own hand. My attempt at transcriptions is below. Dee's work is in some fiendishly difficult code, which I confess baffles me. I can only guess at its meaning, and find it endlessly frustrating. . . . But the man certainly had some secret knowledge of the dark mirror I have obtained and which he names the* Chronoptika.

If only I could find out what it was!

She flicked her eyes sideways. The curator was absorbed in his work.

She lifted her bag onto the table, took out a hand-kerchief, and blew her nose.

He took no notice.

So she slid the tiny camera from her palm and quickly photographed the single tightly written fragment. The camera made the softest of clicks, but in the hushed silence they sounded huge.

She coughed, cleared her throat, had it hidden away before he glanced up, eyes glazed with words, not even seeing her. Then he looked down again.

A desk magnifier stood nearby; she moved it closer and clicked the light on, aligning it over the piece of brittle parchment. Looking in, she gave a great sigh of dismay.

Fiendishly difficult code was something of an understatement.

How could she ever read this? The page was covered with Dee's tiny, black, indecipherable writing. In places it seemed written backward; in others it ran up and down in random diagonals, or curved into the margins. Everywhere, there were diagrams in strange spindly lines, sigils of lost meaning, alchemical signs, formulae, scraps of what might be Latin and certainly Greek. And all over it, as if the man had doodled and drawn and daydreamed his visions too fast to write, was a interwoven web of drawings, of strange landscapes, towers against the moon, edges of castles and corners of rooms, and trees, many trees, tangled and hollow and gaunt as the ancient oaks in Wintercombe Wood.

She stared, fascinated. The confusing perspectives, the slanted worlds, reminded her of something . . .

And then she remembered, with a sudden chill of fear.

The Summerland.

The kingdom of the Shee, in the heart of the haunted Wood.

She frowned, brought the magnifier closer.

In the curved surface she saw her own blue eye, made huge. As sunlight slanted through the window, one of Dee's smallest, darkest drawings held her attention.

Ruined buildings, black and smoking, silhouetted against a lurid sky. Searchlights swiveling like pale cones in the darkness.

Sarah's heart thudded.

Had Dee managed to *journey* into the future? Had he seen what Janus's tyranny had done? That place where her parents were chained, where the black mirror pulsed with uncontrollable power, collapsing endlessly inward to a black hole that was devouring the world?

She blinked, pulling back.

She had to decipher this. This single page might give her the information she needed. It might solve her problem, her obsession, her mission.

It might teach her how to destroy the mirror.

Too agitated to keep still, she turned and gazed down at the crowded court below. More tourists were queueing for coffee.

And, outside the bookshop, she saw a man. A big, stocky man, his hair neatly combed, his coat an old no-nonsense ex-army parka, his scarf the colors of Compton's School.

Her eyes widened. "No! It can't be!"

He was talking to an attendant and she breathed his name in a whisper of dismay.

"George Wharton!"

Jake's tutor was unmistakable. But what was he doing here?

The attendant nodded, as if in answer to a question, and pointed up at the window. Wharton turned and looked. Before she could move, he saw her.

Their eyes met; a second of startled recognition.

Instantly he was running for the stairs.

Sarah jumped up so quickly the magnifier slid over with a thud. She snatched her bag, grabbed her coat, and raced for the door.

"I'm so sorry! Emergency! Just realized. Have to go!"

"What about the papers!"

"I'll be back!"

Shrugging into the coat she ran out, turned left in the corridor and then right, found the stairs and raced down them, praying desperately Wharton wasn't thundering up. She had to get out. *How on earth had he known where she was?*

Since leaving Wintercombe on Christmas night, she had kept herself hidden in London. There was no way they could have found her . . . it must be sheer coincidence . . .

Unless he had been looking for Mortimer Dee's papers too.

She stopped. Far down the stairwell heavy footsteps were thundering up. She glanced over the rail.

"Sarah!"

He was a flight down. His face was lit with satisfaction. "I knew it was you!"

She turned, hit a door marked *Fire Exit* and crashed it open, bursting into a huge echoing space packed with people. Colossal Egyptian statues frowned down at her; she ran between gods with crocodile heads and jackal faces into a gallery so jammed with excited and chattering schoolchildren she had to fight her way between their small warm bodies.

She glanced back.

Wharton was at the door. Over the heads of a class in green blazers he yelled, "Wait! Sarah! Wait!"

She twisted away, shoved on, muttering "Sorry . . . Excuse me . . . Sorry . . ." getting caught in photos, bumping into tourists deafened with audio guides.

Plate glass stopped her, a wall of it. She almost

slammed against it, spread her hands and saw, beyond it, the mummies.

They lay on their backs in gaudily painted cases, blind eyes staring upward, their shrunken desiccated bodies wrapped in tight bands of ancient linen. For a fatal second she stopped, staring in awe, because these were travelers from a time so distant she had no words for it, fragile *journeymen* her father would have loved to have seen, treasures that, despite their dreams, had never made it to the world's end.

Then, over their painted stillness, Wharton faced her.

The crowd hemmed her in; there was nowhere to run.

He yelled something, his breath misted the glass.

Furious, she shook her head. "Leave me alone!"

He found space; he shoved people aside, powering his way around the mummy case toward her. She stepped on someone's foot, wriggled out, found a wall, a fire alarm. Her hand shot out to the small glass disc.

She hit his fleshy palm instead.

"That would be a really foolish thing to do, Sarah," he gasped. "And not at all like you."

She was sweating. Her hair was in her eyes. She felt as if some long wearying effort, some exile had come to an end.

"No," she said. And then, "You know, George, I'm really tired."

He could see that. As she sat in the café drinking the tea he had insisted on buying her, he thought she looked thin and worn, her eyes red-rimmed, her blond hair lank. Hungry too, if the way she demolished the egg mayo sandwiches meant anything.

For a while he let her eat. Then he said, "Where have you been living?"

"A hostel."

"Student?"

"Homeless."

He stared. "Sarah, why . . ."

She swallowed a mouthful. "I'm stuck here now. In this time. I have to find a way to destroy the mirror, and that's the last thing Venn wants. How can I go back to Wintercombe . . ."

"He wants you back. He's been searching for you."

That was an understatement. As he watched her sip hot tea, Wharton thought of the night, four months ago nearly, when she had slipped, invisible, from the window at Wintercombe Abbey and walked off into the night, leaving behind only her footprints in the snow and those last, astonishing words.

Now he said, "Did you think Venn wouldn't move heaven and earth to find you? You told him you were . . . would be . . . his *granddaughter*. Even though his wife is dead and he has no children. You tell him that not only is it possible for him to change the past, but that in your time *he's already done it!* And then you disappear!" He shrugged, and sipped his coffee. "Come on, Sarah. Even for a normal man that would be unbearable. For Oberon Venn, it was like the descent into madness."

She nodded. He realized he didn't have to tell her that Venn had had his strange servant, Piers, virtually chained to the computer, spending every waking second combing every missing persons database, every police record he could hack into, phoning every hospital for miles around for news of her. She was far too intelligent. Nor could he, Wharton, even begin to express the utter relief he had felt seeing her pale astonished face up at the window. Because there was no way they could let her destroy the mirror.

Not now.

"You have to come back with me," he said.

She stirred her tea, put the spoon down with a clink, stared at him over it. "No, I don't. And you can't make me. Nothing you can say will make me."

"Sarah . . ."

"I have work to do here! All Venn thinks about is getting Leah back from the dead. I can't help him with that. That's his problem. I suppose he's been working at the mirror . . ."

"Nonstop. And Jake . . ."

"Yes, well, Jake needs to find his father. They both

want opposite things to me. Selfish things! I have to destroy the mirror, and that means destroying their hopes. Destroying my own existence. We're on opposite sides, George . . ."

"There are no sides. We need you."

"You don't. Just leave me alone."

She gathered her coat and stood, but he put one firm hand out across the table and grabbed her wrist in an iron grip.

"Listen to me. Venn is desperate to recover Leah, but he dare not try yet. To be honest, I don't think he could cope with failure. He needs to be ready. He needs Jake's father, David. So Jake persuaded him to go after David first. Three weeks ago Jake entered the mirror. It was all planned. Piers was sure it would be safe. I was totally against it, but none of them listen to me, least of all my arrogant little brat of a so-called pupil. He insisted on being sent to the 1960s, because David had been there—remember the photograph? But the mirror, Sarah, it's so unpredictable. The damn thing seems to work by emotion as much as anything . . ." He shook his head.

Slowly, she sat down again, seeing all at once the sickening worry in his eyes.

"What? What happened?"

"You've guessed. He hasn't come back. He's lost, just as his father was lost. And the bracelet with him."

"But . . ."

"It's worse than that. Venn is ⟨ . . .⟩ that he's going to do the unth⟨ . . .⟩ ask Summer for help."

"Is he crazy!"

"Probably. But she—Summer, that beautiful, faery creature—she'll say yes, Sarah, you know she will, just to trap him, and God knows what he'll have to promise her in return. I've reasoned with him, Piers has argued with him, but he won't be swayed. The man is so bloody stubborn!" He rapped on the table with a teaspoon. "As hard as that. But he might listen to you. You're like him. Part of him."

She said, "Venn goes his own way."

"Maybe. But also . . ." He laughed, awkward. "*I* need you, Sarah. I need you to help me, because none of them are human, none of them really care, not like we do. Venn is obsessed with Leah, Piers is some hobgoblin, Gideon is half Shee. Flesh and blood, Sarah! That's what I need at Wintercombe. Another human being. Or I'm alone in a world of creatures and machines."

She shrugged. "A girl from the future . . ."

"Is better than no girl at all!"

"You don't have to stay."

"And leave Jake? The truth is, I suppose I've started to care about him. I think you have too. And I'm *in loco*

s, remember? I feel responsible. Help me get
e back, Sarah. Please."

For a moment they both sat silent among the echoing chatter of the tourists and the shrieking of children.

Then she laughed a short, bitter laugh and he knew
he had won.

"George," she said, "you're too much for me. What
time's our train?"

He grinned, modest. "Actually, I have a car."

3

I paced all night, as I believe one is supposed to,
up and down the corridor of the infirmary, smoking
cigars until the air was a fog of blue. Even Moll's
antics, even the search for the snake bracelet, faded
from my mind.

Then, just as the sky brightened and the gas-lamps
were put out, there came a great eerie cry, as if the
whole world wailed.

The nurse came out, wiping her hands. "It's a girl,"
she said.

And I found myself the most astonished of
fathers.

Journal of John Harcourt Symmes

THERE WAS SOMETHING sinister about the three
children. They didn't smile. The lenses of their glasses
were shiny and hid their eyes. Even in this terrible
time of fear and sudden death, their faces were too pale
under the dirt.

Jake said, "How the hell does everyone here know
my name?"

"Not everyone, just us." The boy to the right, his
small face serious.

"Remember us. Remember what we say." Was it the

left-hand one now? Their voices were as identical as their faces.

The middle boy took a worn wooden yo-yo out of his pocket and let it run expertly down and up its grubby string. "We'll be back. Soon."

"Just hang on." Jake took a hasty step toward them. "What do you mean? What black fox? What box? Are you Shee? Do you know Summer? Do you know Venn?"

They turned away. Linking hands, they walked into the crowd on the platform.

"Listen to me!" Jake dived after them, but tripped over a man wrapped in blankets, curled in sleep. A storm of swearing emerged; Jake backed, staggered against a pram; a baby screamed. A women yelled, "Watch what you're doing, stupid!"

"Sorry. Sorry." He scrambled away, trying to edge his way along the platform. Where were they? For a moment he thought he saw them, a little farther on, near the tunnel entrance, but when he climbed over the crowded refugees to get there, the only children were sleeping ones, their weary mothers gazing suspiciously at him.

He stopped, staring around.

Had they vanished? Or had he just lost them in the hundreds, maybe thousands, of people camped down here? Had they been Shee? Those cold faces. That dead stare. It was possible. For the Shee, all times were alike.

Suddenly he was too tired to think anymore.

He had to get some rest.

It took half an hour to find a corner of space against a damp wall. As he lay curled there on the hard platform, his head pillowed on borrowed newspapers, his coat for a blanket, he worried about his predicament. He was in the wrong time, and the only way back was through the mirror. *He had to find it.* However long it took. He quashed the secret fear that it might take him weeks. Months. The newspaper under his ear was dated June 1940. The height of the London Blitz. He'd studied it last year in the module on the Second World War, but he had no idea how long the bombardment lasted.

If he was killed . . .

But he couldn't be, because then . . .

Paradoxes swam wearily through his brain.

And those children . . . those weird kids . . .

Thinking of them, he fell asleep.

He must have slept for several hours, despite the distant crashes of anti-aircraft guns, the heavy thuds that shook dust from the ceiling. Because when he woke, things had changed. There were a lot less people; those left were packing up, folding blankets, heaving bags and small children onto their backs.

Jake groaned. He was so stiff his joints cracked as he stretched; one arm was numb from his weight on it.

He mumbled, "What time is it?"

"Eight o'clock, love. The all-clear has sounded." The woman next to him swept a blanket into a suitcase quickly.

"Where's everyone going?"

She stared. "Work, mostly. Or to see if their houses are still standing."

He thought of the collapsed street, the weak whisper of a voice in the wreckage. That woman . . . Alicia. She was dead now.

He sat up slowly, pushed back his hair and rubbed his face with both dirty hands. He should find the mirror.

Then he reached into his pocket, pulled out the luggage ticket, and looked at it.

He had promised her, and she was dead now.

➤·←

Above ground, London lowered in a dark, rainy dawn.

He walked on the streaming pavements, collar up, soaked. Workers and women, cars, buses, and army trucks hurried past. The past was a place of strange illusions; at one corner he could almost believe he had never even *journeyed,* because the doorways and alleyways were so ordinary and familiar. And then a huge advertisement board for Pond's Cream, or Bovril Meat Extract confronted him like a stark reminder of some alternative reality. Gradually, street by street, he saw how the shops were different—smaller, their fronts shaded by dripping awnings, their windows crisscrossed with protective tape. Sandbags were heaped in great walls down the road. Barriers—were they tank traps?—blocked every junction. There were no traffic lights, no automatic crossings, none of the normal paraphernalia of the city he knew. And then he turned a corner and muttered in surprise, because a whole landscape of rubble lay cold under the rain, and in the middle of it, completely undamaged, one small barber shop flaunted its striped red-and-white pole defiantly, and a few men queued to be shaved in makeshift seats in the debris.

There were other queues. Even this early, patient lines of people had formed outside nearly all the shops. At a baker's, the smell of hot fresh bread made his hunger painful. He had a purse full of pre-decimal coins— part of Piers's safety protocol—heavy in his pocket. He joined the queue.

Ten minutes later he reached the counter.

"Ration book?"

Jake said, "Sorry?"

"Your ration book, son."

"I . . . forgot it."

The baker stared at him in disbelief. "You what?"

"I just want . . ."

"Whatever you want, there's no chance. Go home and get it. Next, please."

Jake stalked out in cold fury, but there was nothing he could do. This was a different world to his, a world where he barely existed, and he had to get used to it. A few streets on, he managed to buy a small dried-up apple from a street stall, and chewed it sourly as he hurried on through the rainy dawn.

Tottenham Court Road was quieter than in his time; the cars and trucks strangely cube-like and slower, the exhaust fumes smokier, making him cough.

There were no signposts, no street names; not wanting to talk to anyone, he summoned up a hazy map of London from his memory and headed north, working his way to the grimy thoroughfare of Euston Road and trudging along it, head down, rain-blinded and cold.

He had been to St. Pancras before, to catch the Eurostar to Zurich—he remembered a huge Victorian station, beautifully renovated. Now it loomed up before him, soot-blackened and oddly shrunken by the barrage balloon tethered above. Crowds of soberly dressed men and women surged out of it, many in uniform.

Inside the vast arrivals hall, at least it was dry. He shook his wet hair and looked around. Trains, people, porters. Echoing voices. The roar of engines.

Near the refreshment room was a window in the wall, the sign LEFT LUGGAGE painted above it in dark green letters.

He walked quickly over.

No queue. Amazing.

He glanced carefully around. A few naval officers sat laughing at a round table; a soldier and his girl embraced over a pile of suitcases. No one took any notice of Jake.

He took the ticket out and went up to the window.

Behind it was a wooden counter, and behind that a keen thin man in a railway uniform who said, "Yes?"

"Come to collect this." Jake pushed the ticket across.

The man read it. "Six fifteen. Did you deposit it yourself?"

"No. It's . . . for my aunt."

"Right." The man looked even more keen, all at once. "Just wait there, please."

He went into the depths of the room. Jake saw hanging coats, boxes, piled trunks, a stack of corded parcels. Behind him a train came in, and he turned in delight at the vast eruption of steam, the hissing brakes of the engine.

"Sign here, please." A small brown suitcase was slid over the counter at him; he turned and scrawled the name *J. Wilde* on the sheet, pulled the case from the man's hand, and walked hurriedly away.

His heart was pounding; he felt as if everyone was watching him, but a quick glance reassured him. Even the keen official was already talking to another customer. Jake walked quickly along the platform to an empty bench at the far end, sat down, and took a silent breath.

So now he was a time traveler and a thief.

No. Because Alicia had insisted. Demanded, with her last breath, that he take it . . .

He lifted the case onto the bench and clicked the fastenings; they weren't locked, and the lid opened easily.

He gazed at the contents, oddly disappointed.

Papers. Letters. Account books. A birth certificate. A red leather photo album. He picked that up at random and opened it. Stiff Victorian portraits, a family group on the grass outside a prosperous-looking rectory. A little girl with a parasol and a tiny dog. Was this Alicia as a child?

He put the album down and rummaged further. Long white evening gloves. A box of chess pieces. A fan, a tiny container with scissors and nail-things. Then jewelry, plenty of it, wrapped in twists of white tissue paper. He opened one; saw a gold ring, obviously expensive. The sad detritus of a dead woman's whole life. He twisted the paper back around the ring and put it away. None of it was any use to him.

As he went to shut the case, something in the bottom slid slightly. He pulled it out.

A black velvet bag tied with cords. At the end of each cord was a tassel of gold threads. He tugged the cords open. Inside was a metal container, circular, a dull gray. He tugged the lid off and saw to his surprise a roll of ancient film, its edges perforated, its frames small and dark. He pulled out a section and held it up but could make out nothing in the dull smoky light. He rolled it back, closed the container, slipped it in, and turned the bag over.

A few letters were embroidered elegantly on the back.

J.H.S.

He stared at them for a second of frozen disbelief, then dived back to the suitcase and scrabbled through the papers, finding the birth certificate and unfolding it with shaky fingers.

It was worn thin, the folds broken through.

He read her name ALICIA MARY. And her father's name.

JOHN HARCOURT SYMMES.

"Symmes had a daughter!" He said it aloud in his astonishment; Symmes, who had stolen the obsidian mirror and got it to work, the man he and Venn had confronted in the smogs of Victorian London. That woman had been his daughter?

Then the mirror would have been in her house.

He hissed with frustration; some papers fell to the

floor. He leaned after them but a hand in a brown leather glove got to them first.

Jake looked up.

The man was thin, average height, his face refined, his eyes dark with intelligence. He wore a long, loose brown coat and a hat Jake thought might be a fedora.

He was obviously, and without question, the police.

"These are yours?" he said.

"Er . . . Yes." Jake flicked a glance sideways. Two uniformed constables waited a few feet down the platform. With them was the keen man from the left luggage office, who said "That's him" with irritating smugness.

The police officer nodded. "What's your name?"

"Jake Wilde." He didn't know what else to say.

"Identity card? Ration book?"

"I . . . don't have them with me."

"Don't you now. Address?"

"Wintercombe Abbey. It's not in London, it's in the West Country. I'm staying there with my godfather." It seemed the time to make an impression. Jake stood and drew himself up. "Look here, I simply don't see—"

"Don't pull the public schoolboy cant with me, son." The man's voice was soft and calmly authoritative. "Don't tell me Daddy is a magistrate. Don't tell me Ma Symmes really was your aged auntie. Just step away from the bench."

Jake didn't move. "And you are?"

"I'm Scotland Yard, son. Like I said, away from the bench. Now."

Jake nodded. He shut the lid of the suitcase and with one quick, fluid action, flung it in the policeman's face.

Papers flew out in a cloud; the jewelry clattered like rain, but Jake was already running; fleeing down the platform at top speed, leaping baggage, ducking a trolley piled with milk churns.

Yells rang out behind him; he sensed the policemen after him, but he was fast; he could outpace them.

Steam gushed, a fog of hot air. The locomotive beyond was preparing to move, carriage doors already being closed. He flung himself forward, grabbed one, hauled it open.

Leaping in, he slammed it behind him, gasping, then brushed his hair back and walked firmly along the corridor into a first-class compartment, sat down, and smiled breathlessly out of the window.

The train shuddered, shunted, stopped. A whistle blew.

Trying to appear calm, Jake craned his neck to see out. Only steam swirled on the platform.

Then with a crash, the compartment door slammed open.

A red-faced sergeant burst in, grabbed him, and forced him up. "You're a bleedin' tricky little beggar, and no mistake."

"Let go of me. You can't do this!" Jake struggled

fiercely, but the man's grip was iron. He was swung quickly around.

Standing in the compartment doorway, the man from Scotland Yard looked hardly out of breath. His glare, though, was steely.

"My name is Inspector Allenby. I think you'll be coming to the station to answer a few questions, Mr. Jake Wilde."

"For what? What have I done?"

Allenby shrugged. "Attempting to travel without due and proper identity, obtaining goods under false pretenses, resisting arrest, and very possibly, high treason. Take your pick. You're in a heap of trouble, son."

He stepped up to Jake and he held the luggage room ticket in his face, the number 615 clear. "I've been waiting weeks for someone to come for this. It seems the old lady was running a bigger network than we thought."

"I don't know what you're talking about." Furious, Jake held himself still.

"Save it. Take him to the van, Joe."

The red-faced sergeant twisted Jake's arm expertly behind his back. "With pleasure. You are going to bleedin' regret making me get all hot and bothered." He jerked and Jake gasped.

"You can't do that! I have rights!" he yelled.

"Oh really," the sergeant growled. "You can tell me all about them. At the Yard."

4

Five men were in the final ascent party on Katra Simba.

There are many rumors about what happened on those terrible slopes, but as only Venn returned, only he knows the truth. He has never discussed it publicly, though he did meet with the families of each of the dead climbers.

If, as is thought, Morris and James plummeted into the crevasse, Venn would have tried anything to save them.

His courage is not in doubt.

Jean Lamartine, The Strange Life of Oberon Venn

SARAH SPENT THE long drive to Devon gazing out at the green woods and the moors.

It was April, and she realized with surprise that the spring was well under way. Hidden in London, she had missed its coming; now she stared with delight at the lambs skittishly running from the motorway's roar, and the white umbels of cow-parsley in the hedges. Every wood had its swathe of bluebells, every tree its small unfolding leaves. Small black horses nibbled the corners of fields.

She knew this country. As the twilight gathered,

Dartmoor began to loom on the horizon, purple-gray receding folds of moorland under the darkening sky. Sleepily she felt the old desire to climb up there, breathe that wild air again, as she used to do with her father and the three dogs. Before Janus came, and unmade the world.

Wharton let her dream. He drove carefully with only the swiftest of glances at her. By Exeter, darkness was closing in. If Sarah hadn't opened her eyes by chance and glimpsed the road sign to Princeton, they would have sped on unknowing into the night. Wharton slammed on the brakes, shunted back, and turned into the lanes, grateful there was no one behind. "Nice one, Sarah. Of course, I was just checking you were awake."

"Right." She wrapped her coat around her, shivering.

"Do you want to stop? Or there's some water and fruit in the back."

"Keep going." She squirmed around to find it. "We need to get there before he does anything stupid."

Urgency seemed to grow in the car as darkness fell. She bit into an apple, gazing out at the black landscape. "So, George. Did you ever get home? To Shepton Mallet?"

"Not yet. I will."

"Then why the car?"

"Had to get something. You know how the Abbey is miles from anywhere." He turned at a crossroads, knowing she was ready to ask the question he had been waiting for.

"What's it been like?" she said quietly.

Wharton changed gear. He glanced out at the passing small squares of light that were cottage windows, the sudden flicker of a pub sign.

"Like? Sarah, it's been like living in a besieged castle, with the enemy all around. For a start, the Shee. You can't see them, can't hear them, but you know they're out there somewhere. Every time you go near the Wood you feel watched. Not only that, the defenders inside with you are silent, preoccupied, and feverishly working at a bizarre and broken machine. I never thought I'd say this, but I'm the only sane man among lunatics. It's as bad as being back at the wretched school."

She couldn't help grinning. "Surely Piers . . ."

"Piers is hardly normal. Besides, Venn works the man like a slave."

She said, "And how is my . . . how is Venn?"

"Obsessed. Sleepless. He scares me. And it's worse, since Jake went."

"Tell me about that," she said.

As he drove deep into the dark land, he was glad to; glad to finally get the story out, to speak it aloud to someone, as if doing that would dissipate it like breath, release the tight hard ball of terror it had become inside him.

"Three weeks ago—on the Wednesday, it must have been—Piers came hurtling into the kitchen where Jake and I were working. As you know, that's the only warm room in the place. He was yelling, tremendously excited. *Come at once, come now, His Excellency says!* Why he gives Venn that ridiculous title . . . Anyway, we ran. Jake first, of course. Turns out they had made some breakthrough—the mirror was suddenly, inexplicably active. They were prepared, though, I'll give them that. The plan had been formed for months— to *journey* to the 1960s—and Piers was so confident they could do it. Jake scrambled into a suit of clothes that was utterly nondescript—it was designed to be unnoticeable for almost any era, and was packed with everything he might need—money, a med kit, a souped-up phone-thing that Piers hoped might be able to communicate with him. And a weapon."

"A gun?"

"I insisted, Sarah. Of course I didn't want him to go, but you know Jake. He put me firmly in my place, the arrogant little sod . . . and then Venn made it clear my opinion counted for less than the dirt on his shoe."

"So Jake put the bracelet on."

The car splashed down toward the Abbey, the headlights picking out ghostly trees, a field gate, a spindly signpost pointing into the dark.

"And?" she said gently, because he was so silent.

"You know better than anyone. It worked all right. The mirror's huge energies erupted, that dragging, terrible pressure, the implosion that seems to suck all your life—your spirit—right out of you. When I staggered up, Jake was gone. Simply no longer there." He changed gear, his voice harsh. "We waited. Time went by so slowly. Time, Venn's archenemy, seeming to mock him, and us. An hour, then two. The night. The next day. Venn just sat there, slumped in a chair, watching the mirror, watching his own dark reflection till he seemed to harden into its black stone. I have never seen a man so sunk in despair. Finally I couldn't bear it anymore. I went up to my room and fell asleep from sheer exhaustion, and because I knew—knew, Sarah—that they had lost him, just as they lost his father. And of course, the bracelet with him."

The bleak anger in him, the cold fury, was so clear she was almost afraid to speak.

For a moment the only sound was the car's tires, slurring down the muddy track; then she pressed the button that lowered the window, and smelled the twilight, rich loamy scents of the fields, the wet decay of the Wood.

"Next morning, about five, a shout woke me. I stumbled over to the window and looked down. Venn was there. He'd thrown the main doors open; he was standing on the top of the steps. It was pouring with rain, and a wind was gusting, but he ignored it. He just stood there, Sarah, a little drunk maybe, and he called her. He yelled *'Come to me, Summer. I need you. Are you listening, you witch!'"*

Sarah shivered. "He must be totally desperate."

"Or insane."

"Did she come?"

"No one came. But they heard him. All the birds of the Wood rose up, starlings and crows and jackdaws, karking and laughing and flapping around the trees. They all streamed off westward. Then Piers came out with an umbrella and he and Venn had one great unholy row. I got out the car and left to find you at once. I just pray we're in . . ."

His voice faded into dismayed silence. The car stopped.

". . . time," he said.

The gates were wide open. Over the familiar lions on the pillars, ivy had grown. Sarah felt the seed of dread inside her grow to certainty.

Wharton blasted the horn, twice. "Hang on!"

The drive had always been overgrown. Now, Sarah thought, it was if the trees had taken a step forward, threatening, closing in. Beneath the faint light from the stars, the Wood seemed darker and denser than before, all shadow and gnarled, silent thickets.

An owl hooted, somewhere close.

She shivered. It was like coming back into a trap waiting to spring and catch her, the snare of Venn's obsession. And it scared her, because if she fell into it—if just for a moment she allowed herself to feel sorry for him, allowed her resolution to waver—the world she had known, far in the future, would be destroyed, and all her life with it.

The car struggled up the drive, jolted around the fallen tree, slurred swiftly over the gravel, and stopped. She looked up at the gray mullioned façade of the Abbey. It was in darkness. No lights showed.

"We're too late." Wharton was already out and racing toward the building. Sarah ran after him; she overtook him and leaped up the steps. The front door was solidly locked.

She rang the bell, then banged furiously with her fists. "Piers! Venn!"

The house stood as dark and silent as a mansion in a dream.

Wharton scowled. "Kitchen door."

They fled around the dark building, through shrubbery and toward the stables; then she stopped so suddenly he cannoned into her.

"Listen!"

A soft creaking sound drifted in the dark breeze. It made the hairs on his neck stir, because it was so alien. He had no idea what it was. A body hanging from a twisting rope? The wheels of a ghostly carriage passing in the night?

"The lake." Sarah was already running, so fast he couldn't keep up.

"Sarah! Wait!" He hurried after her. The Wood was black; he stumbled over briars and brambles, almost pitched into a sudden ditch. Then he shoved his way through bracken out into a dark path tangled with sprouting fungi, the smell foul.

"Sarah!"

Hurtling after her, he came out on the lakeside.

Quite suddenly, as if they had all been lit at that moment, he was blinded by lanterns. They hung from the trees, floated on the water. Some seemed to be carried in the air like small moving stars. And their colors were the most gorgeous he had ever seen—turquoise and orange and emerald, each jewel-bright flame blurring and blending into another. Underfoot, as he hurried down to where Sarah was, he sank ankle-deep in a soft drift that he realized was petals; the heaped petals of a million roses, scattered with the abandon of a wedding. The scent of their clotted richness was so overwhelming that it made him gasp in a stifled breath—the perfume of summer in the coldest of spring nights.

He stopped beside Sarah. "This is trouble."

"Yes." Her voice was hard. "Look."

Venn stood at the edge of the lake, where the bank crumbled. He stood tall, his spare figure silhouetted against the moon. Coming toward him over the dark water was a small boat rowed by four of the Shee, canopied with silk, hung with lanterns, the oars creaking. Seated in it was a young woman, her hair short and black, crowned with flowers. She wore a long white dress, simple as a nightgown, that trailed out behind her in the dark water. Her face was Summer's and her red-lipped smile was sweetly triumphant.

The boat touched the bank. The faery woman stood, rocking slightly, and gathered up her dress. She held out one long white hand. Venn seemed to hesitate.

Then he stepped forward. Their fingers reached for each other.

"NO!"

The yell of fury broke from Sarah before she could think; she ran down and grabbed Venn's arm, forcing it down, physically pulling him away. "What are you thinking? Are you mad? Have you forgotten about Leah? About Leah, Venn!"

Astonished, he stared at her. "Sarah. You came back."

"And only just in time. How could you betray—"

"I don't betray her. I do this to save her."

He had lost weight. His face was gaunt, his eyes colder and bluer in their pain. There was a terrible blindness in them. His hand was a weight in hers.

She dropped it, stood back.

"That's not what *she* thinks."

Summer stood smiling, unmoving. And then in a bewildering instant she was on the bank between them, close to him, and her voice was girlish as she laughed.

"Since when do you listen to children, Venn?"

"I don't." But his gaze was dark.

"You will!" Sarah wanted to push Summer aside but dared not touch her. Instead she walked around her and faced Venn again. "Yes, I'm back. I'm back to work with you on the mirror. To find Jake, get the bracelet, bring back Leah. That's what you want, and that's what we'll do."

"Sarah, you can't . . ."

"You have no idea what I can do! What I know. Maybe I have ways, Venn. Maybe I know things from the future you can't even guess at."

"Such as?"

"I'm saying nothing in front of *her*. Get rid of her. Do you seriously think you can ever trust her? You told me yourself . . ."

"*I have no choice.*" It was a whisper of defeat. It infuriated her.

"*You do!* I've been busy, researching. I've found Mortimer Dee's page—it may tell us how he built the mirror, all the secrets he knew about it. You can have it! Use it. You don't need this dark magic. This danger."

Summer sighed. A breath of breeze rippled the trees. The Wood seemed to stir with hidden unease.

"*Oberon . . .*" she said.

He ignored her. "How can I believe you, Sarah? You want the mirror broken."

"*Yes.* But not yet. That's why I'm back. To get Leah. Remember what I told you. She's my great-grandmother. If we fail, I'll never have been born."

For a moment he stared at her with those ice-blue eyes, a shared intensity, an instant of consideration. Wind lifted his blond hair, flapped the collar of her coat.

Summer snapped the silence like a twig. "She's quite obviously lying. She'll do anything to get her way. Come with me, Oberon. I'll send my people through the Summerland to find Jake. It will be too easy."

He was silent.

"Don't ignore me." Her voice had the tiniest edge of frost.

Sarah's gaze was steady.

Venn looked down. Then, abruptly, he turned away. "I've changed my mind, Summer. You always ask too much. She's right. I'll do it without you."

The faery woman's pretty face did not flicker; her red lips made no pout. But at once, and from all sides, a gust of wind lifted the petals and scattered them high into the darkness like clouds of dark ash.

Sarah backed off. Wharton, close behind her, felt the sudden slanting chill of rain on his face.

Summer stood barefoot on the soaking grass. Behind her the boat shriveled. Its flags became cobwebs, its canopy shredded to rags; the four boatmen lifted their arms and flew away, starling-dark, into the stormy sky.

"Oh Venn," she whispered. "I will destroy your house for this."

Venn pushed Sarah toward Wharton. "Get back inside. Now."

She couldn't move. She stood mesmerized, like a mouse before a swooping predator.

Because Summer was transforming.

As they stared, her eyes darkened, widened, her pale dress shivered into feathers. She fragmented, fell to pieces, her fingers curled to talons, her small red mouth warped into the cruel hooked beak of an owl.

"Move!" Venn yelled. He grabbed Sarah, forced her away. "Run!"

The Wood was alive with crawling shadow. Tree-shapes stirred. A cascade of bats clattered up across the moon.

The wind screamed.

Sarah tore her gaze from the dissolving woman and fled, running blind into the darkness, Wharton puffing beside her.

Venn came last. Glancing back she saw he too was looking over his shoulder; between the trees the lakeside was ablaze, as if all the lanterns had flared into a great conflagration. Lightning, swift as a silver dagger, stabbed from the sky.

A branch above her cracked like a pistol shot; leaves and foliage crashed.

Wharton's hand grabbed hers. "This way!"

Flying leaves blinded her. Then, far over the darkened countryside, thunder came, a low, angry, incredibly sinister rumble that seemed to shake the Wood and the landscape even to the horizon.

"She'll kill us," she gasped.

A snort behind her. She realized it was Venn's bitter laugh. "Not yet."

They floundered through the undergrowth and out onto the black lawns. As suddenly as if all its switches had been pushed at once, the Abbey burst into light, windows blazing, its door wide open, a small figure in a white lab coat hovering anxiously on the threshold.

Even as Sarah ran for the steps, the rain crashed down, a deluge that soaked her in seconds, plastered her hair flat, streamed in her eyes and down her neck.

She scrambled up the wet stones, her hand slipping

from Wharton's, and stumbled into the black-and-white tiled hall.

Breathless, she crouched on the floor.

Wharton was bent double, gasping. Venn crashed in last; the wind gave a wild screech, snatched the door from his grip and slammed it in his face. Breathing hard, he shot home the bolts, top and bottom.

"Do your worst, Summer!" he yelled.

Outside, like a scornful answer, the thunder roared again.

Piers, wearing a wine-red waistcoat under his lab coat, stood gripping his hands together. Venn turned on him. "Where were you? What sort of coward are you?"

"She terrifies me." Piers shrugged. "Sorry. Sorry. But there was no way . . ."

"Shut up." Venn swung on Sarah. "If you weren't telling me the truth . . . If I've just lost my only chance . . ."

"Relax." She stood, wearily, pushing her wet hair back. "Like I told you, we don't need her. I've got Dee's page. Well, photos of it."

"And," a low voice said from behind them, "you've got me."

Gideon sat, knees up on the stairs. He wore the green patchwork clothes of the Shee, and his eyes glinted with their alien brightness. But his ivory-pale skin was human, and his voice was full of scorn.

"If you want Jake found, let me find him. I'll go into the Summerland for you. And out the other side, into wherever he is."

Venn stared at him, intent. "If Summer knew, she'd destroy you."

Gideon looked at Sarah. "Let her. It would be a relief."

"What would?" she asked.

He shrugged and leaned back, and she saw his bitterness was so deep now it burned him.

"Death," he said.

5

Tonight I try again. I have the table set out, and
the cards, and the board. I have the mysteries of the
tarot and the scrying ball. I have my father's black
mirror propped near the window.

One of these things must have engendered the
power, the thrilling, quivering power. After all these
years, to see a spirit! Right there, Jane, in my room!

No one will laugh at me now. The ladies of the
League for Psychic Research will no longer titter into
their handkerchiefs. Oh my dear Jane, my spirit guide
even told me his name!

It is David!

Letter of Alicia Harcourt Symmes to Jane Hartfield

"SIT DOWN."

The interview room held one chair, a stool, a table.

Jake perched warily on the stool.

The night in the cells had been a living hell of noise,
fear, and hunger. He was sore from the straw mattress,
itching from fleas, and had a bloody lip from stupidly
yelling at a drunk to be quiet.

All he wanted was some hot food and a bed.

Instead he had to keep his wits alert.

Inspector Allenby sat on the chair, a lean man in his
neat gray suit. He said nothing. Instead, in an ominous

silence, he took out from his pocket the small wallet they had found on Jake when they searched him. Opening it, he laid the contents out deliberately, one by one, on the table.

Jake watched, trying to look unconcerned.

A comb. Wooden, not plastic.

A purse of money. Safely pre-decimal.

The med kit. Tablets, a small glass syringe.

"What are these?" Allenby's nicotined fingers separated the painkillers and antibiotics.

Jake shrugged. "My aunt's prescription. Some stuff for her heart."

"I see. And this?" Allenby looked up.

The gun.

Jake's heart sank.

It was a lady's tiny pearl-handled pistol from about the 1850s. Piers had found it somewhere in the Abbey's storerooms, brought it down, cleaned it, loaded it. It looked ridiculous but it was deadly, because Wharton had insisted on him bringing a weapon. Jake sat back, silently cursing Wharton to hell.

"Just an antique."

"Illegal."

Jake shrugged. "There's a war on. My aunt wanted it. In case."

"In case of what? Nazi parachutists breaking into her house?"

"I don't know! The blackout. Burglars. Whatever. She was old . . . nervous. She got scared."

Allenby took out a cigarette and lit it. Shaking the match out, he said, "Tell me about your . . . aunt."

Jake didn't miss the hesitation. With a feeling he was digging himself into a deeper hole, he dragged up the snippets of information he had glimpsed in the suitcase of documents.

"Well, her name is . . . was Alicia Harcourt Symmes. She lived . . ."

"I know where she lived. I also know she was an elderly woman of seventy-two and unmarried and an only child. What I don't know is how she suddenly acquired a loving nephew."

Jake was silent.

Allenby leaned forward, curious. "In fact, you really puzzle me, Jake. There's something . . . foreign about you. Something alien. And here we are in the middle of a war."

He slid the cell phone across the table. "What is this?"

Jake was sweating. "I don't know. I found it."

"Found it?"

"On a bomb site."

"Remarkably undamaged. What is it made of?"

"Bakelite?"

"What does it do?"

He kept his voice light. "Absolutely nothing, as far as I can see." Which was perfectly true.

Allenby sat back. He stared at the phone, down where it lay on the table between them. Tapping the cigarette on an ashtray full of butts, he said, "Shall I tell you what I think? Shall I cut to the chase?"

Jake shrugged. It was better to say nothing at all.

"We know what Alicia Symmes was. To all the neighborhood she seemed a dotty old lady who read tea leaves and held séances. Eccentric, well-off, harmless. Middle England in person. Lace handkerchiefs, tea with the vicar, no one you would ever suspect of anything. And yet we had a tip-off that she was the spider in the heart of a spy ring that maybe goes all the way up to the German Secret Police—to the SS itself."

Jake stared. He felt a terrible cold chill down his spine. "Now wait a minute . . ."

"Three days ago she realized we were onto her. One of our watchers got too close, maybe. Maybe the spirits told her. She packed a suitcase and went to St. Pancras. We were following, all ready to close in. Maybe she knew that too, because she didn't get on any train. She put the suitcase in the left luggage office and then went and had a cup of tea at the station buffet. She chatted, knitted, read the newspapers. The bloody infuriating old biddy wasted a whole afternoon of my men's time. And then she went home for tea."

Amused, he stubbed the cigarette out. "I have to say I had a sneaking admiration for her."

Jake shook his head. "I don't get it. You're the police. Why not get the suitcase out . . ."

"Oh, we did. We examined everything in there."

"So you saw. It's just family stuff. Papers. A roll of film . . ."

Allenby shook his head. "The film is too fragile to be playable. Those papers must be in some sort of code. Names, dates, operations. Maybe she wasn't doing anything herself. But she was the center, the contact. We've known for some time that important information was being passed, from the offices of the Cabinet. So we slipped in some disinformation."

"What?"

"False stuff. Just to see. It got through all right. So we checked for any connections between the ten people who had known of it—ministers, secretaries. Their wives. Turns out six of their wives regularly attended dear old Alicia's séances." He smiled, bleak. "What better cover? We posted watchers. We found that all sorts of people came to her house every week: civil servants, army wives, members of Parliament. What messages were passed, what information changed hands there, under the tilting table, in the fake voices of spirits?" He laughed. "She was a charlatan, they all are. But worse, she was a traitor."

Jake shook his head, then stood and paced restlessly to the window. "You don't know that. It could have been anyone there. My aunt was just an old woman who thought she could talk to the dead."

"You believe that?"

Jake remembered the word from the rubble. *David.* "Of course not. But she did."

"No. She was a deliberate con artist. She took money from gullible people—well, I don't blame her for that. But treason is another matter."

He was watching Jake with professional calm. When he said, "Sit back down," his authority was complete.

Jake frowned. And sat.

"We searched the suitcase. Then we put it back. We were waiting for you to collect it."

"Me?"

"Someone. Her contact."

"Don't be ridiculous . . ."

"You had the ticket. You knew the code name."

"She gave me the ticket! Passed it to me, through the rubble, in the air raid."

"You said she was your aunt."

Jake thought fast, cursing his own stupidity. "All right. All right, you want the truth? I'll give you the truth. I lied. She wasn't my aunt. I'd never met the woman. I just chanced along the street, right? And this ARP warden made me help him. We tried to dig her out, but there was no way. She was trapped, she knew she was dying. So she gave it to me—that ticket." He rubbed his dirty face with a dirtier hand. "I was going to throw it away. But then I thought . . . there might be something valuable. Not that I'm a thief . . . I was . . . just curious."

Was he saying too much? He had to sound scared and confused, as if he was breaking down. After all, it was pretty much the truth.

Allenby sat back. His brown eyes studied Jake with an inscrutable stare.

"Not so cocky now, are we."

Jake shrugged. "It was stupid. I'm sorry."

"So you never met her?"

"No."

"Never even heard of her."

"Before today, no. I swear."

Allenby put his fingertips together and gazed at his yellow-stained nails.

"I want to believe you."

That was unexpected. Jake sat up.

"Can I go then? You've got no reason to keep me here. I've got rights."

"So you keep telling me. But this is war, Jake. Life and death, for millions of people. And you need to explain something to me."

"What? I don't . . ."

"You need to explain why, when she left the suit-case, three days ago, dear old batty Alicia said to the office-boy *My nephew will call for this. His name is Jake Wilde.*"

Oh God.

Jake stared.

And understanding crashed through him like the bomb through the houses.

He must already have met her—no, *he would meet her.* In his future, and her past. That's how she knew his name, who he was, that he would be there.

"So you see," Allenby said calmly, taking out another cigarette, "that you are in it up to your neck, Mr. Jake Wilde. Of course, you could come clean. Tell us who you work for, how they get the information out, where the transmitter is. Spill the beans on the whole net-work. I'd advise you to do it, because if you don't, our orders are to hand you over to the military. They have a few unpleasant little methods to get their information. And that's before they hang you."

Jake rubbed a hand over his face and closed his eyes. A click on the desk made him open them quickly—

The bracelet lay there.

"Look, Jake. I like you. Talk to me." Allenby put the cigarette down and pulled his chair closer with a scrape along the floor. Suddenly he was animated, his lean face alight. "This bracelet. Not the sort a thing a lad like you should have. Silver. Heavy. Old. And then, these."

He fished out a few coins from the purse and slid them over.

Jake stared at them. A shilling, a sixpenny piece. Piers had made sure they were all safely . . .

He closed his eyes again . . . *Oh hell hell hell. Pre-1960!*

The sixpence, close to his hand, was dated 1957. The young Queen Elizabeth's face looked at him sideways.

"Where do you come from, Jake?" Allenby tapped the coin. "This is the one thing I don't understand. They sent you out all prepared, but with coins dated fourteen years in the future. That's one big mistake. It's almost as if . . ."

A rap on the door interrupted him. He frowned, scraped the chair back, and went over. Jake saw the burly sergeant framed in the doorway, murmuring, sounding anxious. Allenby glanced over. Then they both went out.

Jake leaned back and groaned aloud. How on God's earth had he gotten into a mess like this?

He couldn't sit still; he got up and slammed around the bare brick walls in fury.

It wasn't like the interview rooms on police TV shows—no two-way mirror, no recording device, no responsible adult. But surely he must be entitled to a solicitor? Or had the war changed all that too?

Hang.

That was the word that already was choking him. Sticking in his throat. For a moment he couldn't swallow, coughed in stupid panic.

Get a grip.

Get . . .

He turned, instantly. The bracelet lay on the table. He picked it up and shoved it on his wrist, clicking it shut and pushing it well up under his sleeve. They'd find out, but . . .

Voices.

He jumped back, stood by the chair.

The door slammed open; Allenby came in with the sergeant behind him. They both looked fraught.

"Sorry, Jake. Too late. The military police are here." Jake backed away. "What?"

"They're taking you now. Nothing I can do about it, I'm afraid. Sergeant!"

The big man tugged a pair of steel handcuffs from his pocket. "Come on, son."

"No way!" Jake backed against the wall. He balled his fists.

"Forget it laddy, I've cuffed more prisoners than you've had hot dinners. You wouldn't know what hit you, and I won't even break sweat."

Jake felt the damp bricks at his back. He flung a

despairing look at Allenby. "You can't let them take me like this."

"Nothing I can do about it."

"I'll talk. I'll tell you everything. The whole thing. But I won't talk to them. No one else. Just you."

The sergeant stopped.

He looked at Allenby. Quietly the inspector said, "You might just be bluffing."

Jake forced himself to stand up straight. He unrolled his fists and spread his hands wide. "Let me go and you'll never know. I'll make a deal. Don't let them take me, and I'll spill."

Allenby's scrutiny was intense. "If you try . . ."

"I won't try anything. What can I do?" He stepped forward. "I'm trapped and I know it. I'll give you the biggest spy network in this country. The whole thing. Names, dates, sabotage plans. On a plate."

They looked at each other.

Silent, Jake prayed. Surely he couldn't resist.

Then Allenby shrugged. "All right. This may cost me some groveling. Sergeant, take him to the holding cell. Get this stuff locked up. No one to know about the suitcase but us, understand."

As he spoke, a distant drone rose up through the walls and roof, a hollow whine that made Jake stare until he realized it was an air-raid siren.

"Oh Gawd. Here the beggars come again," the sergeant muttered.

"Get him downstairs." Allenby hurried out.

"No cuffs," Jake said.

"You think something of yourself, don't you." The sergeant sucked his teeth. "I could take you blindfolded."

Jake was hauled up and shoved out into the dingy corridor, down damp stone steps, down and down past a few guttering lamps. Outside, the sirens stopped abruptly. There was a moment of almost breathless silence. Then, far off, a low pounding.

"Bloody East End copping it again." The sergeant grabbed him. "Here." He tugged out a key and unlocked the cell door. "Inside."

Before Jake knew it, he was through the dark slot and slipping on the wet stone floor, the familiar stink of urine and mold around him.

He dived back to the door, pushed his face against the grilled opening. "What if we get bombed?"

"Pray you don't, son. After all, they're your lot."

The grille was slammed shut.

He turned, and stared into the gloom. At least he was still close to the mirror. He wasn't on his way to some military prison the other side of England. And he had the bracelet.

Then he saw the other prisoner.

A tramp maybe. A shadowy figure anyway, lying on the bench against the wall, legs stretched out, wrapped in a coat of muddy grays and greens.

Jake slid down and sat on the filthy floor, knees up. He could just sleep now.

Sleep for hours.

But the figure said, "Not even pleased to see me then, Jake."

He didn't move for a second. Then he raised his head and stared.

Gideon lounged on the bench, back against the wall. His ivory skin was dark with smeared soot. His long hair tangled in the collar of his pied coat.

Jake was too astonished to move. "Where the hell did you come from? How did you get here?"

"Through the Summerland." Gideon stretched his legs out. "And believe me, it wasn't easy."

"But . . . how did you find me?"

"I searched. There are ways."

"Searched? It must have taken you . . ."

"No time at all." Gideon shook his head. His green eyes narrowed in amusement. "You still don't get it, do you. In Summer's land there is no time. *No time.*"

He scrambled up. "Venn sent you? But . . . she . . . Summer . . . my God, what did he have to promise her?"

Gideon looked at the floor. "Summer doesn't know anything about it. It was Sarah's idea."

For the first time in a long time a flicker of hope warmed Jake like a shaft of light. As a bomb fell streets away, shuddering dust down from the ceiling, he grinned.

"So Sarah's back," he said.

As if that could make everything all right.

If you can look into the seeds of time . . .

6

Where Janus obtained the mirror is uncertain. It is thought that among his earliest advisers was a man brought in great secrecy from a high security unit in the environs of what had once been Tokyo. ZEUS has no records of this man, and no images. But with him were transported various objects carefully packaged. The guards who accompanied him were never seen again. The consignment appeared on no flight details and was never reported in any customs document.

The package was delivered to London Central.

Immediately after this the tremors and earthquakes began.

Illegal ZEUS transmission; biography of Janus

SARAH WOKE very slowly.

For a long moment she lay curled among the white sheets, trying to hold on to the flavor of her dream, but already it had dissolved to frail, wispy remnants.

Of kneeling here, in this room. In her own time, with the sky raining on her through the charred rafters, and ivy smothering every wall with its glossy leaves. She had been hiding treasures in the small space under the floorboards—a seashell, a doll, a child's drawing of a red house and a yellow sun crayoned with spikes of light.

She sat up in the bed and gazed around.

In that End Time, over a hundred years from now, the Abbey would be a burned-out ruin, oaks growing through its tiled hall and up the broken staircase. She and her parents had lived—no, would live!—in a small cottage of salvaged stone and charred timbers, built into one of the corners of the cloister.

It was a bitter memory. It hurt her. She swung her feet out of the bedclothes and dangled them over the side. The room was dim; she slipped down and padded to the window, tugging back the heavy velvet curtains, wanting light, and air.

The morning was still.

The storm Summer had created had raged all night. The bright spring was shattered. Bluebells lay broken, new buds and catkins torn down by her spite. The morning was dark with cold rain, the trees gloomy through the drizzle, boughs tossing in the wind. Sarah saw again how the Abbey was a tiny sanctuary in the heart of the deep Wood; how the oaks and beeches rose up on each side, so that only from up here, high in the attic, could you glimpse the hills beyond, and Dartmoor, a gray shadow in the north.

She took down the old red dressing gown Piers had lent her and tugged it around herself. Then she climbed on the window seat and opened the casement.

Cold wind gusted in, rippling the curtains with its salt tang of the distant sea.

She allowed herself a wry smile.

She was glad to be back. Because after all, she was a Venn; this was her country.

This was her house.

Under her foot the floorboard creaked. She looked down at it, and another fragment of the dream broke in her memory. Her mother cooking. Her father outside, chopping wood. And then Janus's voice had come suddenly from the old wind-up radio, breaking the music. He had said *"I own the world now. I am the world now"* and her mother had turned it off with a shudder, saying "No! Never!" but that hadn't stopped him; he had crawled and squeezed out of the radio as it had transformed into Wharton's small red car, and there he had stood in the kitchen, a lank-haired man in blue spectacles, his uniform dark and neat.

"I'm afraid the time has come," he'd said.

And the last few trucks in the world had roared up the drive, a convoy of them.

She always woke up then. It was as if her mind wouldn't let her see the horror that followed. Her mother being dragged away, her screams. Dad running full pelt round the corner of the house with the axe still in his hand, face-first into the stun blast that sent him crashing.

The bruising thud of his body onto the mud.

And the careless way they had carried him, one arm dangling down.

She set her lips firmly and turned away from the window. This wasn't helping. Her parents were alive, would always be alive, somewhere in that distant future. And only she could help them.

She bent quickly, before she lost courage, and opened the hiding place under the boards. There was the small black pen she had brought from the future, and the gray notebook. These and the diamond brooch she had given Venn and the half of the Greek coin Summer had taken were all that remained of that world. She took the pen out.

On its cap was the enigmatic letter Z. The members of ZEUS had used these for their secret correspondence, but no one was left to answer her.

None of her friends.

She uncapped the pen. For a long moment her hand hesitated; then she wrote quickly, savagely.

Is anyone there?

Janus's reply was so prompt she drew in a sharp breath.

I WAS HOPING YOU WOULD BE BACK SOON, SARAH. I'VE BEEN WAITING SO PATIENTLY.

She loathed this. It felt like betrayal. But she had to know.

What's happening there? The black mirror.

. . . HAS NOT YET DESTROYED THE WORLD! AFTER ALL, YOU HAVE BEEN GONE ONLY A FEW MOMENTS, SARAH.

She stared at the scrawled lines on the paper.

Another appeared, swiftly unraveling.

I DON'T WANT YOU TO BE LONELY IN THAT PAST LAND. ALL BY YOURSELF. SO I HAVE SENT YOU MY CHILDREN.

"Sarah!" Wharton's knock made her drop the pen with a start. "Are you up? Piers says breakfast."

"Fine. Be there now."

His footsteps creaked away along the corridor.

She wrote: *What do you mean?*

WHY DON'T YOU LOOK AND SEE.

A sudden gust of wind rippled the pages and made the casement bang open.

She leaned out and grabbed it, and then stopped, astonished.

On the lawn, just at the edge of the Wood, three children were playing. Three small boys, dressed in old-fashioned school uniforms, their faces identical. Triplets. As she stared, one bent down, the others leap-frogging his back. Then they all stood and looked up at the window, a silent threesome.

"Who are you?" she said. "Where . . ."

They turned, as one. Even as she called "Wait" they

were gone, walking calmly into the Wood, though the last one turned back as he ducked under the dark branches.

And waved.

→⋅←

"Stand back!" The sergeant's key turned quickly in the lock. "And stop that bleedin' racket!"

As he burst in, another bomb hit so close that the walls shuddered. Dust and plaster crashed from the ceiling.

"Right Wilde, move. All prisoners evacuated."

The cell was dim.

A flicker in the corner of his eye. He turned, and swore. Because there was the boy spy. And next to him, like his shadow, a spirit so pale and thin the sergeant thought at once of his own dear dead brother, Albert, glimpsed years ago cold as marble in the narrow bed.

Then they were on him. He opened his mouth to yell—a filthy gag was shoved in. He fought furiously but the beggars were fast—and the spy knew a few fiendish Eastern tricks too, because his feet were knocked from under him by a savage kick, and his arms whipped back and bound even as he struggled.

They trussed him tight.

Then Jake sat on his chest and said, "Keep still. And listen."

The drone of aircraft, high above.

"I'm sorry to leave you here. I hope you'll be okay.

But I have to go. I want you to tell Allenby that I'm not a spy—he's got it all wrong. I just walked in on this. Understand?"

The sergeant swore again, furious and indistinct. Then his eyes slid with fear. Gideon leaned over him, a strange flint knife in his hand. "Why don't we make sure he stays silent."

"Are you crazy?" Jake stared in disbelief.

"If he gets free . . ."

"You've been with the Shee too long. You're turning into one of them."

"I'm as human as you are, mortal!" Gideon's eyes were bright and fierce as a bird's.

For a moment he and Jake shared a bitter doubt.

Then Gideon stood abruptly. "Do what you like. But let's go."

In the doorway Jake winced as the building shook again. He was worried about leaving the man here during the air raid, but there was no choice—he had to get away. "Sorry," he said. "Really sorry."

He slammed the cell door, and locked it.

Then, after a second of bitter hesitation, he turned and tossed the keys in through the grille.

"What are you doing!" Gideon grabbed him. "He'll untie himself . . ."

"I'm being human. We'll be long gone. But first, I have to find that suitcase."

Wharton strolled into the kitchen just as Piers was saying ". . . must never know anything about it. But the teacher—"

"What about the teacher?"

Standing by the fire, Venn glanced up. His cold, clear gaze was an icy chill; it seemed to weigh Wharton in a second's acute scrutiny. Then, surprisingly, he said, "I think the teacher is a man who can be trusted."

Piers sighed. He was sitting on the inglenook bench, absurdly cross-legged, wearing a white chef's apron splashed liberally with what looked like tomato sauce. His small alert face was twisted in thought. Then he shrugged. "Your call, Excellency."

"Trusted with what?" Wharton demanded.

Venn didn't answer. Instead he went to the door and opened it, looking cautiously up the dim paneled corridor. He shut the door and came back, one of the seven black cats pacing behind him. Striding to the fire and staring at it, his back to Wharton, he said, "There's something you should know. Unless . . . Has Jake ever spoken to you about the coin?"

"What coin?"

Piers scrambled up. "I'll make some tea. Or coffee?"

"He hasn't told you." Venn turned. "So he has some discretion."

Wharton went and sat at the table. He pushed the

unwashed dishes aside and said, "Coffee please, Piers. So maybe you should tell me, then."

Venn was wearing his usual dark jacket; his hair was dragged back with an easy carelessness that Wharton envied hopelessly. To Wharton's surprise, he came and sat opposite, leaning his long arms on the table, his fingers interlocked.

"The night Sarah left. Christmas Day. On that night the man called Maskelyne told Jake and me something important about the mirror."

Wharton nodded. "The scarred man. He's a strange character. He knows more than he's letting on."

"I agree. Clearly his connection to the mirror is an old one. He owned it before Symmes, remember. He traveled through it unprotected—with no bracelet— and just about survived. He hungers to get it back."

"Have you seen him since then?" Wharton asked.

"Not a sign." Piers put a steaming cup of coffee in front of him. "Not a whisker. Not on the cameras, not on the estate, not even in the village. As if he's vanished from the earth. And that girl, Rebecca, with him."

"Never mind her." Irritated, Venn watched Wharton add sugar and stir, savoring the aroma. "Maskelyne told us that the obsidian mirror cannot be destroyed. *Not by force or fire, by wind or water. There is only one way to destroy the mirror.* Those were his very words."

Wharton frowned, sipping. "And that is? By the way, mega coffee, Piers."

Piers smiled, modest.

"For God's sake! Will you pay attention!" Venn's frail patience snapped. "He told us that there is an artifact shaped like a golden coin, a Greek stater with the head of Zeus on it. This device contains enough energy to destroy the mirror. He said that the coin had been cut in half and the halves separated in time and space, so that they might never come together accidentally. God knows what happened to the left half. But the right half is here."

Wharton was staring now. He put the cup down so sharply it clunked in the saucer. "Oh my God. The one Sarah had? On a golden chain?"

"Precisely." Venn's fingers tapped the table. "She brought it with her from the World's End. It was the same half coin that Symmes was given, to lead him to the mirror."

"But . . ." Wharton was so agitated he had to stand up. *"But she gave it to Summer!"*

The stark horror of that statement seemed to hang in the air like a wisp of smoke.

Piers sighed. "She doesn't realize its power. Didn't know."

"And she never must." Venn stood too, facing Wharton. "Sarah's mission is to destroy the mirror. I can never let her do that. If she should find out about the power of the coin, she might . . ."

"But if the other half is lost . . ."

"That won't stop her looking for it. I must have the mirror safe. Or I'll never see Leah again." Venn swung away. For a moment Wharton glimpsed the tension in the man, wound so tight a hasty word, a forbidden thought might snap it.

The cat on the windowsill stopped washing and gazed over.

Venn took a breath, dropped his voice. *"Sarah must never know.* And neither must Summer."

Wharton sat down again slowly, trying to consider this calmly. "What if Summer knows already? She demanded the coin as her reward, after all."

"Then we're in worse trouble than even I feared." Venn walked to the window. "Let's assume, for the moment, the Queen of the Wood has no idea of the power she wears round her pretty white neck. In that case, my plan is—the only plan possible is—to get it from her. But with Summer nothing is simple. Nothing is easy. If she had any notion how much I want it, she'd take great delight in keeping it from me." His face was set and hard. When he spoke again it was in a bitter whisper Wharton had to strain to hear. *"Is this my punishment, Leah? . . . As soon as I command the mirror I will come for you. I swear."*

He turned, abrupt. "I need a plan, Piers."

Piers looked worried. "Tricky."

"And you"—Venn turned to Wharton—"must never breathe a word of this. I'm only telling you because I may need you. You might be useful. That's the only reason."

The man's arrogance made Wharton ball a fist with annoyance. "Don't talk to me like that. He may be your slave, but I'm not."

Venn shrugged. "Fine. Then go. Get out of here."

"I go nowhere until Jake is safe. As for Sarah, I don't like deceit. I'll decide what I say to her."

"About what?" Sarah's sharp question alarmed them all; turning quickly Wharton saw her standing there in the scruffy jeans she had worn in London, her hair washed and clean, her eyes curious.

There was a silence so pointed it hurt. Venn's arctic glare was fixed on Wharton. They were all looking at him. What could he do? His bold words still echoed, but at once and to his own dismay, he knew his first priority had to be Jake's safety. The mirror must be preserved. He pulled a face. "Well . . ."

Venn watched him sidelong with the attention of a hawk on a scurrying rat.

Piers seemed to be holding his breath.

Sarah said, "Well what?"

Wharton squirmed. Then he licked his lips and

murmured grimly, "Only that there's been no word. From Gideon. Or from Jake."

>→·←←

The police station was deserted. Jake ran down the dusty corridor "We need to find his office. Allenby. The name's on the door."

Gideon shrugged. "Then you'll have to read it."

Jake glanced back, astonished. "You can't read?"

"Learning wasn't for the son of a hovel, great magician."

The sarcasm was bitter. As Jake found the door and burst through it, he spared one thought on what Gideon's life might have been in that long-lost far-off century; then he was ransacking the drawers and flinging open the filing cabinets. One was locked. He grabbed a metal ruler, slid it in, and forced the drawer hastily. It swung wide.

"Got it!"

The suitcase had been propped inside. He had it out and open at once. At the door Gideon watched the grimy corridor. "Listen!"

The whine was distant and alien, the metallic howl of a strange beast. Gideon had his flint knife out, alert, but Jake said, "It's just the all-clear. It means the air raid is over."

Gideon listened a moment. "I don't understand what's happening in this time. This war—is it fought with machines? Do the machines make war against each other, or against the men?"

"You don't want to know." Grim, Jake was rummaging through the contents of the case. He found the birth certificate and stuffed it into his pocket.

Gideon frowned. "I can hear voices. People coming back."

Jake couldn't hear a thing, but he knew the changeling's senses were Shee-sharp.

He tossed aside the photo albums and the letters—fascinating, but no time—and just as a door slammed far down in the buildings his fingers touched the softness of the black velvet bag. He pulled it out.

"Ready?" Gideon turned.

Jake had the bag open. He tipped out the metal film-case. What was on this? Was this what she had wanted him to see?

"Jake. Jake, we have to go! Now!" Gideon locked the door and crossed to the window. Even Jake could hear the shouts now, the banging on cells, the sergeant's furious yell.

The window was barred; Gideon shivered at the touch of the metal, but climbed up and had slithered lithely through before Jake realized what was happening. "Wait! I'll never fit."

"You have to."

Voices in the corridor. The door handle turned, was rattled angrily. Allenby yelled.

"Wilde! Open this door."

"Take this. Get them back to Venn."

Jake thrust out the velvet bag and the papers into Gideon's pale hands. Then he climbed up and gripped the bars and slid his arm, then his left shoulder through. Turning his head sideways he breathed in, sweating, willing himself between the rods of steel.

The door shuddered.

Gideon grabbed him.

"Don't! Don't pull me! I'm stuck!"

He was thin and agile, but the bars were too close. They squeezed his head. He was caught in a vise. He would never get free.

Panic gripped him. There was no way on, no way back. "I can't do it! I can't!"

"You can!" Gideon grabbed him, fierce. "Push."

"No! It's too late."

Something crashed and gave. For a second he thought it was him, that he was out, then behind him the lock burst. Pinned halfway to freedom, he slipped off the bracelet and flung it at Gideon, who caught it with astonished speed.

"To Venn. *Not Summer! Promise me!*"

Hands grabbed him, hauled him out from the bars

with careless, brutal force, knocked him down. He crashed into a black circle of boots.

The window was empty.

Gideon was gone, and if he answered, Jake didn't hear it.

7

What doth my mirror show?
It showeth not what a man looks like but what he is.
Not what he sekes for but what he hath found.

From The Scrutiny of Secrets *by Mortimer Dee*

The diary of Alicia Harcourt Symmes:

After the strange demise of my dear papa, and now that I am truly his heiress, I think it would be a suitable tribute for me to continue his diary. His name was John Harcourt Symmes, and he was a Victorian gentleman of science, in those distant days when the study of the occult could still be scholarly, and respectable. Unlike now, where I am called a foolish woman and people smirk at me behind my back.

I knew hardly anything about him until the day the letter came.

I was a young girl of 19, living a quiet life with my aunt and uncle in the rectory at Charlecote Thorpe in the county of Yorkshire. It was a remote, windy hamlet on the moors, the nearest town ten long miles away. I had lived in that dingy and depressing house since I was eight, the year when my dear mama passed over to the Other Side. She had separated from Papa very early in her marriage, and no one ever told me why. I was kept in complete ignorance. It was never even spoken of by my aunt and uncle. I could only suppose there had been some terrible scandal, some wonderfully thrilling disgrace. Mama had even reverted to her maiden name of Faversham, though in secret I practiced my true forbidden name over and over in my books in childish handwriting.

Alicia Harcourt Symmes.

It had a refined sound to me, even then. It made me feel like a different person, as if I had some hidden dark mirror image of myself.

I was an isolated child. Not ill-treated but certainly unloved. It was clear to me my aunt had only taken me in out of duty to my dead mother. I had only my dolls to play with, as the village children were thought too rough and uncouth to come to the house. Sometimes I used to peep at them from between the heavy velvet curtains, as they ran on the moor and small scruffy dogs chased after them. I envied them their wild fights, their screeching arguments, their real families. Because, though I seemed outwardly a quiet and reserved child, respectful and silent in company, the truth was that I was seething with rebellion.

I loathed my life!

Maybe that was why I was fascinated to learn more of my father. Once, coming very quietly into the room, I heard my aunt in conversation with one of her cronies, the curate's wife, and she was saying: ". . . My dear, he experimented in the occult, in fiendish, terrible things Of course, he was a most depraved and villainous creature. How my sister came to fall under his spell remains the sorrow of my life. Do you know, they say at one time he even kept a girl from the streets and she actually became . . ."

Then they saw me, and fell silent.

How I pondered those words in the curled cave of my bedclothes! How in secret I would imagine and dream of my father! Depraved and villainous! I shuddered with delight. I pictured him tall and devilishly handsome, with a curled mustache, and I prayed that one day he would come in a great carriage and whisk me away from the tedium of the dull dark house, to Paris, to Rome, to London!

But he never came.

Instead, on my twenty-first birthday, the letter arrived.

Sarah spread the photocopies of the Dee manuscript on the kitchen table. Piers had enlarged them, so that the page of scribbled drawings, the tangles of coded words, could be seen more easily.

Venn picked one up and examined it.

"Total and utter gibberish." Wharton turned a copy, not even sure which way up it should go. "I mean look at this. A tower, a bird-mask, some sort of crane? Then an equation. Then a scratchy picture of what might be, well . . . a man on a horse?"

"A centaur," Venn muttered.

"Well, maybe. But what does it all mean? How can this help us get Jake back?"

Venn flicked a glance at Piers. "Any idea?"

The little man looked at the page almost hungrily. "Not yet, Excellency. But I'd love to have a go. Puzzles! I love puzzles."

Venn frowned. "Be quick. We need the information."

He turned to Sarah and she faced him. That sharp blue gaze they both had, Wharton thought. How hadn't he seen before how similar they were?

Venn said, "So. My great-granddaughter."

Sarah knew there was one question that had burned in him since their last meeting; she asked it at once, unflinching. "Is it true that Leah comes back?"

She looked away. "In my history, she didn't die in a car crash. But I don't know details. All our family documents were lost in the fire, or Janus took them. But that painting of her—the one you have in her room? We still had that."

"So I'll succeed." He seemed numb with relief, dizzy with disbelief. He glanced at Wharton, then back at her. "If only I knew how. As for what happened with Summer . . . I'm trusting you, Sarah. You have to help me. When Leah is back, I don't care about the mirror. You can blow it to smithereens if you like."

He turned and went to the door.

"What about David?" she said.

He stood stock-still, as if he had forgotten the name. "Yes, David. David too. Of course." He went out. A moment later they heard the front door slam.

"He's not going to the Wood, is he?" Wharton said anxiously.

Piers shrugged. "The estate has many footpaths. He'll roam up on the moors for hours."

"That Summer creature gives me the creeps." Wharton turned to Sarah. "Come on. We need to check the mirror."

On her way out, she looked back. Piers had seated himself at the table. He had poised a lamp over the papers and was making hasty notes with a long red pen. From nowhere he seemed to have found a green visor to shade his eyes.

"Looks like a newspaper hack," Wharton said.

She smiled. As she closed the door, three of the cats jumped up and sprawled on the table, mewing for food.

"Get lost," Piers said absently.

➤·◄

The house was silent and musty. As they walked its corridors, they passed through slants of pale light from the windows, watery with tiny running raindrops.

"It seems so empty without Jake," Wharton said.

"Yes."

To her it seemed as if an air of hopelessness, of damp decline, had invaded the place. She paused beneath a pale square of paneling. "There was a painting there Christmastime. Surely?"

"Venn sold it last week. Piers boxed it up and I took it to the station. It's being auctioned in Christie's."

"So he's short of money."

"Sarah, he's out of money."

She shook her head. As Wharton led the way up the wide, curving staircase, she thought of how the Time-wolf had once slunk up here, its eyes sapphire fragments. On the landing, the ancient floorboards creaked.

The Long Gallery stretched before them.

They walked down it, but Wharton stopped abruptly before a bedroom door. "Reminds me. There's something you might be able to help me with, because the damned beast won't even look at me."

He led her inside.

Jake's bedroom.

It had been his father's, and he had moved in there. His clothes lay on chairs, on a heap on the floor. His laptop sat on the mahogany dressing table.

Wharton pointed up. "Horatio. Quite lost without his master."

She saw the marmoset. It was huddled in a heap of misery on the very top of the great curtain rail. It spared her a miserable glance, its tiny face screwed up.

"Horatio!" She reached up, her voice soft. "Come on. Come down."

The creature turned its face away.

"Just won't eat," Wharton said gloomily. "If Jake gets back and finds him dead, there'll be hell to pay."

Suddenly he turned to her. "Though what if he never gets back, Sarah. What if . . ."

"Don't panic." She kept her voice firm. "Of course he will. Pass me that chair."

It took ten minutes to coax Horatio down, but the grapes she found proved too enticing, and finally he jumped into her arms with a screech and snatched the fruit.

"Brilliant." Wharton was delighted. "I knew he'd like you."

She clambered down. The marmoset's fur was soft and lustrous. It looked up into her face and chattered. Then it took another grape, held a handful of her hair, climbed onto her shoulder, and sat there, sucking. Its tail was a soft tickle around her neck.

She turned. "Right. Let's go to the mirror."

At first she was amazed that Venn had left it unguarded. Then, as she ducked through the viridian web that was spun about it, she noticed the new bank of security devices, the alarms and laser-thin beams of light that Wharton held her back from.

"Venn is more and more afraid of theft. Getting paranoid. There's the control panel, and they've wired it up like the crown jewels. If there's any sign of Jake coming back, the whole house will probably explode with alarms. This is what the portraits are paying for. We can't go any closer than this."

Sarah hissed in frustration. "Crazy."

"Maybe. But that thing scares me . . . It seems to have a life of its own."

The obsidian mirror.

It leaned, facing her, a dark sliver of glass in its jagged silver frame. In the angled shadowy surface, she saw a slanted image of herself, and her own face looked different, subtly altered. The mirror showed her herself, but for the first time a stab of doubt pierced her—

did it show what was there now, or were its reflections warped and rippled through by time, so that she might be seeing herself seconds ago? Or did the mirror show not only the outward form but how a person felt? Their emotions? Their soul?

Wharton was talking. She dragged her attention back.

". . . can do about any of it. I never thought I would miss that infuriating, arrogant wretch."

She realized he was talking about Jake.

"Jake can look after himself."

"So could his father. But what if we never see him again, Sarah?"

She patted his elbow, and walked as near as she dared to the network of lights. "Don't worry. Keep believing. Gideon will find him. He promised."

Wharton snorted. "If Summer knows that, Gideon might be torn into pieces by now."

"You really have to . . ." She stopped. *A brief glimmer, like lightning.* "What was that?"

"What . . ."

"Did you see!"

She felt him hurry beside her. "I can't see anything except . . ."

The mirror flickered.

For a brief, terrible moment it was not even there. They were in a place of utter darkness, the air a choking dust; all around them and over their heads, a crushing, suffocating mass of rubble and brick.

Sarah gasped.

Wharton swore.

Then the mirror was clear.

"What . . . *where* was that!"

Sarah stared at the obsidian glass, seeing her own eyes, wide and startled. She stared into the fear that the black hole had reached even here to engulf the world.

"That was death," she whispered.

Jake sat on the wooden bed and gazed around the cell.

This was no police holding room—this was prison. They had brought him in a black police car, the bell on the roof jangling, and at least four heavy metal gates had clanged behind him. The air was stale and sour, the muted sounds of voices and the clatter of dishes marking other distant prisoners.

But it was still too quiet. Prisons should be noisy. He wondered if the military held him now, or whether Allenby had managed to keep him in his own custody, whether the blurted promise to tell all had tempted the man.

He scowled up at the cobwebbed ceiling. What a mess. What could he say? If Alicia had been running a spy ring, what the hell did he know about it?

He felt weary and out of ideas. His head ached and

he was bitterly hungry—the empty plate by the door hadn't been filled for hours. He would have given real money for a hot shower. Clean clothes. Even a tooth-brush.

He scowled.

This was useless. All he needed to do was examine the room, learn the routine, make plans.

The prison that could hold Jake Wilde hadn't been invented yet!

→→←←

Ten futile minutes later he knew that it had.

And that he was in it.

→→←←

On a gray day in early June my uncle summoned me to his study.

He said, "Well, my dear. It seems that today you finally come into your inheritance."

I was astonished. "My inheritance?"

He cleared his throat. He seemed a little ner-vous. "Indeed. You see, it is exactly ten years to the day that your father had his, er, unfortunate demise."

"He died? On this day?"

"Well . . . that is . . . An experiment must have gone wrong. The room was quite empty after the explosion. He could never have survived, of course, but his body must have been . . . entirely . . . My

dear, I do not wish to distress you. Such details are not for ladies. Let us say his body was never found. Which made legal difficulties, as you must know."

I sat tense with excitement. "I don't know. No one has ever told me this before."

"Er . . . yes." He was very uneasy. My uncle was a small man, usually quivering with self-importance. I began to feel a strange hope creep over me.

He glanced down at a cream vellum envelope that lay on the desk. "A letter has come for you. I of course opened it, as your guardian."

I gripped my hands together in anger. "I will take it now."

"There's no need. I will explain . . ."

I stood up. "I will take my letter, Uncle."

He looked a little startled. I took up the missive and opened it eagerly. As he strode to the window and stood with his hands behind his back, harrumphing at the dismal scene, I read these fascinating words.

Messrs. Queenhythe and Carbury
Solicitors at Law,
Staple Inn, London

Madam,

I beg to inform you that my client, your father,
Mr. John Harcourt Symmes, is from this date
legally declared deceased and that his estate,
house, and chattels now revert to you.

Should you or your representative care to apply
in person to our premises, we will supply you with
all further details.

May I offer my congratulations on your good
fortune, and commiserations on your loss.

I remain, Your most humble and obedient servant,
Marcus Queenhythe

I held the paper with trembling fingers. I could
nor believe what I was seeing. My dull life of
drudgery was over. I was an heiress!

My uncle turned. "I will of course set off immediately. The London house will need to be sold,
and any money—"

"No," I said quietly.

"I beg your pardon?"

I drew myself up. This was a moment I had dreamed of for years. I was not going to lose it now.

I said, "No, Uncle. I shall take the train to London myself tomorrow."

"You! You've never been out of Yorkshire in your life . . ."

"Then it's time I did." I folded the precious letter. "As for my father's house, it will not be sold. I intend to live there."

He gaped. "A single woman! In London!"

"I will be quite able to afford a servant."

"I utterly forbid it!"

Coolly I pocketed the letter and looked straight at him. "Uncle, you may bluster as you please. I often wondered why you took me in, when it was clear you had no love for me. Now I see that you must have been waiting eagerly for this day all along, thinking to obtain my father's money. Well, I thank you both for all your . . . care . . . over the years. Rest assured I will repay all the debts you may have incurred on my behalf. But tomorrow, by the first train, I will leave."

The years of humiliation and timidity and boredom were over!

As I marched to the door and closed it firmly

I looked back and saw him mop his bewildered brow with a white handkerchief. "Bless my soul," he breathed.

✦

Needless to say I lay awake all night in a trembling terror.

But next morning, bag in hand, my heart quaking with fear and excitement, my head held high, I climbed aboard a train for the first time in my life and set off.

For London!

Immense, brilliant, terrifying labyrinthine London!

8

. . . It is told that there was once a man of that
district named Oisin Venn. And that late one night
of February he rode home from the wars, and
wandered from the path, and long was he lured and
mired by feylights and willows o' the wisp in the
marshy places of the moor. And he came to a deep
wooded Combe and though he sensed somewhat of
the danger, he entered that place.

And he became aware of the eyes of dark birds
upon him, and of the malice of laughter.

Chronicle of Wintercombe

REBECCA DROVE CAREFULLY up the rutted lane.

Where it met the edge of the copse of firs, she parked
and climbed out.

The wind from the sea was cold; she pulled her coat
tighter, then hauled out her wellies. Pulling them on,
she turned and trudged up the narrow track, the bag of
groceries slung on her back.

Why he had to live out here, she had no idea.

There were cottages in the village for rent. Even on
the Wintercombe estate. But then, he was working feverishly on this spell-thing, and he needed quiet.

As she came to the top of the track and opened the

bleached wooden gate, she thought of Venn, down there in the ancient house, working equally obsessively with the obsidian mirror. The mirror that was Maskelyne's. Had they gotten it to work? Had Venn already changed time to bring back a dead woman? Had Jake found his father? She hadn't heard from Jake for weeks. The silence was unnerving.

A lapwing called and flew up, out of the gorse. The bushes were just starting to come into their mustard-yellow flowers, but something had frosted them hard. Term was half over. And she had so much work to do!

Trying to ignore the familiar guilt, she walked up and rapped on the back door. The cottage was a low, lopsided building, a Devon longhouse, once maybe the home of some medieval yeoman and his few animals. In the summer it was a holiday home for artists and romantic couples.

Now Maskelyne was camping out here.

"Come in, Becky."

She ducked under the lintel.

"Brought you the food. And . . ."

She stopped. "So you've finished, then."

Maskelyne was sitting at the oak table wearing an old overcoat, his chin propped on one hand, staring down at the peculiar pattern of discs before him. As he looked up at her, she caught that abstracted darkness in his eyes that seemed to be there more and more lately, since he had come so close to the mirror again. And the scar that disfigured his left cheek seemed deeper and more raw.

"I didn't hear you come up," he said.

She took off her coat and squeezed the rain from her long plait of red hair. "Too wrapped up in the spell."

"I told you, Becky, it's not a spell." He gestured at the discs. "It's not anything, yet."

She could tell by his barely hidden despair that it wasn't working. After a lifetime of watching him flicker like a ghost into her life, she knew the degrees of his anguish. She pulled a chair over. "What else would you call it?"

"A configuration. Have you finished your assignment?"

She shrugged. "Almost. The Wars of the Roses seem a long way off."

Maskelyne sighed. "If my problems affect your degree, I will never forgive myself."

She glanced around the room. "That's my business. I told you, it's fine."

The room was almost cozy today. He had drawn the curtains against the rain, and a small bright fire of furzewood crackled and spat in the open grate. From the rafters hung great bunches of grasses and herbs she had no names for; their pungent dusty leaves desiccating into dusty scatters on the floorboards. The room smelled of charred wood and damp.

On the table were the discs. He had spent every hour since Christmas working on them, and now, finally, twenty-four were laid out in a pattern of six by four.

They were a few centimeters across, and each was of a different material. Some were stone—she recognized granite, limestone, basalt brought from the moor, some greenish shale from the river. Others, like the white discs of chalk and the black one of coal he had had to search farther afield for, in Wiltshire and Wales, sometimes staying away for days. A flint disc lay roughly chipped in the center. She touched it lightly. Beside it lay circles of wood, brass, silver, steel and copper, of glass and paper, cork and cotton, various plastics cut from a credit card, labels, a shiny CD. Others that disturbed her more were cut from skin, fur, fleece. Some were materials she couldn't even identify, but certainly the central disc was of solid gold, resting in the center like a coin. It had cost a lot of money, some of it from her savings. This was the one he touched now, renewing a slow, silent process of moving the pieces, as if in some secret checkers game with himself, played endlessly, day and night.

"What will it do?" she murmured.

"It will bring them." His husky voice was patient. "It will bring Venn."

He moved a piece, sliding it with the softest of touches.

She went and put the kettle on, then came back, leaning closer.

Each of the discs was marked with a symbol. Some she recognized—the zodiac signs of Scorpio, Gemini, and so on. Others looked like warped letters.

She reached out to touch one.

"Don't!" he said quickly.

"What does that one mean?"

"Mercury. The planet of speed and quicksilver. The thieves' planet. This is Mars. This, Venus."

She nodded. The disc made of silver had a moon-crescent; the central gold one a rayed circle that must mean the sun. "Astrology? Alchemy?"

He smiled, even as he moved the discs. "Both and neither. A science so ancient only ghosts remember it."

She frowned. He rarely spoke about his life before he had leaped into the mirror. Jake had told her about Symmes's diary—how Symmes had stolen the mirror from Maskelyne in some dingy opium den, sometime in the 1840s. But before that, who had he been? How had he come to possess the mirror? She wanted to ask. Instead she said, "You should have something to eat. I've brought some stuff."

"Not yet." His nervous fingers touched a clay disc, then slid a copper one, lightly. She went to the kettle, lifted it off the stove, and was pouring the hot water when she stopped.

She looked up. "Something's happening," she whispered.

The room had changed. There was a new dimness in the corners, a delicate sparkling haze. She put down the kettle and turned.

Shadows.

They were drifting, flickering over the walls and ceiling. Like the flicker of the faintest black-and-white film, people barely there, ripples of silhouettes.

"What is it?"

He didn't answer. She crossed quickly to the table, scared by his silence. "What?"

The discs were moving.

With a sigh of satisfaction Maskelyne drew his fingers away, and still they moved. Their pattern was rapid, hard to see, a swift, silent rearrangement as if the elements themselves had taken up the dance, moving with purposeful gravity.

"How is that . . ."

"Hush. Watch."

As the colors formed and re-formed, Rebecca wondered if they were making themselves into galaxies, into a set of concentric circles like some ancient diagram of the cosmos, some drifting clockwise, others counterclockwise, around the golden coin of the sun.

Maskelyne watched, tense.

The room darkened. The discs seemed to glow, marble and plastic and metal.

Then they stopped.

Breath held, she stared at the new configuration. Through the gently shimmering smoke she said, "Have you done it? What does it mean?"

Maskelyne sat back in the chair. For a moment he seemed too exhausted to speak. He said, "It means they'll come, Becky. They'll need me."

Then to her surprise, he picked up the central disc and rapped it gently three times on the tabletop.

Knock. Knock. Knock.

"Oh hell and damnation!"

Piers flung down the pen in irritation and jumped up. Whisking off his apron, he struggled into his dark tailcoat, buttoning it hurriedly over his scarlet waistcoat as he half ran down the corridor.

The tiled hall was quiet. Wharton and Sarah were up with the mirror, probably.

But who could have gotten through the locked gates and up the drive?

He flitted across the hall, reached the front door, threw it open, and looked out.

The steps were empty.

Beyond them the overgrown drive was blurred with

rain, the tall grass of the lawns rippled with broken tulips in the cold breeze.

No one.

Piers put his hands together, flexed them till the knuckles cracked, stepped back, and closed the door.

Inside, he stared at its dark wood, thinking hard.

Because he had definitely heard them.

Three soft knocks.

Gideon ducked under oak boughs, breathless. The very air kept changing. He was lost in the tilted, angled, colliding worlds of the Summerland.

He stopped for breath, fighting down panic.

Here was an empty piazza, a dry fountain at its center. The air shimmered with heat.

He crouched down, wiping sweat from his face. He knew better than to trust his eyes, because only a few paces away, the sunlit square had a shadow slanting into it, rising at a bizarre angle to a glass skyscraper.

A pigeon fluttered down; his whole body jumped.

Any bird could be Shee.

Any snake, any lizard, any cat.

Any narrow face at a window could be Shee.

In this Otherworld, the very stones and trees might be spying on him. And with a surge of panic he realized the bracelet would draw them. With his Shee-sharp sight he saw how it glowed on his wrist, heard how it sang. It pulsed with power, it smelled of pollen and honey, and the Shee would swarm to it like wasps.

He had to get out!

Taking a breath, he raced through the piazza into a meadow. Beyond it a blue ocean stretched, with tiny islands green as jewels. Crashing down the hill, he saw dryads twist into olive trees, a kraken dive into the waves. Gideon ran onto the beach, up the gangplank of a moored quinquereme, its slaves oiled with sweat, then leaped an oar and landed swaying in the sudden roar of a train corridor rattling through streets and factories. Grabbing the window rail, he edged down the aisle, unseen by passengers, opened a carriage door, and walked into a golden field of barley.

Gritting his teeth, he waded through the waist-high crop.

These were the secret ways of the Shee, their unseen paths through the world, barely glimpsed by mortals, except in certain, potent intersections—a fairy ring, a haunted room, a crossroads at twilight, notorious for generations as places of danger. He was deep in the Otherworld, and any moment the whole scene would reset as if someone had shaken the pieces of a kaleidoscope. It was a place of madness, and he knew every time he traveled in it, it contorted his very reason.

He felt a tickle on his wrist and looked down. A

tangle of white bindweed had slid around the bracelet. The green stem explored, curious.

He shook it off quickly.

Out! Where was out!

In the center of the field, as if it had crash-landed from space and been half buried by the impact, tilted at a crazy angle, was a castle.

He climbed through the ruined barbican and came to a great wooden gate. It was locked, but in it was a smaller postern, cut so tiny he had to kneel to open it.

He squeezed his head and shoulders through.

Instantly, as if they had been waiting for him, bees swarmed down.

Gideon beat the buzzing things away, scrambled through, and ran. Through an orchard, ducking under apple trees, into a silent and deserted school where the classrooms slept in summer heat, out through a rabbit hutch, where three identical rabbits watched him with huge eyes.

Then a corridor, stark, gray, one fluorescent light strip buzzing overhead. As he looked up the strip came apart, and became the swarm again, bright electric bees that clustered around him, stung him, so that he ducked and twisted with increasing panic, flung a door open, threw himself through.

Venn grabbed him. "Down!"

Gideon collapsed, gasping for breath. Venn gave

one ferocious yell at the bright buzzing swarm. "Leave him! NOW!"

His voice was savage with wrath.

Instantly there was nothing there to shout at.

Gideon slid to the grass and sat there, stunned. When he could look around, he saw a small glade of bluebells. Above, oak trees, just coming into tiny new leaf.

He was at the edge of the Wood.

He was back.

"Listen," he gasped. "Jake . . ."

"Not here!" Venn hauled him up, then noticed the bracelet on his wrist. With a cry of joy, he slid it off and gripped it tight. Then he ran out of the Wood, up the path and through the small metal gate to the cloister, its threshold protected with an iron strip, its bars hung with charms.

Gideon followed, limping and sore. Passing over the iron made him shiver, but he felt nothing of the peculiar jagged pain it seemed to give the Shee.

"Venn, wait."

He was irritable with stings and scratches. Venn dragged him to a bench, flung him down, and stood over him. "Right. Tell me. Is Jake alive?"

Sarah burst out through the cloister door, a glass of water in her hand. She pushed it into Gideon's trembling fingers. "Take your time."

The cold water was blissful. He gulped it down so fast it almost choked him. Then, looking up, he saw Wharton was there, behind her, looking as if he had aged ten years.

"Where's Jake? Where is he?"

"Don't blame me." Gideon put the glass down. "I tried to get him back, but he's so . . . stubborn. And then the bars in the window . . ." He stopped, trying to get his thoughts together because the Summerland did that to you, shattered your mind, left you in pieces.

Deliberately he said, "Jake is in a city where a war is happening. Metal is falling from the sky and smashing the houses. He said to give you this."

He put down the black velvet bag and out of it took the steel film canister.

Sarah picked it up. "Film? Of what?"

"And is Jake all right?" Wharton demanded.

Gideon drank the last drop of water. "He's fine. Except that he's in a dungeon. And likely to be hanged."

9

Jake has charm if he cares to use it. He can be most persuasive. His academic ability is not in doubt. He has spectacular confidence in his own judgment—which is often at fault.

He seems to trust no one but himself. Frankly, I think he'd make a good politician.

Or a spy.

End of term confidential report; Compton's School; G. Wharton

London!

I had never imagined a place so frantic. My soul thrilled to the motor cars, trains, horses and carriages! The thronged pavements of people— beggars, thieves, duchesses, bankers—all strolling among a bedlam of street vendors who cried every ware from violets to soap to ointment that would remedy hair loss for the modern gentleman.

But when I finally walked under the ancient archway of Staple Inn, I found myself in a sudden haven of quiet; an old stone courtyard surrounding great trees, their leaves just budding in the spring sunshine.

I was ushered into the offices of Messrs.

Queenhythe and Carbury, Solicitors at Law, to find a very tall young man with a walrus mustache who introduced himself as Marcus Queenhythe. I must have looked terribly tired from my bewildering journey, because he instantly poured me tea from a brown china pot.

"And you walked all the way from Euston? My dear Miss Symmes . . ."

"I had no idea which omnibus to take." I drank the tea thirstily. "There were so many."

"Of course. Well, we will have a cab to your house. That is if you wish me to attend you."

"Oh please. I would so like it."

Your house.

My heart beat with quiet pride. I sat up straight and tried to look like a woman of property. But I could not help but be aware that Mr. Queenhythe seemed unaccountably nervous. He stroked his mustache with inky fingers. "There is a little . . . that is . . . you may be a little disturbed by the . . . er, state of the property."

"In what way?" I tried to sound confident, but my heart sank, as if at some hidden dread.

"It has been unoccupied for many years. And your late father was a noted eccentric. There are heaps of books and papers . . ."

I was relieved. "Oh, papers. I can deal with those."

"And . . . um, machinery. There seems to be some sort of peculiar invention. In the study. Wiring and such. It fills the room."

I waved a hand. "It can be dismantled and sold. Shall we go now?" Because I was burning with impatience.

He sent the clerk for the keys, and sat at the desk. He did not meet my eye. "I think . . . If I may be so bold as to advise you, Miss Symmes, perhaps a hotel would be better. Until . . ."

"No hotel." I rose, so he had to scramble up, startled. I kept my voice firm. "I intend to sleep in my own house. Mr. Queenhythe, may I ask what it is that you are not telling me?"

I detected a certain panic in his voice. He stood, turning his back and arranging his cravat in the mirror. Finally he said, "In point of fact, Miss Symmes, though I consider them foolish, there are rumors about the house. We have found it impossible to keep a servant there. They all leave very quickly. They say . . ."

His hand shook a little on the tie. ". . . that the house is haunted."

He watched me anxiously in the glass.

I must admit to a certain cold shiver around the heart.

But I drew myself up. "Ghosts, sir, do not trouble me."

⇥⇤

However, when the cab arrived before the dilapidated frontage, I admit to being a little daunted. The house was a fine Georgian building in a grand square, but trees had been allowed to grow and overshadow it, and the shutters were closed and dark, like blind eyes. Ivy obscured the upstairs, and strange scorch marks starred from what must have been the study window. As I climbed the steps and waited for Mr. Queenhythe to undo the padlocks, I felt as if my mysterious father was still here, gazing down at me curiously from some attic. When I glanced up, the panes were dark.

We entered the hall. A peculiar smell of charred metal seemed to hang there, even after so many years.

"This was the drawing room. The dining room is in here. The morning room. And this was Mr. Symmes's study, I believe."

He opened a door onto a room crowded with dark masses of sheeted furniture. I put a hand out and touched an armchair. My fingers came away covered with a film of brown dust. "Does no one clean?"

"As I said, we have had problems. The last cleaner refused to return. She spoke of footsteps. Movements where no one was."

I opened the shutters. Pale daylight fell on my father's desk, his chair, and revealed by it, suddenly, there in the corner, I saw her. A gangly awkward young woman, drably dressed, her face thin and pale, her glance startled. I moved, and so did she. And then I realized this was no ghost but myself, reflected, and I put a hand to my cheek in dismay, because for a moment I had seen myself as a stranger sees me, a lost girl, away from all the certainties and fixtures of my life.

I recovered myself because Mr. Queenhythe was observing me, and stepping forward, removed the rest of the sheets.

To reveal the mirror.

It was tall and made of some curious glossy black glass.

It reflected the room as a slanting, warped space, the walls distorted, the windows bulging outward. Coils of wiring led from it into the heaped and piled corners of the room. I picked one up, and it curled in my hand with a strange *friction that made me drop it, quickly. Behind me, the mirror showed Mr. Queenhythe laying a pile of documents on the desk.*

"These are your father's will, his diaries and letters. If you would care to sign here, and . . . just here, our business is concluded."

He wanted to be out of the place. I could sense his nervousness. I crossed the room and signed the papers with what I hoped was a defiant flourish. He put the keys down on the desk, gathered his effects, and hurried into the hall. I trailed after him.

"If there is anything you need," he said, his look suddenly intent and urgent. "Anything at all, Miss Symmes, please don't hesitate to contact us. At any hour."

Rather unnerved, I put out my hand and he shook it.

At that moment a soft sound startled us.

Knock.

Knock.

Knock.

It echoed through the empty hall and dusty stairwell.

We looked at each other. "Now who can that be?" he said. He marched to the front door and flung it open.

There was no one there.

Mr. Queenhythe stepped out and looked up and down the street. The pavements were empty. But I thought I heard, as if from somewhere far, the giggle of children.

"Some scoundrel playing tricks," he said. "Well. I wish you the best of luck, Miss Symmes. The very best of luck."

It was only when I had closed the door on his hurried departure, and turned to face the dark stair and the silent house, that I allowed myself a secret smile.

Ghosts were just what I needed.

I was my father's daughter, after all.

❧⚜☙

Allenby took another pull at the cigarette and stared at Jake through the coil of blue smoke. "Let me get this straight. You want me to take you—a prisoner on remand—out of here, across the bomb craters of London, to a smashed-up house in a street that no longer exists?"

Jake nodded.

"You really have a nerve, Wilde."

Jake leaned back. "It's the only way. If you want Alicia's spy network, you have to take me to her house."

"Her house is in smithereens!"

"Not all of it." Jake leaned forward. "Come on. Your

men must have been digging about in there. They've found it, haven't they. You know they have. The mirror. The machine."

He made his voice as confident and enticing as he could, but in truth he felt sick and desperate. He had barely eaten for days—the muck they gave him was inedible—and his brain was weary and fuzzy from broken sleep, because at night the cells were crammed with drunks and infuriatingly noisy women. But at least they were keeping him here. There was no sign of the military. Allenby wanted the credit for this for himself.

Allenby crunched the cigarette in the ashtray. The door opened; the sergeant came in with two mugs on a tray. As he set them down, he gave Jake a particularly filthy look.

Jake grabbed the tea with both handcuffed hands and drank it gratefully. The hot sweetness was a glorious comfort.

Allenby watched. His calm, alert face was hard to read.

"What is this machine?"

"I told you. Alicia used a very strange device. It won't have been destroyed. It looks . . . appears . . . to be made of glass. Black glass."

A flicker. Hardly anything, in those steady eyes. But Jake was sure.

He put the mug down. "You *have* found it."

After a moment Allenby said, "Let's say we've recovered . . . something. Something we don't understand. But . . ."

"Take me there. I'll get it working for you."

Their eyes met across the table. It was a game of chess, Jake thought, with London the board and himself as one of the pawns, the smallest of pieces. But it had to work, because if Gideon failed him, he certainly wasn't going to be stuck here for the rest of his life.

Allenby sighed. Abruptly, he scraped the chair back and stood. "I must be a bloody fool," he said.

⇢·⇠

Sarah said, "You can't do it, can you?"

Piers, sitting on the floor among a pile of wiring as big as he was, looked at Venn.

"It's not that I can't do it exactly," he said warily. "I mean, given time, given a bit of leeway, I could. But to be honest, I'd rather work on that page you brought."

"Jake needs us now!" She scrambled up and walked angrily to the mirror, staring into its enigmatic curves.

The mirror slanted her own gaze back at her. She knew Piers and Venn had been up all night re-aligning it. Once, they had tried to activate it. At four o'clock a shudder of noise and energy had rippled terrifyingly through the house, waking her and sending her racing out into the dark corridor and crashing into Wharton's startled panic.

"What the hell was that?" he'd yelled.

Now he lay in an armchair dozing, his maroon dressing gown tied tight over a pair of ridiculous pajamas with little anchors all over them.

She looked at the film canister. "Can we see this?"

"I'll have to find the old projector," Piers said, not looking up.

She frowned. Then she touched the bracelet. Gideon had told her about the Blitzed world. And Jake was there, locked up in some cell, fuming with restlessness and fear. She knew how that felt.

"Where's Gideon?"

"Gone back to the Shee." Wharton yawned. "Everything needs to seem normal. If Summer knew . . . Really, sometimes I fear for that poor boy's sanity."

Venn had said nothing for ages. He watched Sarah, his glance sharp and cold.

She said, "Listen to me. We can't just work in the dark. We don't have any more time to experiment and get things wrong over and over. If we make a mistake, we could miss him by years. We could be too late." She turned to face him. "You know what to do, and you don't have any choice about it. There's only one man who can possibly help us now, and that man is Maskelyne."

Venn, leaning on the filing cabinet, stood upright.

He walked slowly into the very heart of the labyrinth and stood beside her, and the dark glass showed her his face, subtly warped. He said quietly, "How can I trust you, Sarah? How can I ever be sure of you? What we want is so different."

"What we want is the same." She turned on him. "Jake back. David found. Leah saved."

"And then?"

"Then you give me the mirror."

He smiled, remote. "You make it all sound so easy." He gazed at the dark reflection of the room, the mess of machinery, Piers sitting exhausted and cross-legged among the tangle. "You! What do you say?"

"I think she's right, Excellency."

Venn took the bracelet from Sarah's hand and held it up in his frostbitten fingers. She saw how its silver enigma angered him, how frustration and despair were eating him away. Without looking at her, his voice a low snarl, he said, "Do it."

She turned fast, grabbed Wharton, and shook him awake. "George. Get dressed. Get the car. Quick."

→⤝

High on the moors, the air was frosty in the dawn. The sun was barely up, struggling through a great bank of cloud in the east, and as the car rocked and bounced along the frozen track, she had to grab the map to keep it open on her lap. "Be careful!"

Wharton drove grimly. "What about my suspension! Are you sure it's up here?"

"So Piers says."

How Piers had found out where the scarred man was living, she had no idea. But the rutted track led to a gate tied with rope, and as she jumped out to open it, she saw the stunted trees of a small pine copse, and beyond, far on the horizon, pale as a diamond, the sea.

She stopped, astonished.

"Sarah?"

She had never seen a sea so beautiful. She stared at it in utter delight. Wharton got out of the car and came up behind her. He said quietly, "So how is the sea different at the End of the world?"

"It just is."

"You could tell me." He sounded fascinated. "You should tell us, Sarah, about how it is there. About what Janus has . . . will do to the world. Maybe the mistakes need never be made . . ."

She glanced at him then, at his wide-eyed curiosity, thinking again how naïve these people were, in their green world with their clean water and ancient buildings and comfortable, convenient lives. How to them the future was something that they would never see. A story, nothing more.

For a fierce, angry moment she just wanted to shock him violently out of his complacency. But she made herself shake her head. "Not now, George. I couldn't even begin."

Before he could answer, she had unlooped the rope and pulled the gate open, lifting its heavy metal bars out of the stiff mud. "Leave the car. This track's too narrow."

He took the keys and let the door slam, loud and alien in the silent morning. The track was lined with gorse bushes, their furzy branches already green, and small sturdy bluebells lurked in the bottom of the scrappy, sheep-gnawed hedge. Walking down, Sarah felt the soft rustle and brush of the rough grass against her legs calming her, the wind whipping her coat wide.

Wharton came behind, watching her. He knew she had almost told him something then, had been on the edge of some revelation, and drawn back. The girl who could become invisible still held so many secrets. Now she was pointing into the wind. "That must be it."

A small Devon long-house of whitened stone, its lichened roof below them in a fold of the hills.

"It looks quiet."

"Not empty. The chimney."

A thin wisp of smoke dissipated as he looked.

They hurried down the steep track. Opening the gate, Sarah walked up to the door and raised her hand, but before she could knock, it was opened.

Maskelyne stood there, winding a scarf around his

neck. He wore a dark coat. She saw the livid scar that disfigured his face, and behind him, in the gloom of the interior, a table set with scattered pieces like an abandoned board game.

"I've been waiting for you," he said, his voice choked with eagerness. "Let's go."

10

I will arise when the Three shall call me.
And when the Wood shall Walk.

Tombstone in Old Wintercombe Churchyard

IN THE POLICE van driving across London, Jake was chained to the burly sergeant and squashed against the window. It was raining, a cold relentless downpour, and the streets were sloping sheets of gray, of tilted umbrellas and glossy slick awnings.

He had seen this era in black and white so often its colors surprised him now; the soft reds and greens of women's clothing, the huge advertisements painted on walls, the navy uniforms of a file of schoolchildren crossing the road. The last in the line, a little boy, turned and stared at him.

"Shouldn't those kids . . . children, be evacuated?" Jake said.

"Some of 'em come back. Others never left. Can't stand the quiet." The sergeant too was gazing out in a silence. Finally, shaking his head, he said, "Bloody war. God knows how it will end."

Jake kept still. Like God, he did know how it

would end. Looking at the shattered houses, the bombed streets, the weary defiance of the people, he was tempted to say something, to offer comfort, to just mutter *It's all right. You'll win.* It surprised him; usually he took care not to feel sorry for people. Also, it would be stupid, and just provoke the man's scorn. So he kept his mouth shut and concentrated on his plan. Get close to the mirror. And then . . . if somehow he could activate it . . . But if Allenby was there, if Allenby saw . . .

He shrugged. Nothing he could do about that. Allenby would see a boy disappear into a pulsating blackness and hopefully would never know how it was done.

And then what? He would have *journeyed* blindly, without the bracelet. He thought of Maskelyne's terrifying story of being stretched endlessly across centuries, of arriving agonizingly slowly, atom by atom, into a new and unguessable place, while time sped past him like a film on fast-forward. That would happen to him. He could end up anywhere.

He fidgeted against the big warm body squashed in beside him.

"Keep still," the sergeant muttered. "Bloody nuisance."

In the front, Allenby turned, the leather seat squeaking. "We're nearly there. You look worried, Jake."

"So would you," he growled, "facing the gallows."

It was hard to recognize the bombed-out street. He remembered it from Symmes's time, a neat square with a garden in the middle where he had hidden with Moll. Now the place was a wasteland of bricks, a broken chimney sticking up, small bent people moving slowly over the surface, heads down, picking up anything they could find.

Jake said, "Her body . . ."

"Not found yet. Right, stop here. This is it."

There was hastily erected white tape around part of the site. Three policemen stood guard. Inside that, over part of the demolished house was a green-gray camouflaged tent, its door fastened shut.

As Jake struggled out, rain spattered on the roof of the car, and far off over the dome of St. Paul's the sun came out in a splash of blue sky between the floating barrage balloons.

The sergeant looked at Allenby, who shrugged. "Unlock the chain. Keep the handcuffs."

Jake watched as the link between them was undone, tugged out, and disappeared into the sergeant's pocket.

Allenby watched too. "This is your last chance with me, Jake. One more mistake, one more stupid escape bid and it's out of my hands."

He knew that.

They stumbled and picked their way over the bomb

site. Jake glanced around, rapidly trying to take in everything in sight. Where was Gideon? Where was Venn? They had to be here. They had to be trying to save him.

The doorway to the camouflaged tent yawned before him like a dark portal.

He hurried toward it, eager, thinking he glimpsed within the black slab of the mirror.

Something smacked into the side of his face.

He turned, furious. "Hey!"

A small blue football bounced away into rubble.

"Sorry." A small boy in gray shorts and a school blazer stood there gazing at him. Just behind, knee-deep among the bricks, two of the identical triplets smiled.

Jake stared. "You!"

The sergeant scowled. "Clear off, you kids."

"No . . . Wait!" Jake made a move toward them. The handcuffs clinked. "You were the ones in the Underground shelter . . . You said . . ."

"Hello, Jake Wilde. Don't forget the Black Fox."

"You said that before. What does it mean . . ."

"Or the Man with the Eyes of a Crow."

The third child came so close he could have touched him. "Or the Box of Red Brocade."

Jake dropped his voice to a whisper. "Who are you? Where are you from?"

The tiny boy put his bullet head on one side and

smiled up at him, spectacles bright with the clear, daunting stare of infancy. "Don't you know, Jake?"

"Are you from Summer? Are you Shee?"

The boy smiled pityingly. He reached up on his highest tiptoes and put his lips to Jake's ear; Jake had to bend to hear the words. *"We are Janus, Jake. That's who we are."*

He jerked back, heart hammering. The child nodded, poised and secret. "You see, Jake. We know all your problems. We can give you what you want, Jake. We can give you your father."

Jake kept still. Made himself say: "And in return?"

The children drew together and held hands. They sang:

Don't let Sarah destroy the mirror
destroy the mirror
destroy the mirror.
Don't let Sarah destroy the mirror
ee I ee I o.

"Clear off, you kids!" the sergeant roared.

They fled, laughing and giggling across the brickfield.

Jake stared after them. Then he was grabbed and forced inside the camouflaged door.

→·←

Maskelyne walked into the brightness of the labyrinth and stared around, at the mirror festooned with cable, at Piers in his white coat, at three of the black cats sleeping in the tangle of malachite-green webbing.

Piers eyed him, sour as acid. "Oh great. So you're back again."

"You can't do this without me." The scarred man crossed to the desk and picked up the bracelet. He turned it, and in his fine fingers it seemed almost to move and rotate with delicate precision. "It's about time you realized that."

Venn was standing in an agitated stillness in the shadows. He came forward and faced Maskelyne, his hair a blond brightness in the strong lights. Maskelyne seemed a shadow before him, a dark copy, a reflection, thinner, barely there.

"Did you create the mirror?" Venn breathed. "How did it come to you, all those years ago, before Symmes stole it? Did you really dig it from some forgotten grave?"

Maskelyne did not answer. Instead he said quietly, "It knows I'm here."

"Good Lord," Wharton muttered, eyes wide.

Because the silver frame of the obsidian glass was indeed strangely alight, the slanted silver inscription no one could read running with ripples of energy.

The lights flickered. One of the cats sat up and spat.

Piers muttered, "Output has just increased. One kilowatt, and rising."

Venn didn't move. "Do you know," he said, his voice arctic, "how to get to exactly *when* Jake is?"

Maskelyne lifted the bracelet. "I think I could find out," he said.

→→←←

Well, it was just what I wanted.

A haunted house!

I cleaned it, had the furniture repaired, engaged a maidservant and a cook, had such fun buying some new carpets and curtains in the smart new department stores of Oxford Street. I opened the shutters and the windows and let the foggy air of London in to invigorate it.

What I did next will surprise you, though. I had posters and invitations printed, on pale violet card, with gilt letters. They read:

Madam Alicia
Spiritualist and Medium.
Do you have a loved one on the Other Side?
Madam Alicia can help you.
Séances, scrying, the tables and the cups.
Respectable and reasonable rates.
Discretion guaranteed.

It may appear amateur now, but at the time I was delighted with it, and thought myself the height of fashion.

Because of course I had to have some source of income.

And I had always wanted to see ghosts.

It was my secret. I had never told anyone, certainly not my hideous uncle and simpering aunt. But always, as far back as I can remember, I had desired desperately one glimpse of the supernatural. I haunted graveyards and crossroads, hoping for a vision of a girl faint as a cobweb, a headless horseman, a faery funeral crossing the road between the muddy carriage wheels. The idea of ghosts did not frighten me. On the contrary, I burned for such an experience. It seemed to me as if they must be still all around, like the echoes of people, doing the things they had always done, for years, barely knowing they were dead, still absorbed in their lives. An old man who lived in the village had a reputation for second sight, and once I managed to ask him about it. He told me he saw many spirits. Some were easy to see, he said, or even speak to. Others—the older ones, in ruff and gown and breeches—

were so very pale they were nothing more than a disturbance of the air, like the ripple above a hot plate.

And their voices, he said, were like the rustle of the breeze in oak leaves, a high whisper that no one but him could hear.

I had read all the Gothic novels, every weird tale. I had no talent to make a living out of, no accomplishments. But as soon as I had seen the house, with its fine paneling and stately rooms, I had had the idea.

I would set myself up as a medium, and become rich! London was full of such practitioners. It was the height of fashion for ladies to visit séances or mesmerists, to be thrilled when the glass moved on the tabletop and spelled out mysterious messages. It would be easy to arrange such things, to deliver messages—true or false—from the dead.

There would be a delicious and necessary degree of deception, of course. But maybe one day, if I sought and practiced hard, a ghost would truly come to me.

I gazed at myself in the dark mirror, proud and hugging myself in delight.

What could possibly go wrong!

→→←

"Are you sure?" Venn leaned over the desk, intent.

"As I can be. Operate this"—Maskelyne indicated a small switch—"and the mirror will allow us to see where he is."

"We'll be looking *through it*?" Wharton too was fascinated. "How?"

"The bracelet has been there. The mirror remembers."

At the back of the huddle Sarah glanced at Piers. The small man was officiously tidying away all the tools and wiring he could find. Catching her eye, he muttered, "I would have worked that out. Eventually."

"Of course you would," she said, soothing.

The aggrieved look died instantly. "You think so?"

"Yes. And Piers—no one will solve Dee's ciphers but you."

He seemed to swell with pride. One of the black cats stopped licking itself to watch, its green eyes slants of scorn.

Venn straightened. Without another word, he clicked the switch.

They saw a dim, greenish interior, its walls rippling.

"What is that?" For a moment Sarah had no idea.

"A tent," Wharton breathed, "and look!"

The door was opened and fastened back. Beyond it they saw the bombed street, a glimpse of devastated wartime London.

Jake was shoved in. He was dirty and unkempt and there was a desperate look in his eyes that scared Sarah at once. His hands were cuffed together.

"Right." Venn turned at once. "This is what we do."

→·←

To see the mirror again sent a thrill of relief and purpose through him.

Its tilted black surface looked exactly the same— there was no scratch, no crack in its perfection, its dark depths showed nothing. Even the silver frame was here, dented and battered, but recognizable.

Jake looked his weary reflection in the face. How to do this?

Allenby, behind him, said, "Is this it?"

"Yes." He turned. "I want the handcuffs off. And no one in here but you and me."

The inspector considered him. Then he turned. "Evans, outside."

"Guv . . ."

"I can handle this. Stay in the street. No one comes past the roadblock."

With one last glare at Jake, the sergeant marched out. They heard him clambering awkwardly over the rubble.

Allenby brought out the leather fob with the key to the handcuffs. But he held it tight.

"First, explain to me what you're going to do."

Jake took a deep breath. "You're in over your head,

Inspector. Alicia wasn't a spy, she was a double agent. Both she and I work for British Intelligence."

Allenby's gaze didn't flicker. Did he believe it? Jake let his imagination race. "The mirror is a highly secret communication device and must not be allowed to fall into enemy hands. I can use it now . . . this minute . . . to contact . . . my superiors. Unlock me."

Allenby didn't move. But he lit up a cigarette and his yellow fingers were shaky. "How do I know . . ."

"You don't know. I've had enough of this. Unlock me. Or your career is over."

In the silence Jake was aware of the vast and wounded city outside, the hundreds of thousands of people all around him, working and injured and scared, not knowing that here, in its heart, was the black hole that could eat them all.

A car door slammed.

Voices argued, somewhere close.

"All right." Allenby seemed to decide all at once. He stepped close to Jake. But before he could unlock the cuffs, the door was flung open. Two men in uniform barged in. They wore red caps and each carried a revolver.

The military.

Jake swore. Allenby turned.

"What's going on? This is police business. You have no right . . ."

"I have every right." The tall officer stared at them both with icy authority. "You sir, will leave now. Wait at the roadblock with your men."

"You can't order me. I'm not under your command."

"This is war, sir." The revolver was raised, just a fraction. "Step outside."

Allenby glanced at Jake. He drew himself up. Very formally he said, "I'm sorry Mr. Wilde. There's nothing I can do. Good luck." He reached out and dropped the key into the officer's outstretched hand.

Then he ducked through the tent flap.

At once they moved. Venn grabbed Jake tight. "George! Stand close! *Close!*"

Jake took one last look around. Wharton was staring out at the street, his eyes wide. "This is amazing!" he was muttering. "Bloody bloody bloody amazing."

Venn grabbed him and yelled at the mirror. *"We're coming now, Piers!"*

The sound rang out like a gunshot across the bomb site. Allenby swore, threw down the cigarette, and ran, all his men stumbling after him.

He flung open the tent door and stared in astonishment.

The mirror stood in its tilted splendor. Apart from that, the tent was empty.

Gasping behind him, the sergeant's breath was hot on his neck. "Bloody hell! Where did they go!"

Allenby had no answer. "More to the point," he said, grim, "where did they come from?"

→→←←

"Are you all right?" Sarah hurriedly unlocked the handcuffs as Jake stood on the floor of the lab as if in a daze.

"Fine. I gather Gideon got back, then."

"Eventually. You must have been terrified."

He wasn't listening. Instead, so slowly and deliberately that it scared her, he reached out and took the greasy key-fob that had been Allenby's out of her fingers and stared at it. It was old, well-worn red leather. On it was the metal image of a fox, with a mouse dangling from its grinning mouth. *Johnson's Car Repairs,* it said, *Black Fox Lane, High Holborn.*

"What?" she said, anxious.

He looked at her, disbelieving. As if he couldn't trust what he saw.

"The Black Fox will release you," he whispered.

Cans't thou not minister to a mind diseased,
Pluck from the memory a rooted sorrow?

11

Of course my marriage was a failure from the
start. Moll saw to that. Moll with her cheeky
urchin ways, with the run of the house, with her
increasingly bold plans to find us a bracelet, to travel
to the future, to find Jake Wilde.

I had also grown far too fond of the little scrap.

When my wife said, "She goes or I do," I'm afraid
it was not a difficult decision.

Diary of John Harcourt Symmes

SARAH SAT ON the end of her bed and stared at the
open pages of the notebook.

Downstairs, in the sleeping house, a clock pinged
three silver chimes.

With the black pen she had scrawled:

What's happening there? Tell me!

No answer. The writing faded before her eyes.

This was the third time tonight she had begged him,
increasingly despairing, and she knew he had read it.
Far off in time, surrounded by his empire, powered by
the ferocious energy of the mirror, Janus was tormenting her with silence.

She flung down the pen and went to the window. It

was a wild, windy night. Since Summer's furious tempest, the weather had been a constant gale; now the lawns of Wintercombe were silvered by a moon half hidden in streaming cloud.

Tugging the dressing gown around her, she hugged herself, staring out stonily at the storm. Janus was the future, but for everyone else, he didn't exist yet. For Jake, Wharton, even for Venn, that world was only a possibility, something that didn't need to be thought about. For her it was real.

Her past.

Her life.

Her parents.

It was as real as standing here, or that Blitz-shattered London Jake had told them about around the fire last night, his hands, still red from the manacles, tight around the battered mug of coffee.

She thought about this house in that century to come, its ruined state, the collapsing wings, the charred timbers of the fire-blackened roof. That was Wintercombe too.

And in that time the mirror was consuming the world.

She turned, alert.

From the corridor outside had come the very faintest of creaks. Holding her breath, still as a shadow, she listened.

Someone was padding, very quietly, past her room.

She crossed barefoot to the door, opened it, and put her eye to the slit.

It was Jake. He was wearing his gray striped dressing gown and had the monkey on his shoulder. As she watched he stopped at Wharton's door, tapped on it softly, and slid in.

She didn't hesitate. Deep inside her mind was the switch that would make her invisible. Janus's gift, that she hated to use. But now she let it operate, felt its warm *itch* flare in her skin.

She slipped out quietly.

Wharton's bedroom was the last in the corridor, near the servants' stairs down to the kitchen. Crossing the landing, under the owl-faced grandfather clock, she felt a cool draft from the dark spaces below move against her bare legs.

The bedroom door was not quite closed. Voices murmured inside, but even with her ear pressed against the gap she couldn't hear what they were saying, so she edged it wider, turned sideways, and slipped in.

Wharton was sitting up in bed looking bleary. "For God's sake Jake, can't it wait . . ."

"I can't sleep! I have to talk to someone."

"Tomorrow . . ."

"No, *now*!" He dumped the monkey irritably; it jumped into an open drawer of the tallboy and began to rummage through Wharton's carefully matched socks.

"Oh stop that," the big man growled.

Jake was a shadow on the window seat, crumpled and morose. Wharton clicked on the reading lamp and looked around sleepily. As his glance swept across her, Sarah flinched, but it was clear he saw nothing.

So she slid down and squatted by the door.

Wharton said, into the silence, "Must have been tough for you in that place. Locked up. Handcuffed!"

"It's not that. I could handle that."

Yeah right. Wharton allowed the thought to yawn through him. "Don't be so ridiculously heroic, Jake. You went through a terrible experience and it would have been hell, not knowing if you'd ever get back. There's no shame in that. I tell you, even the brief half hour I spent in . . . the mirror . . . shook me to the core."

He could hardly believe it even now, the alien, oddly wrong smell of the wartime past, the disconcerting loss of certainty there, the utter disbelief that had almost frozen him.

Jake snorted. "Where did Venn get the uniforms?"

"Piers produced them. I don't know where he keeps all that stuff."

"Piers has a lot of abilities we don't know about."

Jake's whisper was low and grim. "It's clear he's some sort of Shee himself." He stood up and came toward Sarah so abruptly she knelt up, alarmed, but he just closed the door firmly and turned the key in the lock. Then he went back and sat on the bed.

"There's something I didn't tell the others. About the children."

"What children?"

"Three kids. Three identical boys. They looked about ten. They were in the Underground station where I slept. There was something really weird about them. They knew my name."

Wharton sat up wearily, starting to pay attention. "Go on."

"They said . . . each of them said . . . a sort of prophecy. As if they could see the future. And then just before you lot turned up, I saw them again on the bomb site. This time I asked them who they were."

"What does it . . ."

"They said *We are Janus.*"

Wharton's eyes widened. Then his gaze flickered to the door, as if somehow he had sensed the jolt of shock that had made Sarah clamp spread fingers over her mouth.

"Janus? But Venn killed Janus . . ."

"Venn killed a replicant of him. But in that weird future Sarah never talks about, Janus controls the mirror.

So who knows what he can do with it? Or how many copies of himself he can make? Anyway, that's what the kid said. And then he . . . it . . . laughed."

Wharton shook his head. He opened the bedside drawer and took out a jumbo bar of fruit and nut chocolate, and snapped some off. Cramming it into his mouth, he muttered, "Great. As if we didn't have enough problems."

At the rustle of the silver paper Horatio dropped like a stone from the chandelier in a shower of dust; he sat on Wharton's stomach, huge eyes wide.

"Get that thing off me."

Jake took the chocolate, pulled out a nut, and gave it to the marmoset.

"Hey! My secret stash!"

"It makes you fat, George." Jake snapped off a generous chunk for himself. "It's for your own good."

They ate in silence. Sarah decided to try and get closer. She reached out a hand.

Horatio's eyes went straight to her.

She froze.

The monkey chattered and shrieked.

"That's all, greedy." Wharton threw it a raisin. "Okay, so these Janus-children told you things. What things?"

Jake pulled the bedside chair over and sat in it, feet on the patterned quilt. "The first one said: *The Black Fox will release you.*"

"And what sort of nonsense—"

"Not nonsense." He took the greasy key fob out of his pocket and threw it on the pillow. "That was Allenby's. The key unlocks the handcuffs. The prophecy came true."

Wharton, after a moment, picked up the keys. He ran a thick thumb over the worn emblem. "Coincidence."

"No." Jake stared straight through Sarah, unseeing. "And if the first one came true, the others might as well."

Wharton drew his knees up under the bedclothes. "And they were?"

"The second kid said: *Find the Man with the Eyes of a Crow.* And the third: *The Broken Emperor lies in the Box of Red Brocade.*"

Wharton sucked a nut. "Sounds like . . . Hang on. The Broken Emperor. Do you think that might be something to do with the Zeus coin? The broken half of it Sarah gave Summer? That can . . . you know . . ."

Jake stared. "You know about that?"

"Venn told me."

Sarah put her hand carefully down on the worn carpet and inched forward. A board creaked under her weight.

"Turns out leaving it with the Shee was such a bloody stupid thing to do!" Wharton stared gloomily.

"If Summer finds out the mended coin has the power to destroy the mirror, then BOOM. End of all of us."

Sarah's heart gave a great jolt in her chest She wanted to cry out with the shock.

"Keep quiet. It's not safe to talk about." Jake got up and paced to the window, staring out at the fleeting moon over the Wood. He had intended to tell Wharton all of it—the children's stupid rhyme that kept going around and around in his head.

But something made him keep that treacherous offer locked tight inside him. He folded his arms, annoyed, staring at his own reflection, the rain running down his glassy face. "So what does it all mean?"

"Search me. Maybe we should tell Venn . . ."

"Not yet." Jake turned. "Horry. Come back here."

The marmoset had skittered to the door. It was scrabbling at something nearby, on the floor, and then with a small spiteful grin it screeched, loud in the still house.

Jake dived over and snatched it up. "Shut up! You'll wake the place."

Then he noticed the door was unlocked.

"Hell!" Very quietly, he opened it and peered out. The corridor was a long silhouette of silent shadow.

He stepped back. "I was sure I locked that."

Wharton lay down and rolled over. "Place is the

draftiest hole in the world," he muttered. "Go to bed now. Talk tomorrow."

For a moment Jake was still. Then he went out, and padded silently down the corridor. Above him the recesses of the ceiling showed faint watery reflections of the rain, pattering loudly down the drainpipes outside.

At Sarah's room he paused. It was unlikely, but . . . Very carefully he tried the handle.

It wasn't locked.

He opened it and peered in.

She was lying in a curled huddle, her blond hair on the pillow. Moonlight caught her closed eyes, her easy breathing.

For a while he stood still there, holding Horatio, watching her. He was tempted to say something, to stand there and say, *Was it you? Were you listening?* But then tiredness came over him, and a sort of sadness, as if he didn't even want to know, and he backed out and closed the door with the softest of clicks.

→⋇←

Sarah did not open her eyes.

She lay in her curl of bedclothes and listened to the thud of her heart, the drag of her breath. Her hands and feet were numb with cold, and so was her mind. All she could think of was one phrase.

The coin has the power to destroy the mirror.

What a fool Janus must think her.

What a fool she was!

Her hand clenched tight under the sheets.

At least now she knew exactly what she had to do.

And who her only ally would be.

12

Her fury brought the lightning
her fury brought the rain.
Her fury took the buds of spring
and frosted them again.
She drowned the blackbird on the nest
the rabbit in the burrow.
Drowned all happiness and hope.
Turned all joy to sorrow.

Ballad of Lord Winter and Lady Summer

GIDEON LAY ON the grass and stared at the cloud-less blue sky.

Outside, in the world, in Wintercombe, the rain had been falling for days, but it never rained here. The end-less blue bored him; he longed for the sudden brilliant spark of an airplane to cross it. He loved to see those bright metal birds, with their arrow-straight trails of . . . what? Steam? Smoke? Sarah had told him people traveled on them, high above the world, and at first he had laughed harshly at that, because he was only too used to mischief, the torment of lies.

Jake said it was true.

He wished he could fly so high, so far.

Then he gave a gasp. Summer was smiling down at him.

"Did I scare you?"

He sat up quickly. "Of course not." Never admit weakness, not to Them.

"You look tired."

"I'm not."

She touched his hair lightly. "It must be wonderful to be tired. To sleep. They say in human sleep there are pictures and visions. Is that true?"

"No." *She would never find out about his dreams.* Dreams were the only place he could go where he was safe from her. Where They couldn't touch him.

"Do you dream about your childhood? When you were small, in that cottage at the edge of the wood?"

He shook his head.

"I'm so pleased. It was so miserably dark and dingy. And yet you seem all *not* and *no* today, my sweet." Her fingers carefully rearranged his hair. "All so quick and touchy. Are you hiding secrets from me, Gideon?"

He pulled his head away and stood up. "Of course not."

"Again!" Summer's small red lips sweetened to a smile. She sat back. "Answer me a question then, without *no,* or *not,* or *never* . . . can you do that?"

He recognized the trap. Hugging himself, he shrugged. "Summer . . ."

She held up a hand. "Did you bring something for Venn. *Through my kingdom?*"

"N— Would I do that?"

Fear. It made him clench his fingers tight. She saw that, her beautiful eyes missing nothing.

"Because if I thought you had, Gideon . . . If for a moment I thought you could do that, you see I would be so, so angry." She tapped him lightly with a long white finger. "So . . . implacable."

"Summer, of course I didn't. What could I . . . ?"

"Something from some other time. Something in a small"—she tapped him again for each word—"black, velvet bag."

He glanced down in horror. His right hand was shriveling. As he stared he felt it contract, the fingers merge, flesh meshing, bones knitting. Nails hooked to claws. The pain of shrinkage shot through him.

"No."

Her finger on his lips. "Not that word, Gideon." She kissed him, her lips soft.

His coat, green as lichen, rippled. The sleeve became feathers, dark and glossy. He felt his skin crack and sprout, his bones hollow out, become frail as twigs.

"I didn't bring anything for Venn. I swear! Not Venn. Venn wouldn't even . . ."

"Then who?" Her eyes were close against his, unblinking as an owl's. "Who?"

"Jake. It was just . . . Jake . . . had *journeyed*."

"What did you bring?"

He hated himself. He hated her. He wanted to die but there was no death. There would never be any death.

"The bag. There was some sort of plastic film inside."

"And?"

"And . . . the bracelet."

"Indeed." Summer smiled, and her smile was cool and the terror grew strong in him. "So you helped them without telling me. Without asking my permission. Do you know what I will do, Gideon, for that?"

He knew. He had been a bird before, wind-blown, buffeted, pecked by the hosts of the Shee from one end of the Wood to another. He had been a fish, caught suffocating in a net; he had drowned endlessly in his own terror till he had torn himself free, and then the stabbing beaks of herons had caught him and thrown him and tossed him back. He had been a stone in the path, without a voice, without eyes, feeling only the pain of the Shee horses that rode over him. He had been trapped in the trunk of a tree, screaming in silent agony for centuries of no time.

He knew exactly what she could do to him.

He made himself stand tall. "Let me make up for it then. Tell me what you want, I'll get it."

His arm was a wing now. She stroked the feathers. "Anything?"

"Anything. Just . . ."

"I want the silver bracelet, Gideon."

Gideon stared. "Venn wears it all the time."

"Not when he comes here."

Aghast, he said, "No. Then he leaves it locked in an iron safe. But . . ."

She leaned against him. "I want the bracelet. Iron holds no pain for you."

Feathers broke out down his back, splitting the skin, tearing sinew, reworking his body. "Yes," he gasped. "Yes, I'll get it, please, just don't . . ."

She stepped back, turned, her voice bored now, cold as stone, as the Shee descended in screeching flocks through the branches. "Until you do Gideon, no more sleep. No more dreams. Gideon shall sleep no more." She clapped her hands.

"Come now, my people! Shall we hunt the wren? Shall we play?"

→✦←

I should have known it would not be easy.

I did try. My advertisements brought many curious seekers, and I soon learned how simple it is to fool people. At my séances voices were heard, lights flickered, ghostly invisible hands drifted across the faces of my guests. In my trances I moaned and murmured and spoke in their own voices comforting messages from dead husbands and lost children. I read palms and consulted the tarot, I gazed long into crystals and traced out names and dates on the lettered tabletop.

I soon had a reputation and a growing clientele.

But after about two years of this I was restless and dissatisfied. Certainly I was making money. I dressed well, and wore the latest hats. But perhaps my conscience was beginning to trouble me, because although comforting the bereaved starts as a warm glow in the heart, it ends as the cold lies of a practiced charlatan.

It was late one evening, after a particularly troubling session, that I entered the room where my father had worked. It was not a room I frequented, being small and dark, but that evening it seemed charged with a strange, silent expectancy. The maid had gone to bed—by now she was a trusted accomplice in my business—so I lit a small fire myself and then sat on the green ottoman by the window looking down at the street, the few late travelers hurrying home out of the dark and cold.

The clock struck three a.m.

At that moment, for no reason I can relate now, I turned my head. As if a voice had called me.

The obsidian mirror stood facing me.

In it I saw a figure, dark and warped. I was wearing the robe I often wore for séances, a fabulously exotic caftan of purple and turquoise velvet; my hair turbaned and fixed with a brooch of kingfisher wings.

But with a chill of certainty I knew this reflection was not myself.

My heart was beating so loud I could hear it; sweat broke out cold on my back.

Was I, at last, seeing a ghost?

I resolved not to be terrified, and managed to stand. There was a lit candle on the sill; I took it up, and came closer to the glass.

The figure seemed to retreat from the light. I saw it was a man, in some dark, perhaps monkish robe. The candlelight threw strange, brilliant streaks of flame across the black glass.

"Who are you?" I whispered.

He came closer. I saw a man of average height, his face obscured by a hood, and behind him, as if in some other place, stone walls, a wooden bench, a table all laid with paraphernalia and alchemical apparatus.

A sudden idea stabbed me with joy. "Are you . . . are you my father? Father, is that you?"

He drew off the hood. "No," he whispered.

He was younger, brown-haired, stubbled, worn

thin with anxiety. "Where are you?" he whispered. "And when?"

"London. The year is 1904."

His shoulders sagged; he looked haggard with disappointment. He sat on the bench and behind him, through a small window, I saw the blue sky of some hot climate.

"Are you a ghost?" I asked, quivering.

He looked up. "I don't know what I am anymore," he said. And then: "My name is David Wilde."

>-<

It was Sarah who answered the door to the repeated, angry knock.

Rebecca stood on the steps under a dripping, striped umbrella. "He's here, isn't he?" She pushed past into the tiled hall. "What's happening? What the hell have you done with him?"

Sarah glanced out into the rainy afternoon. Starlings were rising from the Wood in flocks.

She shut the door and bolted it. "If you mean Maskelyne, yes he's here."

"Why on earth couldn't he call me! I've been waiting at the cottage for an hour."

"There's no signal here. Besides, he's busy. With the mirror."

The tall girl closed her umbrella. Sarah saw how her

long red plait of hair was soaked, the way her anger had suddenly thawed to a bleak resentment. "The mirror. Always the mirror."

Sarah nodded. But she didn't move, checking quickly there was no one around but one of the replicated cats, washing its tail on the dark wooden table. Then she ventured:

"If it wasn't for the mirror, he wouldn't be here."

"He never is here!" Rebecca dumped the umbrella in the rack; a pool of water trickled from it across the tiles. "All he thinks about is how to reach the thing, and now he's done that. They need him and he needs it."

"To do what? *Journey?*"

Suspicious, Rebecca shrugged. "What's it to you?"

"Nothing. Except . . ." Sarah came closer. Rebecca always made her feel small, ridiculously petite. Folding her arms, she leaned back against the table and said, "Except that without the mirror, you'd have him all to yourself."

As soon as she'd said it, she knew it was too crude. She cursed herself silently.

Rebecca's suspicion became indignant certainty. "Don't involve me in your crazy plots, Sarah. I know all about you, and where you've come from. Maskelyne says you're dangerous, that you want to destroy the mirror. You'll get no help from me. Now, where is he?"

She stalked across the hall head high, and Sarah let her reach the corridor to the kitchen before saying, "Yes, I'm dangerous. But I'm not your enemy. The mirror is your enemy. Your rival. The fascinating, endlessly powerful Chronoptika."

Rebecca stopped, but didn't turn.

Sarah went on, relentless. "Venn, Jake, Maskelyne. They all think they need it. But they'll become slaves to it, and believe me, I know that's true, because I've seen it happen. I've seen how the mirror can devour people, mind and soul, how it can swell and pulsate with its own power, how it can become a darkness that can—will—devour the world." She took a step across the hall. "I'm going to stop that happening. You could help me."

Rebecca's braid dripped rain on the tiles. Her jacket was patched with damp. She said, "Leave me out of this, Sarah. I'm not like you. I don't care about saving the world. I'm just a girl in love with a ghost."

The cat stopped washing and gazed at them both; Rebecca scooped it up and ran her hand over its black purring fur. Then she walked down the corridor, carrying it.

The cat stared back over her shoulder.

Sarah followed, thoughtful.

The seed had been planted.

It would have to be enough for now.

Piers had set up the ancient film projector in the drawing room, and had cleared the wall of its paintings to use as a screen. He wound the restored film reel in expertly, humming, his red brocade waistcoat a cheery brilliance under the dirty lab coat.

Venn paced. "Ready?"

"Almost, Excellency."

Wharton was sitting on the leather sofa, feet up on the coffee table. "Like a Saturday matinee, this. Should have some popcorn, Piers."

As the two girls came in, he nodded at Rebecca in surprise. "Hi."

"Hi," she muttered.

He also saw how Sarah had what he had come to call her "plotting" face on—he raised his eyebrows at her now and she smiled quietly, sarcastically back.

"I don't remember inviting guests," Venn said.

Ignoring him, Rebecca went straight to Maskelyne. The scarred man stood near the window, his dark eyes on the silver bracelet Venn wore around his wrist.

Quietly to Rebecca he said, "You should be in Exeter."

"Not when I don't know what's going on."

"Nothing is going on. Except that my magic game worked."

She nodded, dumping her wet coat. "And you were too busy even to tell me."

"Right." Piers flexed his fingers. "Are we all ready?"

"Where's Jake?" Sarah said.

"Here." He came in with the marmoset on his shoulder; it leaped to the curtain and raced up.

To Sarah Jake looked tired, and strangely older, as if time in the past had moved differently, as if he had lived longer than the few days he had been there. But he wore his expensive clothes carelessly, and threw himself down next to Wharton.

"Right." Venn turned. "Get on with it."

Piers clicked the projector on, and the reels began to whirr. "Just to say this was almost impossible to get back. Corroded almost to nothing in places."

The room was dim; rain patterns moved on the windows. On the wall, shadows began to blur; Piers muttered and played with the focus, producing a rapidly shrinking fuzziness that made Wharton say, "What *is* that?"

"People." Jake watched, intent.

"One person." Venn came forward, his eyes fixed on the screen. "Sort it, Piers."

"Doing my best. Like I said, it's in bits . . . How about . . . that."

With an abruptness that silenced them all, a man loomed from out of the darkness and was there looking out at them. A man in a dark place, wearing some sort of brown ragged robe.

His outline flickered, vanishing briefly, reappearing with a jerky flicker slightly off center.

Wharton sat up. Sarah stared.

Rebecca looked around, wondering why they were all so silent.

"Who is that?" she muttered.

Rain pattered on the window.

No one answered.

Until Maskelyne said in his husky voice, "That's Jake's father."

13

Janus has everything. We have nothing.

He has spent years perfecting his knowledge of the Chronoptika—his hunger for its secrets is destroying us all. We believe that seconds before the final catastrophe he will enter the mirror and journey to a refuge he has carefully prepared. He will live on, safe in the past.

Only we can break this cycle of despair. If we destroy the mirror, we destroy Janus.

Illegal ZEUS transmission

IT WAS DAVID'S idea to make the film. It might have been on our third time of speaking—or channeling, as I was delighted to call it.

He insisted that he was no ghost, and I have to admit a slight sinking of the heart about that, because, after all, dreams are dreams. But when he explained to me that he was a man from the future, a man who had traveled in time, and had even once worked with my dear father, I was more than mollified.

I was thrilled!

"How is that possible?" I breathed.

He shrugged. He always seemed to stand very

close to the glass, to be almost able to reach out through it, but when I touched the obsidian surface it was hard and smooth as ever.

"The mirror makes it possible," he said. There was an anger in his voice. "If it wants to."

"Then . . . might I also journey?"

"You don't have this." He raised his arm and I saw he wore a silver bracelet, curiously carved and worked, with an amber stone embedded in it. "It was what your father never had."

"But . . . you do. And you must have this mirror . . . so therefore . . ."

The logic bewildered me. Was he gazing into the very same mirror as I was, but in some other age?

He nodded. "Yes. I found the mirror again here, in Italy. Three journeys after I left your father. Three journeys the wrong way. Always backward. Always further in time from everything I loved. I dare not try again. And yet . . . I dare not stay here!"

A ghost should not be anguished. But there was such pain in him that I felt as if the mirror somehow amplified his sorrow and his fear.

"And . . . how is it you can talk to me?"

"I don't know." He turned and paced, restless within that dark, curtained room. "Perhaps because I worked on the mirror with Symmes. Perhaps because you're a medium, or some sort of sensitive. It's crazy. In my own time I would have laughed at such things."

My heart swelled with pride. I had told him of my séances, though not of my deceptions. And yet surely—surely!—this proved I was indeed a true clairvoyant, a seer of spirits!

Seconds after that, as he was about to speak again, his image faded. It left a mark in the mirror that I saw for days, a faint dissolving smudge in the glass.

I sat on my divan that day and the next, watching the black enigmatic mirror, ignoring my clients, hoping and praying that he would come back, that it had not all been some illusion of my brain.

But nothing happened.

Gradually, I came to wonder if indeed I had ever seen him. To doubt myself. Until, two weeks later, on a rainy afternoon I came in from the theater, took off my hat and mackintosh, said, "Tea please, Edith," and turned my head.

There he was. As if he had never been gone.

Perhaps, for him, there had been no gap. No interval of time. Because he spoke as if we had never ceased the conversation. He said, "I have *a son, Alicia. A son called Jake, who will be searching for me. There is also a man, Oberon Venn, who needs me. So this is what I want you to do."*

→→·←←

"Turn the volume up," Venn growled. "Jake, sit down."

He couldn't. He was standing close, his silhouette black against the flickering indistinct image. "How can it be him? *How can it?*"

Wharton's hand tugged him gently back. "Sit down, Jake. Let Piers get it right."

The image had frozen; now in the attentive, silent room it jerked to life again, became Dr. David Wilde, looking tired and haggard, unshaven, his eyes red-rimmed, his clothes a dirty surcoat of brown.

And then he spoke.

"Are you ready, Alicia?"

Jake swallowed. The voice was a shiver of memory.

Then a reply, faint on the soundtrack.

"Quite ready, David. The machine is operating now, though I have no idea if I'm doing it right. Cinematographs are such new, awkward things, and this great contraption clatters so . . ."

Jake drew in a sharp breath. Even at this distance, through the hiss and static, he knew her voice.

The woman in the rubble had sounded just as quavering, just as self-assured.

Piers said, "This is the very best I can do. The film is grainy and the sound quality—well, I have no idea what she was using or where she got it, but these were extremely early days for sound recording. It's not synchronized—I can't do anything about that."

Sarah glanced at Jake. He was transfixed, his eyes never leaving his father's face. Venn too stared with a grim intensity.

The man in the mirror stood looking out. When he spoke again, his voice was a whisper of static.

"Are you there, Venn? Are you seeing this? I have to assume you are. I wish I could see you. You and Jake. Hi Jake . . . I wish I could be there with you, back at the Abbey, if that's where you are." He stepped closer, his voice coming seconds after his lips formed the words.

"Is it winter there? God, I'd love to see some snow! Or just good British rain." He lifted a hand, as if to the glass. "Just to walk across the moor again and breathe the fresh sea air! Instead of the endless scorching heat here, the humidity, the filthy mosquitoes that breed fevers and . . ."

He stopped. Lifting his chin, he smiled, but it was a weak attempt. "Sorry. Getting maudlin. Talk to myself too much these days. You need facts, so I'll get on."

"And the tape is running out so quickly!" Alicia muttered, louder on the soundtrack.

"He looks ill," Jake whispered.

More than that, Sarah thought. He looked like a jaded, worn, weary man.

"Venn, listen to me." David came and gripped the frame of the mirror, looking through it with a determined stare. "After I left Symmes I *journeyed.* Three times. Each time I found the mirror, adjusted the bracelet, was as sure as I could be that I was doing everything right. Each time I ended up going backward." He shivered. "A rat-infested tavern—sometime in the Civil War. I was arrested as soon as they saw me, because I appeared out of the air in a crowded place. They had me down for a sorcerer and a witch . . . Haven't time to explain how I got away. I managed to bribe the magistrate, get to the mirror, and just *journey,* fast . . . I found myself in York, about ten years before that date . . ." He shrugged. "God, I wish I could see you."

Jake folded his arms about himself, tight. His eyes gleamed wet. "So do I, Dad," he breathed.

"The third jump brought me here. It's Florence, the year is 1347-ish. I can't tell you what . . . how it is here. Fascinating, yes, but the heat, the squalor, the casual violence! Life is so short, so . . . hard.

"I thought . . . I decided . . . not to *journey* again. There's no point flitting through time—you'll never find me. The plan was to stay here, to wait for you. To find a way of contacting you. I've got the mirror—at least I have access to it. It's in the palazzo of the warlord I've had to pledge myself to serve."

He grinned. "I'm his doctor. He's vicious and dangerous, but while he lives, I'm safe. I even pull his teeth. I'll bet you find that funny, Jake."

No one laughed.

"I've been here three years, local time. Tried over and over to contact you. Spells and scrying and anything I can think of, but I have to be so careful! They burn witches here." He looked away, then back. "All that time I saw nothing in the Chronoptika but my own warped reflection—and then, God knows how, a woman. Alicia. She's Symmes's daughter. She's recording this and that's crazy . . ."

"It's brilliant," Venn breathed.

". . . but it's all I can think of to do. You have to find this tape! You have to find me!"

He came close to the glass again, and the whisper of his words jarred against the hurried movement of his lips. "It's plague, Venn! *The Black Death*. I've been waiting for it; now I've seen two cases and I know the signs. This is the year it swept over Europe like fire. Two in every three people died. Realistically my chances are zero. If you don't find me I'll have to *j* . . ."

The film juddered and stopped, the screen startlingly black. The reel flapped and rattled.

Piers switched it off into an appalled silence.

→·←

For a moment only the rain pattered. Then Jake turned on Sarah, his face white as paper.

"So what happens? Does he die there? Because you're from the future, you should know!"

Wharton murmured, "Jake . . ."

"But she should! She should know the answers to this nightmare." He stepped close to her. "Does my father ever come back?"

"I don't know." Sarah kept her voice calm. They were all looking at her, Maskelyne curious, Venn's eyes blue as ice. "If I did, I would tell you, Jake, I swear . . . But I'd never heard of David Wilde before I came here. Please believe me."

He turned on Venn. "We have to go for him! Right now!"

"No." Venn's voice was low. "Not until Maskelyne is sure . . ."

"Give me the bracelet. Let me try! If—"

"Jake." Wharton came up to him. "Think. We can't risk it. As soon as we're ready . . ."

"You too?" He stared around at them all. "Look at you! All of you! Paralyzed by fear! And my father might be dying back there. But you don't care about him, do you, you just care about Leah, who's dead, and you, Sarah, about a future that hasn't even happened yet! I loathe and detest the lot of you! And if I have to, I'll get him on my own!"

He slammed out of the door.

Wharton sighed. "Sorry, everyone. Sorry, Sarah. He's just . . ."

"I know." She went and stood in front of the dark and silent mirror. "I'd be just the same if it was my father. But believe me, I don't have the answers."

Piers cleared his throat. "Well. Do you want me to run it again?"

"Once was enough." Venn went to the fire and thrust another log on, gazing down at the resin bubbling and crackling through the gray ashes.

He stood there, thinking for a moment, then said, "At least we know exactly where David is. If we could be certain of configuring the mirror accurately, of being as exact as we were with the Blitz, we could get in there and pick him up as easily as we did Jake."

He turned on Maskelyne. "You're the expert. What do you think?"

The scarred man had turned and was standing silently by the window, his dark eyes fixed intently on the rain-beaten lawns and the dark tossing trees of the Wood. Now he said quietly, "It's not that easy. Accuracy decreases exponentially as you go back. 1940 was recent enough to be sure we would arrive within days, at least, of Jake's whereabouts. A date seven hundred years before, that is almost impossible to hit. A journeyman might arrive years later or before, and the difficulty of retrieval is . . ."

"I don't want the problems," Venn growled, "I want the solutions."

Maskelyne gazed out at the rain through the reflection of the lit room. Then he turned and faced them. "These are my conditions. I have completely free access to the mirror. I have a room here in the house, and I work without any hindrance or interference from anyone."

Venn's eyes narrowed. "Not the bracelet. That stays with me."

"Agreed, for now. Piers gets me what I need. And when I succeed, and we get David Wilde back, and your wife, I take both of the bracelets and the mirror as my reward. I take them, I go, and you never see me or them again. That is my price."

Wharton pulled a face. Sarah scowled.

It was Rebecca who said: "Sounds fair to me."

Venn snorted. "Does it." He tipped his head and gazed at Maskelyne with cold curiosity. "You think the mirror will respond to you, more than anyone else? That it recognizes you?"

The scarred man laughed, a light, soft sound in the dim room. "I know it does."

"Then you'd better get on with it." Venn turned.

"My conditions . . ."

Venn spun back and glared at him with cold fury "If you can get David and Leah back alive, then as far as I'm concerned, you can have the whole damned estate and the souls of everyone in it! But if you're lying to me . . ." He stepped forward. "If you're wasting my time for your own selfish—"

An enormous clang made them all jump.

Piers had dropped the film reel onto the floorboards. "Oops," he said, deadpan.

Venn gave him a venomous glare. "Have you got something to say?"

"Just . . . well, let's not get hasty. Remember the Dee page, Excellency. I've been working on it and I think there may be things to help us there. Mortimer Dee may not have invented the Chronoptika, but he knew many strange things about it."

Maskelyne's whole body seemed to be shocked into sudden movement; he came straight from the window in two steps. "Dee? You've found his papers?"

"Sarah found them," Wharton said, thinking that would please her.

It didn't seem to; she glared at him. Then she said, "One page of unreadable mess. Scribbles and drawings."

"That might be just what I need! Where is it?"

Piers raised an eyebrow at Venn. "In the safe. But . . ."

"Give him a copy." Venn watched as Maskelyne made eagerly for the door. And as the scarred man reached it, Venn said icily, "But the bracelet stays with me, and if you fail, I'll throw you to the Shee and let them torment you for all eternity."

Maskelyne paused. Then he went out.

"Oh goody," said Piers, picking up one of the cats. "And now lunch, I think?"

Wharton went to find Jake.

He was in the cloister, the monkey clutching around his neck. It was chattering right into his face, but he was taking no notice of it at all.

Wharton took one look, then flung him his coat. "Forget Piers's cottage pie. We're going to the pub."

Jake didn't move. *"The Black Death,"* he said.

He was white and still with fear.

Wharton, his arm halfway down a sleeve, paused. Then he pulled the duffel coat roughly on and did the toggles up, concentrating on them too carefully. "Don't give up, Jake."

"I'm scared. Is that so strange?"

"No. Not strange at all. But you're Jake Wilde. You're the crazy kid who stabbed Patten in the wrist just to get out of the school. You don't give up. That's why you're such a pain. And that's why you'll succeed. We've got Maskelyne on our side now. He's a strange man—I don't know what to make of him. But he knows about the mirror. Let me tell you about the deal he's made with Venn."

Jake nodded, barely listening. Then he stood, and Horatio screeched and swung upside down in relief. "All right. Let's get out of here. I need to think."

Sarah watched the car start and judder into gear and slur down the flooded avenue. She sat knees up on the broad sill of the study window, until the bare black branches of the elms hid it from sight. For a moment a flicker of pain went through her. They hadn't even asked her to come.

Jake's outburst had hurt. He was such a spoiled kid! He had no idea of what she had seen, of what lay in the dark future, and she couldn't even tell him, not about Janus's terrible experiments, or the secrets of the ZEUS organization. He only thought about his own problems. And Venn was just as bad.

She shook her head, finished tying the laces of the walking boots Piers had given her, and pulled on the red raincoat, a little too big, that he had found. Forget them. The coin. That's what she should concentrate on. *Getting the coin.*

She slipped out of the house by the side door to the

sunken garden, closing it carefully so that the row of metal shears and bars hanging from it clinked only softly. Piers had a camera here, but she knew he was too busy cooking to be checking it now, and she ran quickly along the gravel path, around to the back of the house.

Wintercombe Abbey led into a tangle of courtyards and outbuildings. In her time, most of them were ruined, but now they still had roofs and odd oriel windows. One, which Piers called the Abbot's kitchen, was an octagonal gothic structure with a vast central chimney, where the long-dead cooks of the medieval abbots had no doubt concocted great feasts at Christmas and Easter.

It stood deep in nettles, its walls smothered in ivy, thick twisted bines loaded with glossy leaves.

She ducked under them, hands feeling for the wall. The stone was wet and crumbling, rain cascading off the leaves onto her hair, down her neck.

She shivered, groped farther, found emptiness, and slipped under a pointed arch, crawling through the leaves, breathing hard.

Then she stood up, in a shower of drops.

The interior was a damp green space, gloomy with filtered light. Her breath smoked, she glanced around and then up into the cavernous hollow of the roof, where a pigeon fluttered.

"Where are you?"

He didn't answer, but she could hear his breathing.

She took out the flashlight, switched it on, and flashed it around.

Gideon was a dark shape under the hanging ivy that infested the ancient stone chimney. He crouched, sullen in the ruined hearth, and as she stepped closer, he looked up. She gasped.

His face was streaked with blood, his eyes red-rimmed.

The sleeves of his green coat were in rags.

And his fingers were raw.

"What the hell happened to you?" she whispered.

He glared at her as if he hated her. "I was the wren," he said. "They hunted me."

14

When he came forth from the Wood, Oisin Venn was changed. He dressed in fine clothes, laughed a cold laugh. Horses filled his stables, his sheep flocks increased, jewels studded his fingers. At diverse strange hours his house was lit with lights and music and the sound of revelry and merriment rang across the moor.

But the village folk locked their doors and brooded over their fires. For to have congress with unearthly spirits leads only to damnation and the gates of Hell. And they feared for their souls.

Chronicle of Wintercombe

THE SEVEN CATS slept and snoozed along the up-stairs corridor.

The one on the window seat was the first to wake. It raised its head and opened its eyes, slits of green in the black fur. Around its neck on a silver collar, a small disc read *Primo*.

Dusk was falling; beyond the gloomy wood the sky was fading. Already the corridor had shadows moving down the walls, rain-patterns on the ornamental coving, the cobwebbed picture rail.

The cat listened.

A raindrop plopped into a bucket.

The cat's fur bristled. It sat up, alert, and at the same time the other six woke too, and each turned a dark head to stare down the corridor toward the stairs at the end.

Footsteps.

They were as soft as a ghost's; they walked up the wooden treads with barely a creak of the boards.

The cat jumped down; it sat with the others on the floor, a row of wide watching eyes, twitching tails.

The footsteps reached the top of the stairs; they paused, and then began to approach down the corridor, soft as dust falling in a disused chimney.

The cats spat.

In sudden panic they scattered, some behind the curtain, one flattened under the bookcase, another skidding to the dusty alcove behind a table.

The footsteps passed them, bare feet tiptoeing down the hessian matting, past the rows of bedroom doors to the locked room at the end.

Without pausing, they passed through the wall.

The seven replicant cats slid out and stared at one another. One turned and ran fast toward the kitchen. The others, very softly, tails held high, paced in a solemn line down the corridor and sat outside the door in a row.

As if whoever had gotten in should be kept there.

Venn was lying, fully dressed, on the bed.

It was an old four-poster, the curtains removed years ago. His eyes were closed, but he knew exactly when she came through the walls of the room.

He sat up slowly.

Summer was sitting at the dressing table.

The mirror had been removed, but he could still see her reflected, as in some magic looking glass. She smiled at him. "Tired, Venn?"

"Why are you here?"

"I can enter the house now, remember? I thought it would be nice to . . . visit."

"I don't want you here." His voice was a low anxiety. "The Wood is your place. The Summerland. Not here."

She ignored him. Reaching out, she took up the black-and-silver brush, and began to brush her shiny dark hair. "These things are Leah's, aren't they. She had lovely taste."

"Get your filthy hands off them."

"Oh. Not nice, Venn." She put the brush down and opened a drawer. Taking out a jewelry box, she flipped it open. Her fingers danced over brooches and rings.

He came over quickly and shut it. "Get out."

"You've kept her room exactly as it was. How quaint that is! You know, we sometimes wonder about mortals. We laugh and puzzle about them. How it must be to know . . . know all your life, that one day you'll die." She smiled up at him. "The strange thing is, most mortals seem to accept it. Except you, Venn. You won't."

He stepped back. "You know nothing about death. Or love."

"True, but I know about you. And you can't fool me with your talk of love, Venn. You don't want Leah back because you love her. You want her because you will not be denied. You won't be beaten. Not by death, not by time. *You won't give in.* You've never learned how to lose. You think wanting her back makes you more human. In fact, it proves you are Shee."

She stood close to him.

"That's the choice you face, Oberon. The Wood, or the World. To be human, and die. Or to be with us and free of it all. Yet, you know, you'll never be quite at home in either place. How difficult that must be!"

She raised her hand to his face. He stepped back. "You have no idea how I feel."

"Yes I do. Once you were mine. I know everything about you."

She stepped closer. His eyes moved away from her, obsessively, as if by long habit, to the painting where it hung on the wall, Leah's face dark and intent, her eyes watching him as if she saw.

"There she is!" Summer twirled, glanced up. "My

enemy." Then her eyes widened, as if with a sudden brilliant idea. "Do you want me to be her, Venn? Is that it?"

Her hair grew longer, lustrous. Suddenly she was taller, her lips paler. The bones of her skull shifted. Her eyes darkened. "Is this better, Venn?"

"Stop it."

"I can be her. Exactly the same. *You need never know the difference.*"

"Stop!" He backed off, then paused, fascinated. Because, before his eyes, Summer was transforming, and glance by glance, gesture by gesture, the turn of the head, the laughter in her eyes became Leah's, and despite himself his heart gave a great leap of fear and joy.

"Is this better, Venn?" she said.

Even her voice was perfect.

He couldn't speak. He couldn't think. She came and took his head, and her fingers were soft on his skin. Leah's fingers. Leah's lips lifted to his. Touched.

An explosion of knocking rattled the door.

"Excellency! Is anything wrong?"

Venn blinked. He stepped back.

"Excellency! There's an intruder in the house! Are you safe, sir?"

With a convulsive movement Venn pushed the creature away and stalked to the window, dragging both hands up over his face and through his tangled hair. Then he turned, with a howl of fury. The room was empty.

Only a soft perfume and a softer laugh hung in the air.

"Excellency?" The door was flung open; Piers stood there with all the cats behind him like a row of guards.

His small sharp eyes darted around the room. "Is everything okay?"

Venn glanced up to the painting. For a moment he was silent with misery, but when he spoke, his voice was as cold as ever. "Nothing's changed, Piers. Nothing is okay."

>>-<<

Diary of Alicia Harcourt Symmes.

Of course, making the motion film had been such a thrill, I thought of very little else for days after!

David had gone; for a week and then a fortnight I saw no more of him. I dearly hoped he would return—meanwhile I had the film processed and then hid it carefully in a suitcase under my bed with my other precious things.

Because one day a boy from the future might come calling for it!

In the meantime I had a fabulous idea.

My séances were fakes and follies—good

ones, but there was always a danger that soon I would be found out. But the mirror—this magical, wonderful machine!—maybe if I incorporated this into my act I would see more marvels. And make my fortune from them!

Father would not have approved. I was fairly sure about that. And yet in his day he had been a seeker after the occult, a man of secrets. Why should I not have adventures of my own, even me, a querulous and bespectacled spinster whom no man would marry?

And so I had the wiring put in order and affixed to the mirror, though the tradesman I employed had no idea what the contraption was and I heard him say to his mate that the old biddy was bats.

But I knew better.

I had new invitations written, and doubled my fees.

And prepared to see what the obsidian mirror would show my credulous clients.

Sarah dabbed the damp cloth on the cut carefully.

Gideon flinched and swore.

"Keep still."

"It stings!"

She was horrified at his injuries. None was dangerous, none would kill him, and yet the Shee had pecked and torn at him, and his body was a mass of bruises.

"We need to get you inside. Piers . . ."

"Not Piers." He was sour and terrified and shaking with anger. "Not any of those filthy creatures."

She wondered at that. Did he mean Venn too? "All right. We'll go up to my room in the attics. No one goes there."

He was reluctant, but she made him. They slipped in through the side door and up the servants' stairs, quiet as they could past the kitchens, where Piers hummed now and clattered saucepans. The wafted smell of cooking onions followed them.

Once, passing the corridor to the bedrooms, Gideon stopped, with a judder of fear that went right through him. "Summer's been here."

"She can't . . ."

"She has! I can smell her."

Once in her tiny attic room, he sat on the bed with a groan. She brought warm water and a towel and helped him pull off the green coat.

"Don't. I can manage!"

He was savage with pain.

She stepped away, sat on the windowsill, and watched him dab at the cuts. After a moment she said, "Summer found out? About you going for Jake?"

He nodded.

"This is her punishment?"

"Oh, she has plenty of punishments. And it's not just me. She's merciless with any of them." He looked up. "I won't take it anymore, Sarah. I swear, I'll go out now, this minute, and climb the estate wall and jump down into the World. If I dissolve into dust, if I get old and crumble and die all at once, it will be better, so much better."

He tossed the rag into the water, red with blood, and stood up.

"Not until you've listened to me," she said.

"Nothing you can say—"

"*Listen.* Then decide." She looked down at the board under which the notebook was hidden. Janus's unseen words mocked her. But she would win, she had to. She said, "At Christmas, I gave Summer an object I had brought from the End Time. Half a Greek coin, gold, hung on a chain. The face of Zeus. Remember?"

He shrugged. "So."

"I need it back. I need you to help me get it."

"Why? What does it do?" He was acute, she thought. Sharp as a pin. As if living there with them, he knew only how to watch, be aware, avoid danger.

She put her hands together, steepled her fingers. "The coin is powerful. I believe . . . if I can get both halves . . . bring them together . . . it will destroy the mirror."

"The mirror!" He looked up, his green eyes narrow. "That machine! I could throw myself into it. Even without the bracelet I would emerge . . . somehow. Sometime."

"And the Shee would be there waiting for you." She had to convince him. She slid off the seat and crouched in front of him "For them all time is the same. You'll never escape from her without our help. My help. Because where I come from . . . in that future . . ."

His eyes were fixed on her in disbelief. In hope.

She took a breath and said, *"In that future there are no Shee."*

Before he could take that in, she changed, stood, walked briskly. "So. The coin. Do you know where it is?"

Astonished, Gideon watched her. "No Shee? That's impossible. How . . . ?"

"First, the coin."

He shook his head. "Summer keeps all her treasure in her House."

"House?"

"Deep in the Summerland. It changes shape and size and appearance. I'm not allowed there."

She came back and stood over him. "A real house?"

"Sarah, nothing is real in there, not as you know it. It's a place. The Shee talk about it. They say that sometimes it looks like a cottage thatched with the wings of birds.

Sometimes an underwater palace. Sometimes a castle. It is not easy to find and harder still to enter. In its heart is a box. They say the box is red as blood, and she keeps her most precious things there, locked tight with spells. The coin, if she values it, will be in that box."

Sarah pondered. Could she even believe him? "Wouldn't she be wearing it?"

"She has more gold and silver than you could dream. She wears none of it. She hoards it like a dragon. Some of it's real, mortal-made, but other things are from far dimensions, mined deep in the otherworld. Some jewels are faery-forged from leaves or toadstools." He pulled his shirt and coat back on, wincing.

Sarah said, "Then you have to take me there. We have to steal the coin."

Gideon laughed, a sour, low humorless laugh. Then he looked at her. Hard.

"Don't tell me you're serious," he said.

→·←

Rebecca, outside the attic door, stood and listened, her back against the wall.

"So let's see who's fooling who, Sarah," she whispered.

→·←

In the pub Wharton took a long draft of the malty brown beer and set the glass down with a sigh. Froth slid down the sides.

"Fantastic." He glanced over at Jake, then opened a packet of salt and vinegar chips. "Feeling better?"

"I'm fine."

Wharton frowned. He knew that abstracted air, that closed-up, scarily intent concentration. "You're not planning anything crazy, are you, Jake?"

"Of course not."

Now he was seriously worried. But before he could ask, Jake sat bolt upright and said, "Look! Out there, in the street. Can you see them?"

Wharton turned his head. He wiped steam from the small panes of the pub window. The village street was a rainy darkness, the single lamppost a nimbus of orange. "What?"

"The children!"

Jake was staring at the patch of lit street under the lamp. Wharton said, "There's nothing . . . I can't see anything."

Jake was silent. Because there they were, the three replicants of Janus, identical, their school blazers soaked, their gray socks around their ankles, their hair plastered to their small round scalps.

They waved at him, then turned and ran into the night.

Remember, Jake, their small mouths whispered. *Remember us.*

15

Venn has a remarkable physique. He has never been known to be ill and has great endurance. Once, when deep-sea diving off Indonesia for his series on volcanoes, there was a problem and he was underwater too long. Everyone was worried, medics stood by. But when he climbed aboard he was fine.

Later I saw a technician looking at the oxygen equipment, clearly puzzled. "What's wrong?" I asked.

"Oh . . . Nothing . . . must be some glitch." The gauge read *Empty*. "Unless he can live without air." The man laughed.

I did not know how to answer that.

Jean Lamartine, The Strange Life of Oberon Venn

PIERS LAY ON his stomach amid a mountain range of crumpled paper.

He had a pen in his mouth, another in each hand, one behind his ear, and more sticking out of every pocket. He was scribbling numbers with startling speed, referring over and over to the Dee manuscript in its plastic protective cover.

Wharton said, "There was nothing there. But I'm sure Jake saw something. What do you think? Who are these weird children and what do they want with us?"

Thunder rumbled outside. Piers raised his head briefly, then went back to the figures. "Replicants almost certainly. Janus has many, according to Sarah. Why not ask her?"

Wharton nodded. "I will. But I'm worried, Piers. I know Jake. There's something he's not telling me."

"Eureka," Piers said.

"What?"

The small man sat up. "Eureka. Furthermore, hallelujah. Even furthermore: hip, hip bloody hooray with knobs on." He was quivering with a sudden suppressed exuberance. Then he threw a pencil high into the vaulted ceiling, where it stuck in the damp plaster like a small yellow stalactite. "Yes!"

Wharton jumped up from the bench in the inglenook. "You've got something?"

"Words. A few words . . . *mirror . . . a dark wood . . . eye* . . . But it's a start!"

He looked so delighted Wharton felt his own shiver of disappointment as rather a betrayal. And when the small man grabbed the papers and said, "Come with me," and ran, he blew out his cheeks and hurried after him, wondering sourly when he would get any answers in this place.

In the tiled corridor, he glanced out of the window.

It was still raining. Now the lawns were more than saturated; great pools of brown water had spread across them, and the Wood beyond lowered, its dark branches tossing and broken under the drenching downpour.

And from deep below the house he became aware of a sound he realized he had heard all night under his pillow, in his dreams; the roar of the swollen river Wintercombe, in its deep ravine beneath the very cellars.

Hurrying after Piers, he noted rain dripping into more buckets here and there, damp green moldy patches forming on the ceilings. The whole Abbey was leaking and running with water.

In the Monk's Walk, the stonework was wet under his hand, the gargoyles of lost medieval monsters vomiting rain through their open mouths. He sensed all at once the soft timbers, the creaking gutters, the saturated soil under the foundations, had a sudden nightmarish terror of the great building collapsing, toppling, washing away, becoming the ruin that Sarah had hinted at.

Like the houses in that street in the past.

He shook his head, and hurried on.

In the great cellar that was the labyrinth, things had changed. Coming in, he stood, staring.

Maskelyne had brought the mirror into the center of the room, tethering it to ceiling and floor. The maze of green mesh, Piers's crazy invention to stop watchers being sucked into the mirror, had been re-aligned, so now it made a strange long funnel, rather like the concoction of some vast spider, leading straight to the glass.

Symmes's old wiring lay on the floor; Maskelyne stood knee-deep in it, meticulously stripping it down. His head turned, the scar a livid weal in a sudden flicker of lightning.

Seeing Piers's smug grin, he came quickly over. "What?"

"Only started to make progress on the code." Piers laid the papers on the table and stood back, ridiculously proud.

"What code?" It was Rebecca, dusty, with her coat and wellies still on. So she was living here as well, Wharton thought. It was getting quite the commune.

Maskelyne ran his delicate fingers over the manuscript, its clotted figures and drawings. For a moment he seemed almost in pain. He said, "Where did you get it?"

Piers tapped his nose. "You're not the only one with secrets." His malicious glee against the scarred man made Wharton step in.

"We're supposed to be working together."

"You tell him that"—Piers turned, snatching the manuscript back and shoving it into his pocket—"next time he magics me into a china pot."

"For God's sake . . . listen, Piers, what about the

river? It's roaring like a wild beast down there. Has this place ever flooded?"

Piers shrugged, uninterested. "Not sure. Probably."

As he bustled off, Wharton breathed out with exasperation. Maskelyne turned away, the wiring tangled in his hands.

What was it between those two? Were they some sort of enemies? It worried him, but then Rebecca caught his arm and drew him aside.

"Forget the weather," she said in a low voice. "You've got worse things to worry about."

He frowned at her. "What now?"

"Sarah. She's got this crazy plan to steal something from Summer. The changeling's in it with her."

His heart went to ice. "Steal? Steal what?"

She shrugged. "Some coin."

→※←

Sarah was invisible.

The itch in her skin was getting worse; every time she did this she felt as if she was putting herself back in Janus's power; in some way going back to the Lab, obeying him, becoming his creature.

Now, as she pulled on boots and coat and slipped out of the bedroom, she let herself remember the day she had woken from the anesthetic in the terrible white clinic and felt it within her, that new, alien coldness lurking in one corner of her mind. How terrified she had been of it spreading, blanking her mind like snow, flooding her own self, her own memories.

She shook her head.

That would never happen.

She would die first.

The Abbey dripped. No one was in the corridors; as she crept along the Long Gallery she heard faint voices down in the Monk's Walk. The boards creaked as she walked quickly past Jake's door and then Wharton's, past the locked room where Venn brooded under the laughing portrait on the wall.

She came down the stairs.

Two of the cats sat at the bottom like silent, disapproving guards. Their green-slit eyes watched her.

Her heart thumped in surprise. *They could see her.*

Inside the front door she checked the pack on her back. Food, water. A small steel knife.

She undid the bolts, tugged the warped wood open, looked out into the rain.

Then she was gone. Like a whisper.

Like a ghost.

>+<

"Behold," I whispered.

Around the table, a susurration of surprise.

The ring of hands clasped tighter.

Within the silver frame, the mirror stood, an enigma of darkness. Figures blurred through it, a voice spoke a phrase and then faded away. Peculiar rooms showed themselves and were gone.

"Is there anyone there?" I murmured, my voice a quaver of fear. "Is there any spirit that wishes to speak?"

The mirror rippled with shadows.

I convulsed. My whole body jerked. I was good at that; I had practiced it a lot. My eyes snapped open; I saw the assembled ring of ladies and a few gentlemen in dark frock coats gazing at me in fascinated awe.

"I am here." My voice was quite changed. A high piping voice, a child's voice. "Mother?"

At least half the women cried out. Of course, I knew they had all lost someone. And yes, you might think me cruel, to exploit them in this way. But my justification was that I felt, quite sincerely, that it helped them. That it was a comfort.

"Mother," I lisped. "This is your own sweet one. I am happy. I watch over you."

Tears. Sobs of astonishment.

I stared into the darkness of the mirror. I had planned the session to perfection; already I had become a husband lost in the Crimea and the great-great-grandmother whose descendant—a very spendthrift woman—had wanted to ask about a lost diamond necklace.

My next spirit would be the recently deceased aunt of a nervous young man who, my maid had discovered, was deeply in debt. Her will had not yet been found.

I opened my mouth to whisper in an old lady's voice.

And the mirror laughed.

I confess a shudder ran through me.

It was a sound so sinister, so truly dark that it made my imitations sound quite pale and weak.

My clients were utterly still. In the dark room the tiny flames of the candles seemed to dim. In the black glass a shadow moved.

I said, "Who is that? David? Is that you?"

My heart thudded. The fire crackled.

Then he said, quite calmly, "My dear madam. I don't believe we've ever met. My name is Janus."

Jake paused in the tiny dressing room. It lay between his father's old room and the locked connecting door to Venn's. For a moment he had thought he had heard a footstep out there in the corridor, but now as he waited, one hand on the cold marble washstand, there was nothing.

Just the drip of the leaking roof.

He straightened, took another key from the bunch

of keys and tried that. He had stolen the keys from the kitchen half an hour ago, when Piers was far too absorbed in his papers to notice.

This one turned, softly.

He gave a grin of satisfaction, turned the handle, and very softly inched the door open.

The bedroom was as spartan as ever.

Venn lay on the bed. He was fully dressed, wrapped in his dark coat, his boots leaving muddy clots on the black-and-white quilt. He slept as if exhausted, a complete sleep, curled up, his breathing regular and shallow.

For a moment Jake watched him. He knew so little about Venn, about who he really was. All the stories of the explorer, the legendary TV series, the terrible solitary descent of Katra Simba . . . all that was the public face, the famous personality.

But who was this, lying here? This worn, changeable, guilty man? Was he mortal? Or was he Shee? Was he some strange forbidden mixture of the two? Because the Shee certainly felt no sorrow. And Jake wasn't sure if they ever slept.

Venn stirred, murmured. He curled up tighter, rolled over.

Jake forgot everything. *Because he could see the bracelet.* It was fastened around Venn's right wrist, and his sleeve had ridden up to expose its amber gleam.

Jake took a tentative step forward. The carpet in the room was thick; it muffled his steps. He reached the side of the bed, then leaned forward carefully.

The bracelet was surprisingly light—he knew that from wearing it himself. His fingers touched the coolness of its silver, the intricate serpent, the finely delicate clasp. With infinite care he crouched closer, using his very fingertips, barely breathing, unfastening the clasp with a smooth movement he could hardly believe himself capable of.

The bracelet opened.

Jake widened the gap, drew it up, over Venn's bony white wrist.

So softly.

So carefully.

An explosion of knocking at the bedroom door made him leap back in terror.

"Venn! Are you there. VENN?"

Venn woke, rolled, stood.

Jake was already on the floor; he dived under the bed, thick dust in his hair and eyes.

His heart was hammering; he saw Venn's feet on the carpet, the door opening.

"What? What's wrong?"

"Sarah's gone!" Wharton's voice. Jake grinned. Those ridiculous slippers.

"Gone? Where?"

Wharton's answer sounded breathless with apprehension. "Rebecca says she's found out about the coin. I think she may have gone after it. Into the Summerland."

Under the bed, Jake's fingers gripped the bracelet tight.

Venn's fury, when it came, was an animal's fury.

An animal's pain.

→⚜←

"Are you sure about this?" Gideon stood at the edge of the Wood, flint knife in his belt, his ragged coat green as lichen, his skin smeared with whorls and patterns of mud. Leaves clotted his pale hair.

"Yes," she said. "I'm sure. Hurry."

His eyes were restless, constantly glancing into the rain-swept Wood. She wondered, for a second, if he had betrayed her. But all he said was: "Right. Let's go."

The ground was awash, the small streams in the wood bursting their banks. She followed him to the edge, ducking under bare low branches, under the pliant stems of brambles.

Then she paused, tugged up her hood, and looked back.

In the Abbey the lights were lit in Venn's room. Someone opened the window up there and yelled something, a command of anger and fear.

But the wind snatched the words away.

"That was Venn," Gideon said. "I think he was calling you."

She turned her back on the house, quickly, not to hear. "I know," she said.

Tomorrow and tomorrow and tomorrow
to the last syllable of recorded time.

16

With Moll gone, I confess I feel somewhat low.
So I have decided to attempt one last great exploit. I
have no bracelet, and accept I may never return. But
if I succeed I will see what no man living has seen.

Because, since I have spoken with Oberon Venn,
only the mysteries of the future interest me.

Diary of John Harcourt Symmes

HE OPENED THE garage quickly, dragged the
rickety doors wide.

A green tarpaulin covered the motorbike; he had
tugged it off and was pulling the black helmet over
his head when Rebecca's voice came sharp behind him.

"Jake. Where are you going?"

He barely looked around. "The village."

"Now? But Venn . . ."

"Stuff Venn." He felt the bracelet safely inside his
sleeve. Now he had to find them, those three replicants. He had to confront them. Before he left. Before
he went for his father. He was in no mood to talk.

"I'm coming with you." She was already tucking her
long red hair into the other helmet, fastening the chin
strap.

"No way."

She sat astride Piers's bike and looked at him. "Get on."

"Look . . ."

"Have you got any sort of license? Because I have."

He glared at her. "I thought you were busy helping Maskelyne."

"He doesn't need me." Her voice was never this harsh. As she took the keys from him, found one and started the bike engine, he watched her, unmoving. Then, through the roaring revs he said quietly, "Are you really jealous of a mirror?"

Rebecca clicked down her visor so that he saw only his warped black reflection.

"Get on," she said. "And shut up."

❧

Wharton heard the roar of the bike; he ran to a window and saw the dark machine slither down the flooded drive.

"Jake!" he yelled stupidly. *"Jake!"*

What the hell was happening to everyone? Had they all gone mad? He turned and cannoned into Piers. The little man was almost in tears, his small hands clasped together, clutching at his scarlet waistcoat.

"George! Venn's going in after her! Do something!"

"After Sarah? But . . ."

"He'll take me with him, I know he will! *To the*

Summerland! Oh, I can't tell you how much I hate it in there! Last time they almost tore me to shreds! I'm a homebody, George, a brownie, a cook, a pwca that lives under the stairs! I'm not for the big adventures. You have to talk to him!"

"Wait. Let me think." Wharton turned, anxious. "First I have to open the gates. Jake's gone out on the bike."

"MY bike!"

"Will you stop thinking about yourself, Piers, for just one tiny second! Open the gates! Please!"

Piers huffed and turned. He stalked down the kitchen corridor and into the scullery with its rows of surveillance cameras and bells, and flicked a switch.

The gate camera lit. Rain trickled relentlessly across its screen.

"There they are," Wharton muttered.

Blurred and dim, the bike approached slowly, skidding around fallen branches.

"Who's with him?" Piers said. Then: "That girl! Didn't expect that, did you?"

Wharton hadn't, but he made no sign. "Let them out."

"But why . . ."

"The replicants. He's going to find the replicants. He needs to know what they mean."

Silent with surprise, Piers reached out and pressed the button for the gates. Together they watched the metal barrier jerk open, water dripping from the wrought-iron arabesques; watched the grainy image of the motorcycle flash through, speeding up.

Faintly, Wharton thought he heard a yell of acknowledgment.

As the gates closed, Piers said somberly, "I wish I could escape that easily. I wish I could just fly out of the window, like Peter bloody Pan."

"Well, you can't." Venn's voice was arctic.

They turned, and saw he was standing in the doorway, his dark coat on, wearing boots, a small pack on his back. "You're coming with me. We have to find Sarah before she gets to that coin."

Piers clutched his hands together. "Excellency, I beg . . ."

Venn's face was white. He lifted his hand, pushing up his dark sleeve. "Don't you see?"

Piers groaned. For a bewildered second Wharton didn't understand; then Venn said, "She stole the bracelet when I was asleep. It must have been her." He was strangely calm, as if the betrayal was too terrible even to think about now. "You're coming, Piers. I need you."

To his own surprise Wharton stepped forward; Piers ducked behind him instantly.

Wharton said, "You need him here. You can't leave Maskelyne alone with the mirror. And the manuscript—it has to be deciphered."

Venn gave him a ferocious stare. "Who asked you, teacher?"

"Take me instead."

Piers gasped.

Venn's eyes narrowed. "*What?* You're a mortal."

Afterward Wharton never knew if he had said it for her sake or his own.

"So is Sarah. If you're going after her, I want to be there. I don't want anything to happen to her. So take me."

Of course I had to cancel the séance.

I hastily drew the curtain on the mirror, pretended illness, had all lights lit, the astonished and chattering clients ushered out. I was so flustered I could barely speak, so my discomfort at least would have been convincing to them.

Because all the time, even with the black silk veil flung over the glass, I knew he was still there.

The new disturbing apparition.

Watching me.

Finally, when I was alone among the scattered chairs and the discarded handkerchiefs, I locked the door and stood staring at the shrouded surface.

"And who is Janus?" I whispered.

No answer.

So I reached out and removed the veil.

He was sitting in a dark room, sideways to me. A slight man, not old, not young, wearing some neat uniform like a Hungarian hussar. Small round lenses covered his eyes. His hair was lank, just a little too long.

He said, "I have wondered about you. About Symmes. There was a young girl he took to live with him, did you know that? Her name was Moll. . . ."

I drew myself up, indignant. "She was just some urchin of the streets. I am Symmes's daughter."

"So you don't know what happened to her?"

"She probably ran away."

He smiled, infuriatingly calm. "I could tell you. It would astonish you."

"I don't have the least interest."

"Really?" He raised both hands and joined the tips of his fingers together. "Do you know where I am, Miss Symmes? I am so far in your future that I am almost another species. I am no ghost, no vision. I am the ruler of the world."

Such a peculiar apparition. Whatever he was, I found him most unappealing.

He leaned forward. "I calculate that you will

already have received a message from David Wilde. This is known to be the year he spoke to you. What I want to know is where he is and what message he has asked you to pass to his son. A simple request."

I smoothed a stray hair from my brow and managed a vinegary smile. "I am not in the habit, sir, of breaking the confidences of my . . . spiritual friends. Or of obeying the orders of strangers. Certainly not gentlemen who claim to be tyrants in some future realm." I thought that quite a neat turn of phrase, and maybe my complaisance showed, because he seemed to gather himself, drawing back slightly, like a snake before it strikes.

"Where is David Wilde? In what era is he hiding from me?"

I sighed, and turned. "I will cover this glass, sir. As a ghost I find you tiresome, and you frighten my clients away. I trust you will have the goodness to disappear before I return to it."

I reached up and took the dark cloth and it was then, as I laid it deliberately upon the obsidian mirror, that I knew I was lost.

Because his hand came out of the glass and caught my wrist.

"I think not, madam," he whispered.

At first it was just ordinary woodland.

Bare trees under a gray sky, the undergrowth of brambles and bracken, the tiny green points of early spring bulbs hiding at the foot of white willow trunks. Sarah followed Gideon silently, her ears alert for every snapped twig, every fleeting bird.

Overhead the sky was a leaden lid, windblown showers gusting from the moors.

Her boots crunched a frozen puddle; then the bare trees were around her and she ducked under their branches.

Gideon walked warily. The path led downwards, as if the Wood followed some deep hidden combe; gradually she saw banks of exposed earth, hollowed with rabbit holes.

At a turn in the path darkened by a thicket of holly, Gideon stopped.

"What?" she whispered.

He glanced around; she saw his anxiety. "I don't understand this. We should be inside by now."

"Inside?"

"The Summerland."

She remembered the other time she had stepped fleetingly into the Shee dimension, the strange instant transition from winter to a world where the summer never ended. She stared into the trees. "Does it change? Does the border move?"

"Not unless they want it to." He frowned. "Are you wearing anything magical? Anything enchanted?"

She shrugged. "No."

"Leave the pack."

"No! It has food and water in it. If I eat anything Shee, you know they've got me forever."

He hissed in frustration. Then he said, "Let's try this way."

As the Wood deepened, the trees seemed taller, their branches meshing far above the combe. The sunken lane became a knee-deep trough of dead leaves, as if oak and elm and rowan shed thousands here each winter and they never rotted, accumulating through centuries. Sarah felt herself sink into their wet softness, deep, up to her waist, and for a moment before Gideon grabbed her she was afraid that she would fall and be suffocated under them all, like some lost wanderer in a fairy tale. And then the leaves thinned, and the path was a slippery incline of cobbles, rainwater gushing down it.

Gideon's hair was soaked; he turned up the collar of his green coat in silent misery.

"What's the matter with the world?" he whispered.

"Might she know we're here?" Sarah caught his arm, stopped him.

The thought turned him sick. "I don't know. It could be just that the Summerland has reconfigured—

it's always changing, just like she is. Always changing but always the same. And since she got so angry with Venn, the rain has dripped and soaked the whole Wood. As if she wants to drown all mortals."

Sarah frowned. "Come on. We have to keep going."

By the bottom of the combe the path was a streambed they waded through. It trickled into a green clearing, the grass lush and long, soaked with floodwater.

In the very center stood a circular well, the empty bucket tipped by its side.

Sarah stopped. "Seen that before?"

"No." Gideon considered. "So that must mean something."

They squelched across. The grass was emerald, shimmering with raindrops. In each drop was a rainbow. Sarah could smell mint, as if it grew tiny among the roots and was crushed underfoot.

At the well coping, Gideon leaned over and looked down. A small stone stairway spiraled inside, into the dark. Beside him, Sarah stared at the smooth wet slabs, the tiny fronds sprouting from their cracks.

"Down there?" she murmured.

The well took her words and whispered them, around and around.

Jackdaws rose and cawed in the Wood, far off.

Gideon glanced up nervously. "It seems so."

⇥⇤

Halfway to the village the motorbike shuddered. The engine coughed, spluttered, and then died.

Rebecca cursed.

"What?" Jake yelled.

"Petrol. No petrol!"

Inside the dark helmet, he heard the rain pattering in the sudden quiet. "Piers," he said. "He probably magicked it all away." Lifting the visor, he looked around.

They were at the crossroads where three lanes met, at the finger-post that leaned in the hedge and said: *Wintercombe 1. Druid's Acre 2. Marley 5.*

Opposite, roofed with corrugated iron sheets, an ancient stone barn gleamed under the gray rain.

"What now?" Rebecca turned. "We could go back."

"Not yet." Jake took the helmet off; she saw how he was alert, his whole body listening. "Do you hear that?"

She undid the chin-strap and lifted the helmet; immediately the rain gusted cold on her hair. Nothing but its pattering on the leaves came to her.

But Jake had already dumped his helmet and was moving, swift and stealthy, toward the derelict barn.

As she followed him, she heard it too.

A soft giggle, a whisper. And then chanting, the high thin voices of kids, meaningless words, a screech of laughter.

"Jake . . ."

"Keep quiet. It's them."

She crouched beside him. "Who? The Shee?"

He shook his head, impatient. "The replicants. Janus."

Then he was gone, up against the ivy-dark of the barn, a shadow slipping along the wall.

When she got to him, she was breathless. Rain dripped from her fingers. Jake reached the door. It was ajar, the wood warped and ill-fitting; he eased it a fraction wider. They saw inside.

Three small children were sitting around a fire. They had dragged some kindling together and lit it on the cleared floor, and it crackled and spat, as if the wood was wet. The boys were identical, so that as Rebecca looked from one to another it was impossible to tell them apart. Their school clothes were grubby and frayed; they wore small black wellington boots and duffel coats with broken toggles. One had his cap on backward.

Another was stirring something in a propped tin can among the charred sticks; to Rebecca it smelled fishy, like some rancid stew. He was singing:

Round and round the garden
like a teddy bear . . .

Then he looked up. Straight toward the door. "Why not come in, Jake?" he said.

"Out of the rain," the third added, cleaning steam from his small specs.

Jake swore under his breath.

He stepped out, into the barn.

Rebecca stayed where she was. Maybe they didn't know she was there. Seeing them now, she understood that these children were all replicants of Janus. Even at this age they had the calm menace she remembered, the considering stare through the round lenses, the unbreakable certainty of the small thin man who ruled Sarah's far future world.

Jake stood there boldly. He folded his arms. "I've been looking for you. I want to tell you that I won't betray Sarah to you and that I'll find my father myself. I don't need you."

They gazed at him with a detached interest.

"He's crazy."

"He believes it."

"He has no idea."

Jake stepped closer. He was much taller than them; he crouched, bringing his face down to their level, close up. He saw himself reflected in three pairs of round glasses.

"And you have no idea about me. Who I am. What I can do."

They smiled. Secret, closed-up smiles.

"Pride, Jake."

"Comes before a fall, Jake."

The last boy tasted the brew in the tin can and made a face. "Always your Achilles' heel, Jake. Maybe you've managed to find out where your father is. But maybe he's too far back for you to reach. That's a problem for you. Not for me, though. I can reach anyone in all of time, Jake, because I'm not afraid to use the mirror. Already I've made myself many. I will make myself immortal."

"You're the one who's crazy."

"As for Sarah, all she wants is to destroy the mirror. She's not worried about your father."

"Of course she is. Besides, she . . ."

"She's already gone to get the coin."

Jake froze. His mind groped after the sentence with a dread that chilled him. "Gone . . . ? What do you mean, the coin? She doesn't know."

"Yes she does."

"You told her, Jake."

"She overheard you telling Wharton."

He gasped. Behind him, he heard Rebecca stand and hurry forward. But the barn was already empty, the fire cold ashes, the tin cup a tipped and congealed mess.

And the children were only three shadows of himself, crouching on hands and knees, across the floor.

17

Confidential report
Department of Covert Operations
Scotland Yard.
Ref2238198/453
Subject: SYMMES, Alicia
An anonymous phone call was received by a local
station on Weds 6th June 1940 suggesting subject
involved in alleged spy ring.
Status: ONGOING
Priority: A1
Assigned Officer: Michael Allenby

He stood up and still he held my arm.

It was quite terrifying.

And yet after a second I sensed that he would not come through, perhaps could not enter my room.

His grip was cold and painful. I said, "I insist you release me, sir."

He smiled. He let me go, and to my relief, stepped back. He said, "You know, you remind me so much of your father, Alicia. A man full of grand ideas of himself, a naively inquisitive man. He pried into the secrets of time and the universe and thought them no more than parlor tricks. You are very like him."

A sound like a murmured objection came from somewhere behind him.

"I never knew my father. But I am proud of what he did." I withdrew to the safety of the mantelpiece and stared at the apparition. He was in some very large space, a cavernous chamber. It seemed to be lit by a cold white light, and there were no windows to see out of. No furniture was visible but a bare gray desk, on which his hand rested. He wore thin gray gloves.

"Is that the future?" I whispered.

He looked around. "This? It may be. I am beginning to think that there are many possible futures. Perhaps I am just one of them." He smiled. "Maybe I will interfere in your future, Alicia. Maybe I will make you a spy in a war not yet even begun. That would be so easy."

He took his glasses off and polished them on his sleeve, but turned his face away from me, so that I should not see his eyes. When he turned back, the lenses were blank blue circles.

"David Wilde," I said. "What's so important about him?"

"Nothing. Wilde is no one. It's Venn."

I remembered that David had said this was his friend. "Oberon Venn?"

"And Sarah Venn. Sarah, my little invisible girl. My star pupil. She escaped from me, you know, Miss Symmes. She escaped through my mirror, and she is dangerous. I don't know what she's planning."

It was as if he was talking to himself. I had no idea what it meant. And then a noise rose, from somewhere very close in his world, a terrible noise such I could never have imagined, as if the whole fabric of the universe groaned and shook.

My own mirror rippled. I saw the very glass melt and re-form.

A potpourri jar juddered on my mantelshelf; I grabbed it just before it slid down into the fire.

Then all was still, but for my pounding heart.

"What WAS that?"

He sat unmoving. "That is the universe un-making itself. That is the black hole crying out."

"It sounds quite dreadful."

He laughed, dry. "You have no idea. It will suck everything in. The world, the people, the planet, the galaxy. In time it will suck in heaven and hell, every speck of light. Even Time itself . . ." He turned gracefully. "Tell me where David Wilde is, Alicia. And in return I will send you your father."

It was so unexpected. Such a shock! I had no

idea what to believe. But then he stood and went aside and drew a man before me, a large, plump man in a blue quilted smoking jacket stained with soot, a balding, mustachioed man I had only ever seen from sepia photographs.

My heart leaped. I clasped my hands together. "Father?" I said.

My father looked out at me. He seemed hardly to understand what was happening. "Are you Alicia? Good Lord. How you've grown."

"Are you . . . alive? Where are you?"

"Not sure, my dear. Such a strange place. In fact, I'm not sure I'm really here at all."

Janus led my father close to what, I suppose, in his world, was the other side of the mirror. "There he is, Alicia. Mr. John Harcourt Symmes. Safe. Alive. I can send him back to you. This instant. Just tell me where David Wilde is."

Reader of this journal, I suppose you would not have been tempted. I suppose you would have been brave and silent and suffered remorse all your life. I was neither brave nor silent. I said, "He's is Florence. The year is 1347. The time of the Black Death."

After all, what was David Wilde to me?

My father frowned. "Well! Is he really? He certainly gets around."

*Janus's smile was slow, of pure pleasure.
"The Black Death! How very convenient." He
pushed my father toward me. "Thank you so
much, Alicia," he said.*

＊──＊──＊

The steps were treacherous with slime; it slicked the
walls of the well too, and Sarah's hands slid away as she
tried to hold on. Below, Gideon was a shadow.

"What's down there?"

"Nothing yet." His voice boomed in the hollow space.
"Just be careful."

She spiraled down, step by step, faltering into darkness. The well shaft was black, as if it pierced deep into
the earth. Once or twice she glanced up; the sky was
a diminishing gray disc rimmed with ferns, and then
there was something perching up there, a bird, perhaps
a starling. As its silhouette flew off, small particles of
stone dislodged and fell past her.

Something plopped far below.

Her father had told her a story, when she was small,
about a country at the bottom of a well. She tried
to remember it now, as the black walls swallowed her;
there was some witch, and two girls who each went there
to be her servant. The good girl, when she came back,
had had gold coins fall from her mouth every time she
spoke. The bad girl had had toads. Sarah grimaced. That
was the part of the story she had always hated.

The toads.

Something soft grabbed her foot; she almost yelled.

"Don't stand on me! We're at the bottom."

As she jumped down into a squelch of thick mud, Gideon was already feeling the walls around them. His green frock coat was streaked with slime; his fingers lichened with emerald.

Sarah stared up. "There was a bird. Watching us. Did you see it?"

"Yes." He stopped. "Here. Look."

Her fingers groped. It felt like an arch, so low she had to crouch down to peer in. A tunnel sloped away, its floor a mash of mud and leaves. She frowned. "Are you sure?"

Gideon was sharp with listening; he held his face to the air that came out of the darkness and said, "I can smell the Summerland. It's down there somewhere. I can smell the grass and the gorse flowers. I can hear bees." He flicked her a glance from his eyes; green in the dark. "Believe me?"

"I don't think I have any choice."

He nodded, crouched down, and crawled into the tunnel.

She gave one last look back up at the leaden sky of the world, and followed.

>-<

Maskelyne saw them go from a high window.

He saw Venn leap down the front steps of the house

and race into the Wood. Behind, someone else came running; to his surprise it was the big man, the teacher, hastily pulling a pack on his shoulders, wrapping a striped scarf around his neck.

They disappeared into the trees.

"So now it's just you and me."

Maskelyne turned.

Piers stood at the far end of the Long Gallery, a cat sitting upright on each side of him, black as Egyptian sculptures. He said, "Just you and me, scarred man. But I'll be watching you. You may fool Venn, but I know you got back in here by some sneaking sorcery, and I don't trust the hairs on your head or the nails on your fingers. Everywhere you go, everything you do, I'll be watching."

Maskelyne smiled, a little weary. "Quite the three-headed dog, aren't you, Master Piers. But you needn't worry. I'm not here to steal the mirror. At least not yet."

Piers's red waistcoat was striped with black. He scowled. "Just so we understand each other." Then he turned his head, startled. "Is that roar the motorbike? Are they back?"

Maskelyne went to the window, opened it and leaned out. "All I can hear is the river."

Piers turned pale. "Maybe I'd better check the cellars."

"You do that."

When the little man had gone, Maskelyne stayed at

the window. The river must be in high spate, under the house. The floodwaters were rising. And there out over the clustered trees of the Wood, what was that? A gray cloud, rising and settling, splitting and re-forming. Rain? Or birds?

He watched them with a distinct unease.

The Shee were flocking. Something was happening, out there in that tangled wildwood. Something was disturbing the faery people.

Time and the world were drowning, the currents of the earth were streaming with strange energies; he could feel them in his very bones and veins. And deep below the house the black mirror pulsed like a pin-point of dark silence, commanding him to come.

"All right," he whispered. "I hear you."

But still he stared out at the darkening sky.

Where was Rebecca? What was going on out there?

There was nothing wrong with the bike.

Rebecca stared at the dial in bewilderment. "It said empty. It *was* empty."

Jake shook his head. "Let's get back. I've done what I came for and now I'm going after my father."

He grabbed the handlebars and as his sleeve lifted she saw a flash of silver; glimpsed the staring metal eye of the snake. "My God!" she stared. *"How did you get that?"*

He climbed on and kick-started the engine. "Get on."

"Jake! To bring it out here! Are you *crazy?*"

But she had to jump to get on as the bike roared down the lane, and as she gripped her arms tight around him, she knew he was as scared as she was, that the disappearance of the children had knocked all confidence out of him.

They rode fast, down the lanes, under the deep banks of red earth, under tangled boles of hawthorn and ash, past branches that snagged and reached out for them.

Wintercombe seemed strangely distant, as if they had come farther than they'd thought; every time the lane twisted, Rebecca expected the ford, the pair of gates with their lion guardians, but there were only the endless hedges, until Jake stopped the bike abruptly, breathless.

"We're lost. You've taken the wrong turn." She wanted to scream at him.

He said, "No. I think the land is wrong. Summer has done something to it."

They went on, more slowly. She saw that the fields were planes of red water; that trees and gates stood isolated. Sheep had been moved to high ground; cattle were missing. And in the west the sun was already wrapped in great piling clouds.

The gates, when they came suddenly upon them, were still open. Jake turned in and rode cautiously up the drive. He was more worried than he wanted to show because yes, it had been stupid to bring the bracelet out here. If Summer got her hands on it . . .

Even as he thought the thought, the engine died.

The silence was terrible.

They slid to a halt under a great oak that sprawled its boughs over the track. Jake dumped the bike, just as a starling landed on a branch with a bounce. Its beady black eyes fixed on him.

"Move," he muttered. "Quick!"

Rebecca was already running. He flung the helmet at the bird and raced after her, but now the host were coming down like the rain, wings fluttering, beaks shrieking.

He leaped a fallen log, crunched through leaves, glanced back. And then he heard the beat of the drum, deep in the Wood, and his heart went icy with fear.

"Jake." Rebecca had stopped. He crashed against her. She grabbed his hand.

The Shee were all around. They stood silent, an army of curious eyes. Of heads tipped sideways with sharp attention. Of intent greed.

Every bit of it was focused on Jake.

Could they sense the bracelet? Could they smell the silver, taste the amber? Did the snake speak to them in some secret hissing syllables?

"Keep walking," he breathed. "Don't look at them. Don't stop."

"I can't." Rebecca seemed frozen with terror. "What are they?"

He pulled her forward. They walked side by side down the track, between the clustering creatures with their silver hair, their beautiful faces. The Shee were assembling, leaping down from the trees, their wings becoming arms, their claws feet, their feathers fine clothes of dark glossy purples and green. As she walked, Rebecca saw them transform, a male with one wing still, a female face shivering from beak to sweet smiling mouth. Behind, in the thickets, shapes moved, slithered.

"Where's Summer?" she gasped.

"Don't ask." If she came now, they were lost. "Hurry!"

But his feet stumbled; Rebecca slowed. The baneful silence of the Shee was working on them; they felt tired suddenly, so tired, that all they wanted to do was stop, lie down, sleep, be covered in leaves by the birds.

"Rebecca. Keep moving." The words were blurred in his mouth. He slipped; almost fell.

Beside him, she crouched, her head bent.

"Can't," she whispered. "Too tired."

They would fall. They would fall here and the Shee would flock down on them, beak and claw, snatching for the bracelet, for the prize their queen would scream with delight to own.

Jake knew it and he didn't care. He slid to his knees.

It was over.

Until, like a pinprick of light, the voice stabbed him.

"*Rebecca. Jake.* Get up."

It was calm, but the shock of it jerked his eyes open. He saw Maskelyne standing alone on the flooded drive before the Abbey. He saw Piers fidgeting with fear and anxiety on the steps behind.

"Rebecca! Do you hear me?"

She looked up. Dazed, as if he had woken her from death.

Jake grabbed her hand, dragged her up.

And as they stumbled past them, the Shee stepped back, drew away from Maskelyne's voice and Maskelyne's very shadow, and from their angry ranks a terrifying and eerie sound arose, a hiss that made the hackles on Jake's neck prickle with raw fear.

And then they were at the steps, and Piers had run down and was hustling them up, staring over his shoulder at the bird army that rose in dark swirling flocks above the Wood.

They fell into the hall.

Maskelyne came last, and slammed and bolted the door.

Jake turned. "What the hell did you do? We were . . . Why were they so scared of you?"

Maskelyne shrugged. "Perhaps the scar frightened them. They hate ugliness."

Rebecca stared at him. "It was amazing!"

"Lucky." Piers seemed torn between relief and fury. "You were just lucky. Because if Summer had been there . . ."

"But she wasn't there." Maskelyne looked at Jake. "And that's what worries me."

"A well?" Wharton stared down at the black interior, appalled. "You expect me to climb down a bloody well?"

Venn was bending over the shaft. Now he looked up, his face pale with cold, his eyes hard and blue. "You were the one who asked to come. You can see the tracks. They went down here." His gaze strayed anxiously to the Wood beyond. "Make up your mind. The Shee might not let you back now anyway. They're hunting."

Wharton growled in his throat. Then he knotted the school scarf tight, swung himself over, and spread a hand on the slimy bricks. "I thought the Summerland was some paradise of a place."

Already far below in the dark, Venn laughed. "You thought wrong."

The sound echoed, hollow. Wharton frowned. No need to be scared. Whatever he was getting into, it was certainly no worse than a Chaucer lesson with the Lower Sixth last thing on a Friday afternoon. After all, he told himself firmly, what worse horrors could the Universe hold?

So he descended into the pit.

18

The east face is the most deadly and has only been scaled once. This was during the tragic expedition of 2005, with Carl Morris, Edwin James, Heinrich Svensson, Oberon Venn, and Fillipo Montaigne. The mountain is now considered too dangerous to attempt and the Chinese government have, despite international protests, forbidden further expeditions.

"Katra Simba, Deadly Mountain";
Article in National Geographic, *2013*

THEY WAITED BEFORE the mirror. Like guardians.

The black glass reflected them. Seven cats, some curled snoozing, some washing, one on its back fighting a tangled battle with a piece of the sticky malachite green webbing.

The house was silent, with only its drips and damp, the subdued rumble of the flooded river below its cellars, the trees on the steep ravine dripping on its tiles.

Then the front door slammed, was bolted.

The cats listened.

Arguing voices came down the Monk's Walk; the cats sat up, attentive, their green eyes wide with curiosity.

Jake burst into the room. "It's a total waste of time even talking about it. I have to go back there because I already did. Don't you see?"

Rebecca blinked. "What are you talking about?"

"Alicia! She knew my name! She knew me." He realized he was shouting. He lowered his voice and tried to keep it even and calm. He was aware of Maskelyne's eyes, as if the scarred man was somehow weighing him up, making some secret judgment.

"When I spoke to her, there in the rubble of her house, she said *'Only waited to give you this.'* So it's clear we had met before. It's in my future, but it was in her past."

"Oh God," Piers muttered. "My head hurts."

Rebecca shook her head. "But why . . ."

"To speak to my father." He glanced at Maskelyne. "It's the only way, because we can't reach him, can we, in 1347?"

"I think he's too far for our resources yet." Maskelyne shrugged. "But it may be possible to make a relay. To pull him forward, even a few centuries."

Jake stared. "Could we do that?"

"We could try to make a chain. Using our bracelet and the one he is wearing, it might be possible to get him back in controlled stages."

For a moment it almost made Jake too happy to breathe. Then Piers sat on a carved chair and said, "You know that Venn thinks Sarah, not you, has the bracelet?"

"*What?*" He was astonished. "Why?"

"Because he trusts her less than you, I suppose."

"I can't help that." Bewildered, Jake looked up as the marmoset swung down from the door with a screech of welcome and flung its tiny arms around his neck. "And where's George?"

Piers coughed. "Gone to the Summerland with Venn. He volunteered."

Rebecca whistled. "He must care a lot about Sarah."

For a moment Jake felt a sliver of some emotion he could barely register. Was it envy? Jealousy? He snarled, "We need him here! What's he thinking of!"

"Fool has no idea what he's facing." But Piers's scorn was muted, almost admiring.

Jake turned to Maskelyne. "This chain. Let's do it. Now."

The scarred man glanced at him. He went and walked to the mirror, both hands gripping its silver frame. Beside him, Jake saw how Rebecca watched, nervous, chewing the end of her hair.

"Prepare yourself," Maskelyne said. "Both of you."

→⊹←

What happened next remains something of a blank in my memory. There was certainly a tremendous implosion—a whoosh of blackness like a vacuum, so that I had to hold on to the table with both hands, and even then the heavy chenille cloth was dragged away, and a stuffed cockatoo under a glass dome fell and was smashed.

All my breath was snatched. For a moment I understood only that the time was stretched like elastic; that the mirror was sucking in the world, and that I would be sucked in with it, to that grim gray future.

The crash was so loud that I fainted.

I came around to a sweet smell. Someone was holding a handkerchief soaked with drops of eau de cologne clumsily to my nose. I spluttered, gasped, struggled upright.

"Father? Is it you?"

He sat back. "Dear girl. Who else."

I could not believe it. For a start he looked no older than the last photograph I owned of him, which must have been taken only weeks before the tragic accident. "You died," I gasped.

"No! Not at all." He helped me up and we stood face-to-face and there he was, John Harcourt Symmes, the fearless inventor of my dreams. Well . . . perhaps a little smaller and plumper. But he made no attempt to embrace me; he seemed more bewildered than I. "I did not die. I made a very great attempt to use the mirror. Moll, you see, had betrayed me with her devious *little scheme . . . and so I still did not have the bracelet.*" He stood, moved to the mantelpiece and stood there, one arm on the marble sill, the other smoothing his mustache. His voice took on the formality of a public lecture. "*I attempted a great feat, and failed. I seemed to float for whole hours in a terrible, black place of no light or time or gravity. Then somehow that man, the tyrant Janus, snatched me from it. I have no idea how.*" He shook his head. "*I emerged from the mirror into his gray room, and what I saw there . . . That was mere days ago, of course. But . . .*"

Doubt crept into his eyes. He looked around the room, at the mirror, the new curtains, the recently installed electric light. "*Good heavens. I have traveled . . . no, journeyed . . . I have actually journeyed into my own future! How many years?*"

"*Thirty-one,*" *I whispered.*

His eyes widened, and he almost ran to the window. There was a silence as he took in the changed vista of the street. I thought of the motor cars out there. The buses. I watched his back. His voice, when it came, was strangely subdued. "*Good Lord. So the old Queen is dead? And this is the future?*"

"*A possible one.*" *I thought of what Janus had*

said. Then I patted the sofa. "Come and talk to
me, Papa. Tell me about this urchin Moll."

⇥·⇤

Wharton crawled on hands and knees in the dripping muddy tunnel.

The pack on his back scraped the brick roof. Water ran down his hair and behind his ears.

He sneezed. The sound rang like an explosion. He groped for a handkerchief. "For God's sake. How much farther?"

Venn was a dark mass ahead. His voice came back like an angry rumble. "Will you stop asking that?"

He obviously had no idea.

Gritting his teeth, Wharton slopped on. After all, it was no worse than the army assault courses he had sweated through in training. They had come in useful years later, when he had needed to invent a fiendish exercise regime for the boys at the school. Wharton's Workouts had soon sorted the wimps from the . . . er well, boys. Legendary in the staff room. He snorted a laugh.

As if it was some signal, light blinded him. He raised his head and realized Venn had emerged ahead; a bright blue glow was emanating from the end of the tunnel. A cold, oddly silent glow.

He pulled himself along, squelching and cursing, but even as he reached the end, he knew that the mud under his palms was hardening, becoming ridges of ice, and when he crawled to the end and staggered to his feet he stared around with a mixture of dismay and delight.

"My God. Where is this!"

It was a high arctic plateau. The snow plain stretched down before them, blinding in the full sun. Beyond, range upon range of mountains needled the sky, their brilliant tops dusting faint cloud into the pure blue air.

He breathed deep, and the cold entered him like energy. "It's fantastic! Even better than the Alps. But we must be so high . . . Is this really the Summerland?"

Venn was a dark shadow on the snow. He stood looking out, intent, his blue eyes cold as the ice.

When he answered, it was not Wharton he spoke to.

"What are you doing?" he whispered. "What games are you playing, Summer?"

Wharton said, "You know this place?"

Venn flicked a freezing glare. "This is the Summerland. It's also Katra Simba."

As if the word was a signal far off in the mountain heights above them, something rumbled. Wharton whipped around, startled. "What was that?"

Under his feet, the mountain vibrated. "Is that an avalanche?"

Venn looked at him, his face white and weary. "Let's hope not."

"But we can't really be there." He knew all about the mythical mountain. Deep in the lost lands of Tibet, it had never been climbed by Westerners until Venn's own hubristic expedition. And that had gone so disastrously wrong. He couldn't remember the details now, but surely only Venn had gotten out alive.

"We're not." Venn seemed to rouse himself. "We're barely half a mile from Winterbourne. *And I will not be played with, Summer!*"

His yell of fury made Wharton cringe; above them the snow seemed to shudder; he fought the desire to crouch and cover his head, and said, "Surely noise doesn't help. Wherever we are, Sarah must have been here first. If we can find . . ."

Venn pointed. "Those?"

The footsteps were deep, and there were two sets. They led down and Wharton could see them as blue smudges far below, tending toward a ridge of exposed rock.

Without a word, Venn set off after them.

Wharton adjusted his pack, pulled out a woolly hat, and tugged it down over his ears.

Then he trudged into the deep snow, floundering down the slope.

"Is Sarah in the same landscape? Or do they see it differently?"

But Venn gave no answer.

>→·←

Sarah could not believe the cold. It was like breathing in arrows or nails, it hurt her throat and lungs. She had already lost feeling in her feet, her hands were throbbing with pain.

Frostbite!

You could lose fingers like that. She thought of Venn's own left hand maimed by frostbite. Had that happened in a place like this?

Gideon had slithered a little ahead; he waited for her, and when she reached him, she wondered why he was standing there grinning, in this white landscape.

"What?" she gasped.

"Look at it. It's amazing!" He seemed exhilarated, set free. "I've never seen a place like this. As if the world goes on forever. As if you could just travel and climb and walk and run forever. With no wall around you. No one watching you. Free!"

She stared at him, his thin clothes, his lit face. Here his skin was as pale as any Shee's, one hand braced against the rock with its crystal veins. She had a sudden desire to bring him crashing down; she said harshly, "It's an illusion, Gideon. It's just the Summerland. She still has you prisoner."

His face held its brightness for a second more. Then she saw the light go out of it, and he looked down.

She was sorry. She said, "Look there. What's that?"

Below them, on the slope of the mountain, was a

dark cube. It looked like a building poking up out of the deep drifts. Some ancient construction, roofless, its doorway an empty arch.

"I don't know." His voice was dulled. "Does it even matter?"

She pushed past him. "As you said, at least it's there. Nothing else is."

This time she led. As they descended the long flank of the mountain, the snow thickened; it was waist-high now and she was forcing her body through it, and she knew they were leaving a great scar down the white slope that anyone might see.

The building waited for them. Its empty windows watched them come. It was small, no more than a stone sheepfold, she thought, something like the ones you found up on the moor, centuries old, rebuilt and mended over the generations.

It was certainly not the palace of the Queen of the Shee.

When they reached it, something made her stop.

A vibration trembled deep in the earth; Gideon glanced back in alarm. "The snow's moving!"

Still she didn't move.

"Go inside." He shoved her on. "At least there'll be some shelter."

"Is it safe?"

"Safer than out here, surely." He glanced back again, screwing his eyes up against the brilliant light, the reflective snow. "Sarah, someone's up there. Following us. I can hear their breathing."

She turned, and stepped between the black stones of the empty doorway, and vanished.

Gideon stared in dismay. "Sarah?"

The doorway yawned, empty. He could see the snow through it.

But he dared not follow her.

Jake and Rebecca stood together at the mirror. He was wearing the same dark suit as before, now with a cloth cap. Rebecca's hair was caught up in a swirly chignon; she wore a long skirt, a white blouse with a brooch at the neck, a coat with fur trim. She fidgeted with the hat. "Do I have to wear this?"

"Totally necessary." Piers stood back. "Every respectable girl wore a hat. Suits you."

Jake checked the clasp on the silver bracelet.

"Nervous?" he muttered.

"Absolutely terrified." She glanced at Maskelyne, who was adjusting the small monitor he had made. "Why me? I mean, I have no desire to go traveling in time."

"He may need you." It was Maskelyne who answered, but he didn't look up at her, so she left Jake and walked over there, and grabbed his fingers. "Don't you need me?"

Piers rolled his eyes at Jake.

Maskelyne looked up. He seemed startled, his dark eyes wide. He said, "Rebecca, you know . . ."

"I don't know anything about you. I thought I did, because you've been here all my life, but for you it's different, isn't it. For you it was just a few seconds here and there, a flickering into existence, seconds and then minutes that were really years apart. This is all you care about. The mirror. The wretched mirror."

Maskelyne held her gaze. The scar that marked his face stood out against the whiteness of his skin. He said, "That's not true. You are . . . very special to me."

"Special."

"Yes. But I am older than you, Rebecca, centuries older, and more different than you could know. Don't trust me, don't rest your life on me. Because one day you might wake up and find me gone."

She stared at him, bleak.

Jake said, "We need to go. Becky?"

She didn't look at him or answer. But she turned and walked to the mirror and looked in, at the early twentieth-century girl that stared back at her. He thought there were tears in her eyes, but her voice was clear and steady. "Well then, let's go. What's keeping us."

Jake glanced at Maskelyne. "What will be the date?"

"We'll try for 1910. Around the time she films David."

He nodded, grim. "Okay. Do it now."

The mirror hummed.

The labyrinth whipped tight.

The mirror opened, and he saw again the vacancy at its heart, the terrible emptiness that snatched him and devoured him, and for a moment he knew all the anguish that was in it, that it had swallowed his father and would swallow him, and that there was no escape from that.

➤⁓⫷

The mirror howled.

Its cry made Piers crouch and clap his hands over his ears, and gasp; it made the cats flee like seven streaks of darkness.

Only Maskelyne was unmoved, his hands steady on the monitor until the blackness collapsed with a snap and the glass was whole and Rebecca and Jake were gone.

Piers lowered his hands and breathed out. He shook his head and hauled himself up.

"That thing is getting worse. And are you sure you can control it?"

Maskelyne looked up. "No one controls the mirror. Not even Janus. But at least I can monitor it now I've sorted out Symmes's dial."

Piers wiped his hands on his apron. "I don't know how you sleep at night. If ghosts sleep."

He stopped.

Maskelyne was staring at the monitor with a fixed fear.

Piers hurried over. "What's wrong?" He looked at the numbers on the dial, flicking back and back and back. 1900.

1800

1700

1600

He put both hands over his eyes. "Stop it. Stop it!"

"I can't."

1500

1400

"Hell," Piers whispered.

19

*My dark devyse is the portal into which my soule
hath journeyed. I fear I have given myself up to its
mercies as to a demon. As to a dark angel.*

From The Scrutiny of Secrets *by Mortimer Dee*

H<small>E ONLY REALIZED</small> he was standing in the middle of a road when the donkey reared up in his face and whinnied; in an instant Rebecca had hauled him aside, and they both fell into the gutter, crashing against the hot stone curb.

Jake gasped. "Are you all right?"

"Bruised." She was rubbing her elbow, there was dirt smudged on her cheek. Then she looked up.

"Oh my God," she said. *"Jake."*

The heat.

The heat struck him like a blow.

He saw a street too narrow, the houses too high. The bricks were tawny, the roofs red tile. Above them scorched a sky bluer than ever possible in London.

The smell of sewage, of olives, of incense, burst onto his senses. And the donkey cart had a driver, who had leaped down and was kneeling now, crossing himself with terror, screaming out "Demons! Fiends of hell!" in a dialect so garbled Jake could barely recognize it.

Rebecca clutched at him. "Jake."

"Don't talk. Keep quiet. That's Italian."

"You know what he's saying?"

"Dad worked in Rome. We lived there when I was small."

He could not believe this. This was all wrong—and, early, so early! The people who came running from the silent buildings, who flung open shutters and stared down at him, were dark-eyed and olive-skinned. He knew, with a rush of joy and terror, that the mirror had betrayed him again.

"Demons!" the driver screamed.

"No. Please." Jake summoned his Italian. "We are merely visitors. We startled you. Please."

It was no use. He realized that as he saw Rebecca turn and face the crowd that was gathering fast as rumor, as he looked at her ridiculous Edwardian clothes, his own dark suit. Slipping the bracelet as far up his arm as it would go, he said, "Run!"

They turned, dashed two women aside, hurtled around a cobbled corner.

Into a line of armed men.

Jake hit the ground; Rebecca screamed. Scrambling up he saw that one of the men had hold of her, and was laughing at her struggles. Her hat was off, her long red hair whipping free.

The men stared and whistled. They seemed amazed. One made a sign with his hand, against evil.

Jake leaped up. "Leave her alone. Let her go!"

Almost casually, a man dealt him a blow with the flat of his weapon that sent Jake sprawling, astonished with pain. He gasped for breath, got on hands and knees, was kicked flat again.

The crowd roared. Rebecca screeched, "Jake!"

As if her voice had released it, silence fell. Someone spoke, a sharp bark of command. At once the crowd fell back, slipped away, fled. The line of soldiers parted, and through them came a man on horseback, wearing a gown of black and gold and a hat of some red velvet wound elaborately about his head. His hair was dark and glossy; his nose curved like a hawk's beak. He looked as though he had ridden out of some pre-Renaissance painting.

He drew rein and said, "Fall back. Disperse the citizens."

Breathless and aching, Jake scrambled up. Rebecca grabbed him. She looked terrified, but kept silent.

As the soldiers cleared the streets Jake tried to think. They were in trouble here. Dire trouble.

"Who are you?"

The question was calm, but this man was clearly

used to getting all the answers he wanted. For a crazy moment Jake was reminded of Inspector Allenby.

"My name is Jake Wilde, signore. This is my . . . wife. Rebecca."

He registered her tiny gasp but ignored it. "We are travelers from a far country."

"Where? Your speech is most barbaric."

"England."

"Ah. That is a distant island." The man clicked his fingers. "Is the climate there really a constant fog so that the sun is never seen but on the morning of Easter Day?"

Jake risked a small smile. "Almost, signore."

Behind the man now were others, a group on foot. He saw priests, a cardinal in red, a gather of well-dressed men. No women anywhere.

He said, "May I ask whom I address?"

The horseman said, "I am Federico Altamana, condottiere of the army of this city. Why are you here? To trade?"

Jake swallowed. Then he said, "In a sense. We heard of a sickness that has come to this place. We've heard how it spreads."

The men murmured. He heard the words *il morto negro*. Rebecca squeezed his hand in a desperate warning. But he ignored her.

"In my land we have knowledge of many medicines

and cures, many cordials and tinctures. I have come to bring this knowledge to you, and the friendship of my king . . ."

"Edward the Third," Rebecca breathed.

"Edward, King of England and France."

He was exhilarated. He was making this up out of half-forgotten history lessons and both their lives hung on it, and yet the danger, the threat, as always, filled him with a wild, reckless excitement.

The horseman turned his head and beckoned.

Rebecca gasped.

Out of the crowd came a man in the strangest mask either of them had ever seen. Of loose gray fabric, it hooded the face, was slitted for the eyes. Out of it hooked a great beak like some vulture, dark as a crow, sinister and bizarre.

"Where are your medicines?" the signore demanded. "Where are your king's gifts? Your entourage?"

"At Pisa, unloading from the ships. We came at once, before them. We hear that many are dying here already."

He flicked a glance at the masked man. A pair of bright eyes stared back at him.

The Man with the Eyes of a Crow.

The signore nodded. "That is unfortunately true." He considered, then said, "Il dottore will take you to the monastery. I hope you will be able to help us. But this sickness is not so great. It affects only the poor and sinful. It will pass, as all sickness does."

Jake frowned. "It may become a great plague."

The signore leaned from his saddle. "Let us hope not. I await your king's gifts. If they do not arrive, you will pay for your lies."

He smiled amiably, jerked his head to his men, and rode on. The armed men fell in behind and followed, gazing at Jake and especially Rebecca with curiosity. She tucked her hair up into her hat hurriedly.

Only the masked man remained. He beckoned, and turned into a dark narrow alleyway stained with pools of ordure. There he unlocked a small door and bowed; they went through before him, uneasy.

Inside was a dark room, lit by one candle. The bird mask turned to face them, was lifted off, and they saw a gray-haired man with an open, weary face staring at them with undisguised terror.

Jake could hardly breath. He whispered, one word, one syllable, and it was like a light coming back on in his heart.

"Dad."

When Wharton finally slid and floundered as far as the buried sheepfold, he found Venn standing with folded arms looking at it with suspicion.

"Come out," he snapped.

For a moment Wharton thought the man had really gone mad. Then Gideon stepped from the shelter of the dark stone. The changeling was pallid and shivering. His forest-green clothes seemed to have faded; they were gray here, becoming white, like a stoat's fur changes in winter. And there was something fading in the boy too, Wharton thought. As if in some way he was becoming transparent, less solid.

Wharton said at once, "Where's Sarah?"

Gideon pointed at the ruin. "She went in there. She vanished."

Venn said, "What's wrong with you? What's Summer done to you?"

"Stolen my sleep. Stolen my dreams." Gideon sat in the snow and dragged his hands through his tangle of hair. "The only place I could go to get away."

Venn nodded. "She's a mistress of torment." He looked at the ruined byre, touched its black stone, trudged a complete furrow around it in the snow. Then he said, "Why didn't you go in?"

Gideon looked up. "I . . . was going to. Then I saw you."

"Liar." Venn crouched and grabbed him by the collar of his shirt. "You know where she is because you led her here. Summer wants the bracelet, doesn't she?"

"What bracelet?"

"The one Sarah stole from me."

Gideon's blank stare was only too convincing. "She doesn't have it."

Wharton said, "But . . . Are you sure? . . . Then who could possibly . . ."

The silence rumbled. It shivered and shook under his feet. As he and Venn glanced at each other it was as if the earth groaned, the mountain was ready to collapse on them.

"Jake," Venn breathed.

Did the word start the avalanche? Was the weight of that knowledge the tiny trigger? Because as they all turned as one, the white wall of snow was already crashing toward them, coming like a line of foam, like a wave that would flatten and destroy anything in its path.

Venn seemed frozen. Wharton heard him whisper, "Not again." Then he spread his arms wide, as if he would stand there before it, defy it, die.

"Oh no!" Wharton grabbed him and shoved him with all his strength toward the doorway of the ruin. Venn toppled in backward and was gone as if through a plane of light.

Wharton yelled at Gideon, "In!"

They had no choice. As the white mass hit, it filled the world with a roar that smashed them against each other, a tangle of limbs, and clutching of hands, a suffocation of snow as hard as marble. Just before it hit him Wharton felt the momentum alone fling him head over heels.

Into blackness.

→→←←

My father stirred his tea.

He sipped it and then leaned back in the armchair with a sigh of pleasure.

"Cake?" I said.

"Oh my dear."

"Éclair? Or Battenburg?"

"Éclair please. All that lovely squishy cream."

I lifted one with the silver tongs and placed it on his plate. As he munched it and the cream fell on the napkin tucked under his chin, I sat back in my chair with as much satisfaction as I ever remember feeling in my life.

"And so this Moll lived with you for ten years?"

"She did. Little terror that she was. She ate my food and drank my whisky and developed into quite a beauty, if all be told. And she was up to every scrape and trick and strategy under the sun."

I felt a squirm of jealousy, but suppressed it. "And all the time I was buried in that house in Yorkshire."

"Your mother took you away. She didn't trust me, I'm afraid. And then we were so busy searching London for the silver bracelet. We were so sure it must be there! Moll—poor girl—was also convinced that Jake Wilde would come back and take her to the future. But he never returned."

"Did it break her heart?" I said, I must confess, hopefully.

"Perhaps. After a year or so she stopped looking out for him. But I don't think she ever forgot. And then one spring morning she slipped out of my house and never came back."

I sniffed. "Once a street girl, always a street girl."

"Maybe." My father looked thoughtful. "But maybe not. Six months later I received a letter with a roll of banknotes tucked inside it. Three hundred pounds sterling—a mighty sum. The note said simply TO JHS: FOR ALL WHAT YOU GIVE ME. It must have been her. I dare not think how she got it."

"She could write?"

"I taught her. She was a remarkably able little thing."

I had heard enough about Moll. I dismissed her from my mind and said, "I wish you could tell me more about the future."

He seemed uneasy. "I understand now the reluctance of David, when he worked with me, to speak of it. I saw little—Janus kept me in the same room, and I was only there for a few hours. Even so, it was a cold, bleak place." He leaned forward. "Do you know, I do not believe they eat?"

I recoiled in mock horror. "Not eat?"

"Never was I offered one mouthful. I believe they take a pill of some essential nutrients each morning. It would save a lot of time."

I proffered the cake-stand again. "But it would not be much fun, Papa."

He selected a Coffee Kiss. "Indeed not, Alicia."

I sat back, and looked across at the obsidian mirror, where it leaned, safely veiled in the corner of my room. For a moment I had felt that someone was there within it, listening to us. I said, "Do you think I was right, to save you in that way? By telling the tyrant Janus what he wanted to know?"

My father licked coffee cream from his lips and dabbed them with the napkin. "My dear, you had no choice. And from what I know of David Wilde, and what I saw of Oberon Venn, they are men of resource and capacity."

He put the cup back on the tray. "Not to mention the arrogant and cocky Jake."

He looked at the mirror, and smiled a rueful smile.

"Your career has been most adventurous, my dear. Truly, you are my daughter."

I could not help a sigh of satisfaction.

"Will Jake come for the film?"

"I have no doubt he will." He leaned forward and took my hand. "And when he does, we must be ready for him."

There was no interval between the snow and the room, but she felt as though she had traveled miles and centuries to get there.

Slush slid from her shoes onto the deep crimson carpet.

A trickle of icy melt water ran from the ends of her cropped blond hair into her eyes.

Her hands dripped. She felt the chill of the high plateau thaw in her.

The room was warm and silent. It was high-ceilinged, the walls papered with an elaborately flowered design. In the vast hearth a fire roared over logs piled high and spitting.

Portraits lined the walls.

Sarah moved. She hurried to the fire and huddled over it; then she stripped off her soaked coat and scarf and gloves and boots and knelt in front of the flames until they scorched her skin and eyelids. The heat was glorious.

Only when she was warm through did she take a good look around.

Tall candelabra stood in the room, each with dozens of candles burning. They burned with a cool unchanging light. The candles did not flicker, and didn't grow any smaller. The windows were curtained with drapes of amber, tassels of knotted cord.

Around the walls were portraits, in frames of gold. She stood and walked under them, her feet deep in the soft carpet.

They were all of Summer.

Summer in a white dress. Summer in a crimson robe. Summer in a ruff and gown, her face lead-painted like some Elizabethan queen. Summer in a 1960s mini shift of black and white stripes, laughing out of the frame.

Sarah frowned.

Turning, she saw the table. It was laden with food, plates piled high with lobster and fish and spiced meats. A row of tureens stood there; she lifted one, and the vegetables steamed below.

She replaced the lid.

"You know, that is a very old ploy," she said aloud. "It's in every fairy story going."

No answer.

Then, in the corner of the room, she saw it. It sat on a small white table, a circular table smooth as the snow slope had been.

She crossed to it, reluctant.

The table was covered with a scatter of small objects. A bone, an acorn, a gold ring, a pile of white pearls like pebbles.

And among them, on small balled feet, a box.

A small lidded box with a key in its lock.

A box covered with red brocade.

She looked around.

The room was silent, the door closed, the windows shuttered.

She reached out.

She opened the box.

20

Oisin Venn did not age, he did not grow old.

He had wealth and land, and everything he turned his hand to prospered. And yet, late one night he came to the house of the priest and said, "Father, absolve me, for I am a great sinner."

He sat by the fire. The holy man said, "God forgives all, my son."

"He will not forgive me. For she offered me a choice of mortality or to be with the Shee forever, and I could not choose. So I have sworn to her that each of my descendants will face this choice, and that one day, one of them will be hers. I have betrayed all the unborn generations. For I dare not anger her."

Chronicle of Wintercombe

"How far?" Piers almost ran around the table.

The dial remained at 1400.

"I don't know for sure. Far enough." Maskelyne was infuriatingly calm, but even Piers could feel the fear in his stillness.

"Do something!"

"I am." His fingers touched the controls that he had rigged up. Figures rippled across the screen.

"Oh my God." Piers pressed his fists to his face. "We've lost them. Jake. Rebecca. Both the bracelets! Venn will absolutely *kill* me. No, not kill. Kill would be too easy. Imprison me in a tree for centuries. Saw me down and burn me on a bonfire. Grind my every atom into sawdust."

Maskelyne flicked him an irritated look. "Always about you, isn't it, little man."

"You can talk. You think the mirror belongs to you."

"It does."

"You wish! You can't even make it work properly!"

"I could once!" In a flash Maskelyne lost his temper; like a flicker of lightning he seemed to transform to a being of raw ferocity and dark fury. "Before I had to spend lifetimes plunging through time and space! Piecing my memories together again! What would you know about that loss, that terrible descent?"

Piers squared up. His chin jutted. "More than you might expect. I'm not all cooking and cleaning. I have a history too, so you can just—"

A mew silenced him.

He looked around.

A black cat stood there, tail in the air. It snarled at them both.

"Well." Piers took a breath. Suddenly he was a little ashamed of himself. "Well, yes of course, you're right," he muttered. "Not the time. Not the place."

Maskelyne stepped back. The dangerous darkness

seemed to gather inside him; he said nothing, but left the control panel and crossed to the mirror itself, gripping the silver frame with his fine-boned hands.

He stared in at emptiness. "All the world is in there," he whispered. "All possible worlds. And I will *journey* in them all again."

Piers watched him, curious. "Is it alive, that thing? You talk to it as if it can hear you."

"As alive as your replicant cats, little man."

With an effort Maskelyne looked away from the black glass. He stepped back, the reflection of the lab shrinking and rippling. Then he turned, and he was calm again, his voice husky and quiet.

"It seems clear that Jake has managed to *journey* back far enough to reach David. Perhaps their longing for each other reached out and touched, like the snake and its tail. Dee recorded a similar result. He calls it the *Magnetism of the heart.*"

"What!" Piers stared. Then he turned and ran to the desk and snatched up the Dee manuscript from under his pages of notes. "That's it! The heart! Oh my goodness. That means . . . this . . . and then this . . ." He scribbled letters furiously, and Maskelyne came and watched over his shoulder.

Then Piers stopped. "Do you see?"

"I see."

Together they stared at the words that had emerged

from the random mass of symbols like a sunlight through the fog of a wintry wood.

Let it be said the mirror is a way from heart to heart. For Time is defeated only by love.

Like a man who finds a path in a dark wood, and follows it to a lighted window, so is the journeyman.

Let the snake's eye open. Let the hearts reach out.

Piers looked up. Maskelyne nodded slowly. "Yes," he said, his voice husky. "I remember. The snake's eye can be opened."

"What do you mean . . . remember?"

A crash made the cat jump.

Then another.

Three separate crashes, as if a giant was beating at the door until the house shook.

Like the slow rumbling thunder of an avalanche, movement in the roots and depths of the earth itself.

"What's that?" Piers breathed.

Maskelyne listened, alert. "The wood is walking," he said. "Summer's revenge."

"Dad."

The word hurt. He couldn't move. Couldn't breathe.

But to his astonishment the figure in the gray robe exploded into rage. "What the *hell* do you think you are doing, Jake! *Telling him you can cure the plague!* How do you think you can say that! These people are dying, don't you realize! Really dying! Babies, and women and little children, dying in agony of this filthy, endless disease and there's nothing, nothing any of us can do and you, you have the reckless, stupid arrogance to stand there and—"

"*Dad.*" Jake's voice was soft. "Dad, it's all right. We're here now." He stepped forward, giving one glance to Rebecca, where she crouched on a chair, watching with wide eyes. "It's all right."

He reached out.

His father's hands, thin and oddly frail, grabbed him, pulled him close.

His father's face was muffled in his shoulder. He was sobbing, muttering, "Oh God. Jake. *Jake. I never thought I'd see you again.*"

Jake closed his eyes.

Rebecca bit her lip and blinked away tears.

For a long moment in the dark room no one said anything, as if just that holding, that watching, was enough.

Then, slowly, David Wilde pulled back. He managed a weak grin. "Look at me! Stupid. Hysteria."

"It's all right."

"It's been so long. On my own. So hard . . ."

"You don't have to say anything. I get it." Jake gave a wry grin. "God, you look awful."

His father laughed, a rusty, snatched gasp of relief. "Do I? You look great. So much . . . more grown-up."

"I'm sorry about what I said. The plague. I just . . . I get carried away, caught up in the excitement. I know it's not a game. It must have been hell."

David nodded. He cleared his throat, wiped his face with a dirty sleeve, and stepped back. "That's one word for it. The one they would use here." He glanced at Rebecca. "Is this . . . ?"

"I'm Becky." She stood and held out her hand; he took it and shook it, slightly bemused.

"Why are you both dressed like that?"

Jake said, "Bit of a mistake. We were trying to reach you through Alicia. I had no idea we could get this far."

"And Venn? Where's Venn?"

"Gone into the Summerland after half a Greek coin. Look, I haven't got time to explain it all now—we need to get straight to the mirror and get you back home. With both the bracelets we should be able to do it, even in stages."

Jake stopped. "What. What's wrong?"

David Wilde turned and walked to the window. He unlatched the shutter and let it swing wide; immediately heat entered the room on a ray of scorching sunlight. Swifts screamed outside, high over the houses.

"Il signore. His family. I can't just leave them."

Jake stared.

"Don't look at me like that, Jake! I'm a doctor, it's my duty."

"No!" Jake couldn't believe this.

"If I go, they'll die. I've been working day and night. I've managed to prepare a crude antibiotic—it's a tiny amount and the process is almost complete. If I could just . . ."

Before it could come again, the words, the flood of terror, Rebecca intervened. She took his hands and held them, and looked straight into his eyes. Jake was amazed at her strength.

"Listen to me, David. This is not your time. I'm a history student, I know about the Black Death. It raged through Europe and nothing and no one could stop it. It was there, it happened, it's over. It's not your fault, or your responsibility. If you stay, you'll die. And so will we, because I can't see Jake going back without you."

David stared at her. She could see how exhausted he was, how worn to a shadow.

He said, "I lie awake at night and dream, you know. About the mirror. It torments me. What use is a time travel device if you don't use it? I could go back to Wintercombe, get the drugs, bring them here. Perhaps we could stop the epidemic, stop it spreading. Save thousands of lives. Change history. We could do that."

He stepped back, sat down on the meager bed, as if stunned. "Think of what we could do."

She threw a worried glance at Jake. "Get burned for sorcery more like," he snapped, and she had never been so glad of his self-assurance.

"What do we do?" she whispered.

"Get him home. That's all I care about." He went to the window and looked down. The street was deserted, burning in the noonday heat. Only the swifts screeched in the eaves.

"And we need to go now. During the siesta." He came back and knelt at David's feet. "Dad. Where is the mirror? You said you knew."

His father looked at him. He drew a hand over his face and said, "Yes. I know. It's in the old palazzo."

"Can we get there?"

"Il signore lives there. His official apartments are there. With his guards and his torture-rooms." He frowned. "But Jake . . ."

"We go. Now."

David stood, picked up the bird mask, and looked around. For the first time Jake took in the meager poverty of the room, its crucifix, its dusty jug of water, its bleached walls.

"You've got the bracelet?"

"On my wrist, always." His father hesitated. "Jake . . . there's something I haven't told you."

"Is there anything else you want to take? From here?"

There was a wooden chest at the end of the bed. Some garments were folded on it; Jake pulled one out. "Maybe we could use this as a cloak for Becky or . . ."

His voice died.

It wasn't a cloak.

It was a baby's shawl.

A small sharp cry rose from the woolen fabrics. He tugged the topmost blanket aside, and stared.

A baby gazed up at him. Its eyes were blue and wide.

Rebecca put a hand to her mouth.

"Who's this?" Jake whispered. He felt numb now. Dread lodged in him like something unswallowed.

David hesitated. Then he came over and picked the baby up, folding the coverings down around its face.

"This is Lorenzo, Jake. This is my son. Your brother."

Venn felt the snow crash down on him like memory, as it had on Katra Simba, the weight of the past white and blank blotting everything out. It filled eyes and mouth and nose, it filled grasping hands, it swept even Leah's memory away and bowled him backward into the doorway that he knew led to Summer's house.

His whole being screamed out against it, but it was fate, it carried him along, and there was nothing he could do about it except rage.

And in an instant he lay on the floor of a vast hall, snow slopping from him, with Gideon gasping on hands and knees and Wharton sliding far over the tiles, coming to rest with his face flat against the wall.

Venn felt as if his rib cage was crushed. It was a feeling he knew. He sat up, slowly, and looked around.

A hundred images of himself sat up around him.

Gideon stared. He stood, and all the other Gideons stood too, an endless replication of tall pale boys in green frock coats that made him turn and stare and laugh in delight. "What is this place?"

"A hall of mirrors." Sour, Venn scrambled over to Wharton, turning the big man over. "George. Are you hurt?"

Wharton groaned and opened his eyes. "One bloody great bruise, that's all I am." Venn helped him to sit up, and his eyes widened as he looked around. For a moment the multiplicity of people astonished him; he thought there was a great crowd there, crouched, standing, sprawled. And then he saw it was just the three of them, over and over, going on forever in the opposing mirrored walls.

He took a breath. "Where is this? Is this Summer's doing?"

Venn stared around, then stood, tall and icy among the tilted glass. There were mirrors of all shapes and sizes, elegantly framed, fixed to every part of the wall, even the ceiling, Gideon realized, looking up at his own crazily foreshortened head and feet.

"This is Summer's doing," Venn murmured.

Wharton spread his hands. "Then where's Sarah?"

→•←

As soon as the box opened, a bird popped up. It was a tiny wooden bird with bright green and yellow feathers; it spun around and opened its beak and piped a high twittering song, so loud in the stillness she almost jumped.

"Ssh . . . shut up. Go down."

She tried to close the lid, but it seemed locked open.

She flung a desperate glance at the door, the curtained windows, but no one came in.

As suddenly as it began, the song ended. The bird stopped twirling and fixed her with a beady black eye.

All around it, the interior of the box was lined with scarlet satin. It seemed empty, but there was one tiny loop of ribbon that showed where a secret compartment lay.

Sarah took a breath. Then she reached in and her fingers lifted the ribbon loop, careful with the delicate sliver.

She stared into the black hole. It was space, eternal and endless. It was dusted with tiny stars and distant galaxies. Or were they strands of gold and diamonds and rubies?

The bird said, "Nice, isn't it? It goes on forever and ever."

She stared.

"I can't tell you how good it is to be back, though." It spread its tiny wooden wings and waggled them. "I am so bored! Centuries of silence." It whistled again, joyful, flew around the room and came back to perch on the box rim.

Sarah took a breath. "This belongs to Summer?"

"Her treasure box."

Hope was dawning in her like pain. She said, "I'm looking for something that belongs to me. A coin—well, half a coin. It's been cut in two. It hangs on a gold chain and . . ."

"Know the very thing." The bird nodded, self-important. "Just you wait there." It spread its wings, then looked at her again, oddly anxious. "You won't go away, will you?"

"NO! . . . No."

It flew into the box. And as she watched, it was lost among the distant stars.

Night thickens
and the crow makes wing to the rooky wood.

21

He could not lie, he could not sleep.
She stole his dreams away.
She locked them in her darkest hall
with fiend and ghost and fey.
He said, "I will not mercy beg,
I will not bow the knee."
But she smiled and thawed the snow
And set the flowers free.

Ballad of Lady Summer and Lord Winter

PIERS SWUNG THE casement wide and hung out. Rain spattered his face.

"There! See it!"

Over his shoulder, Maskelyne stared. From every window, a cat gazed.

This corridor was at the back of the Abbey, where the building crouched under the great crag called Winter Tor, a range of slate that jutted through the Wood. Far below, in its hidden ravine, the Wintercombe roared in flooded spate. Above, on that steep wooded slope, Piers could see movement.

It was slow. A trickle here, a slither there. A bush would snap, a scatter of earth fall into the river below.

But he could feel its threat in the very stillness of the air, the persistent drizzle of the rain. The whole hillside was slipping, inch by inch, shallow roots straining and tugging up in the saturated soil, until the weight tore them away. Already, a tree opposite the window was leaning against its neighbor, the trunk creaking as if in pain.

"The whole lot could come down on us any minute," Piers breathed.

He jerked back inside. "What do we do?"

Maskelyne did not seem too concerned. "If it falls, it damages the house. But the mirror is safe in the Monk's Walk. That part is more ancient and built of stone. It would survive."

Piers gaped. "It might, but I won't! Have you any *idea* what Venn will do when he comes back and finds his house flattened! Have you any notion of the utter misery . . ."

Maskelyne shrugged gracefully and walked away down the uncarpeted corridor. A trail of cats followed at his feet. "What can I do?"

"Plenty." Piers pattered along behind him. "You have . . . means."

Maskelyne stopped.

"Means?"

"Abilities. Oh, I don't know for sure who you are, Mr. Scarface, but I know what you are. Nobody bottles me up in a jar unless they have magic stored up right to their fingertips. I never felt a spell as strong as that, and I've been around some sorcerers, let me tell you. So maybe a moving forest would be easy-peasy."

Maskelyne smiled, shaking his head. "Piers! I think you must have me mixed up with someone else. I can't stop the rain."

Piers folded his arms, stubborn. "Maybe, maybe not. But if the house is flattened, what's to stop the Shee picking the place clean, mirror and all. Think on that, Mr. Ghost."

Maskelyne slid him a dark glance and then resumed his stride toward the stairs.

Piers watched him go, smug. That was telling him. No pulling the wool over Piers's eyes.

He puffed his chest out and grinned, and then saw the cats watching him and the grin went.

"Well? If I don't guard the place, who will? You lot?"

They slunk away, except for Primo, who rubbed against Piers's ankles. The little man scratched him fondly; the cat arched, then sauntered to a bedroom door and sat outside it, giving one piercing mew.

This wasn't a corridor Piers got to often in the rambling house—he could tell that from the dust. Now he opened the door and saw the attic room he had given Sarah.

"What?" he whispered.

The black cat advanced graciously in and padded across the worn rug. Just under the window it stopped. Its paw creaked a loose plank.

Then it leaped up onto the windowsill and began to wash.

Piers came and crouched. The plank was completely loose; he pried it out and found a dark space beneath the boards.

He looked up at Primo. "She hides her treasures here then, does she? Should we be looking?"

The cat licked on. Piers leaned in, groping.

He pulled out a small notebook and a black pen held tight to it by an elastic band.

The pen was from the future. He could tell that by its smell, and the big *Z,* as if for Zeus, on its clip. The notebook was gray. When he opened it he saw it was full of messages, written by Sarah and someone else, someone who wrote in capitals, a jerky, amused, bitter handwriting.

Who signed himself *JANUS.*

He read the last one.

I HAVE SENT YOU MY CHILDREN.

Piers put his lips into a whistle shape but no sound came.

"Oh that's bad," he whispered instead.

→·←

David sat on the narrow bed, the baby in his arms. He said, "There was a woman. She was pretty and young and . . . we started as friends. She was . . . the only one I felt safe with. Then . . ."

"I don't want to hear the whole sordid story," Jake growled.

He had gone back to the window and was standing in the shade. Gazing out.

Rebecca said, "Jake."

"Stay out of this. This is not your business."

His arrogance infuriated her, but she could hear the raw pain too, so she just reached out to David. After a moment he handed her the baby; she was surprised at his warm weight. Then he went over to Jake and stood behind him.

"Don't hate me, son."

"I don't hate you. But . . ."

"It just happened. She told me she was pregnant. We got married."

"You're already married! You're married to my mother!"

"She's a thousand years in the future in a country not even discovered yet." He tried to smile. "She never need know."

Jake spun. "This is not some joke!"

"No." His father's tired eyes held him. "No. It's not. Not when Gabriella was carried home from the market and I saw the first black lesion on her neck. Twenty-four hours, Jake, that's all it took. Twenty-four hours of agony from a healthy woman to a corpse suppurating with dark sores."

He gripped Jake's arms. "I couldn't save her."

Jake said, "The mirror. You could have . . ."

"And spread the pestilence to some other age? Not even for her."

They were silent. Outside, a church bell began to clang for Mass, somewhere far across the city.

Rebecca shifted the weight in her arms; the baby made a small contented noise.

Jake took a step back. He said, "Okay. Look. Whatever happened. Whatever you did, doesn't matter. We have to go. Now."

"The baby comes. He has no one else."

They stared at him; Rebecca said, "Can we . . . ?"

"Two bracelets. Together. We can try."

Jake breathed out, hard. Then he nodded. "Right. All right. Let's go."

→·←

Ten minutes later they raced down the stairs. David had replaced his doctor's mask, Jake wore an old apprentice robe. Rebecca had a cloak swathed around her and the baby was tied in it. "You'll have to carry him," David had breathed, fastening the swaddling. "It will look more natural."

"Will it?"

She had felt ridiculous, but as if he knew, he said, "You would have been married here for years, Becky. You'd almost be old."

It scared her now. Running down the dark stairs, she wanted to flee, suddenly afraid that the life she had always thought was in front of her was over. The thought of that other girl, who had gone from beauty to corruption in a day, terrified her.

At the street door, David peered out. Then he said, "Walk behind me. Close. Don't speak. Put your arm around her, Jake, as if she's sick. Everyone will stay clear."

The streets were deserted. They hurried, but the heat was like a great hand on their chests, a film of sweat on their faces.

Above them the narrow tawny buildings rose, castellated houses and towers, each with a barred wooden door at the base, the windows fixed tight against contagion. The city stank of its own dying, as if it was already a silent graveyard. With a sudden shock Jake recognized it—these were the scribbled towers on the manuscript Sarah had brought—turning a corner he came face-to-face with a statue of a man on horseback.

"Dee," he whispered

Rebecca was desperately trying to remember all she

could about the disease that had wiped out a third of the population of Europe. Had it been spread by fleas? She held the baby tight and slipped between the pools of ordure and tried not even to breathe.

Like a knife-edge of darkness, the shade ended. They came to a small piazza, shimmering in the heat. Opposite it was a gray stone building with a narrow tower. It looked ominous and heavy. Two guards leaned wearily at its single door.

David glanced out, then drew back.

"That's it. The Bargello. Town prison. Take a look up there."

Jake looked. Two masses of bone and clothing that might once have been bodies hung from a window on the second floor. They turned, slowly, in the rancid air.

"God," he muttered.

"Il signore's holed up here while the plague is running." David wiped sweat from his face. He managed a weak grin. "Visited it in 1986 on holiday once. Had an ice cream in a café just about here." For a moment bewilderment seemed to flicker through him as if he no longer knew where he was. Then he turned back, and stepped out.

They climbed the steps slowly. The guards straightened. "Dottore . . . ?"

"New patient." He waved at them. "Stand back, well back."

They couldn't do it fast enough.

Jake, his arms around Becky and the baby, hurried past. He had hoped it would be cooler inside, but the stone chamber led to an open courtyard, with a stair running up the side. David puffed up. "First floor. Hurry."

They pattered around an open loggia stacked with stores and chests, as if the signore had had all his riches dragged in here too. Ignoring them, David ran into a stone flagged hall, its high windows wide so that the sun made slants of burning molten light across the floor.

"There," he gasped.

At first Jake didn't see it. Only sculptures. Gods and angels. Great painted chests. A table laden with an unfinished meal.

Then, in a shadowy corner against the marble wall, it leaned like a dark doorway.

The obsidian mirror.

→→·←←

The bird was a speck. It grew slowly, circling toward her, and when it came out with a rush of speed, she drew back with a gasp.

In its beak it held the broken coin.

Sarah held out her hand. The coin was in her palm.

"Now," the bird said, "don't make the mistake of running off with that. All I have to do is screech and

→※ 293 ※←

the whole host of the Shee will come crashing in down the chimney and through the walls. I wouldn't like to think what will happen to you afterward."

She swallowed. "So you threaten as well."

"If I need to." It preened a small yellow feather back into place.

Sarah looked at the broken coin. The halved face of the Greek god stared out past her, and she felt a stab of guilt, because she was forgetting them, forgetting the whole horror of that distant bleak future, all that the group had planned, all their sworn friendship, forgetting Cara and Max.

"You're not crying, are you?" the bird said. Its head tipped, sidelong.

"No," she lied. "Look . . . I have to take this. It belonged to me—I gave it to Summer . . ."

"Oh, don't say her name." The bird seemed to shrink; at once it was tiny, a shiny miniature. "She'll hear!"

"Now I'm taking it back. It's vital. I can't explain why. But . . ."

"Are you one of the Venns?"

She didn't know what was best to say, so she nodded.

The bird whirled on its axis with an agitated rattle. Then it grew, just a little, and said, "I've seen him, you know, Oisin Venn. A handsome man. She torments him wonderfully."

"It's not Oisin anymore. Now it's Oberon."

The bird made a shrug in its depths. "Oberon, Oliver, Oscar. All the same. To her, that is. She's like the weather and the earth. Ageless and pitiless. Come closer."

Sarah approached, pulling the chain around her neck. "Look, I've got to . . ."

"She did this to me." The bird fixed her with its bead of an eye, and she thought that deep down inside it, there was a spark, like a flame. "Imprisoned me in here. Turned me into this contraption of twigs and feathers."

"Why?"

"Disobeyed her once. There was a place in the Wood—a trap. It looked just like any other piece of grass. But if a mortal stepped on it, they'd be stuck there while time went by without them. A step that would last a hundred years. Her idea of a joke. So everyone waited for one to come along."

Despite her fear, Sarah was interested.

"Everyone except you."

"I . . . well." The bird preened. "Sort of felt . . . mischievous. I wanted to annoy her. The mortal was a real yokel—spade over his shoulder, right off the fields. The Shee were all clustered round like flies. So I warned him off. Whispered in his ear. You should have seen him run!"

It gave a soft, sad whistle. "Then she found out."

Sarah said, "I'm sorry for you. But I have to go."

"With that?" the bird gave a cheep of scorn. "You'd never get out of the room. Unless . . ."

"What?" But she already knew what.

"Take me with you. Put the box in your pocket. I'll guide you all the way out of the Summerland. Refuse, and I SCREECH NOW."

Sarah almost laughed. The pompous pride of the tiny thing was almost funny.

Then, outside, there was a crash. She whirled. "What's that?"

"Nothing good, be sure."

She decided. The mirror's destruction depended on it. Without a moment's hesitation she grabbed the box and slid it into her pocket, and even as she turned, the door opened.

→⊷←

There was no door out. Even the one they had come through was gone. There was nothing except the repeated surfaces of the obsidian mirrors, all identical and all, Wharton thought, illusions. He said, "She's trapped us here. If we step through any of these, without a bracelet . . ."

"It doesn't matter." Gideon was gloomy. "We won't be going anywhere. All this is in the Summerland, and that goes on forever."

Ignoring the paradox, Wharton stared at himself. Really, he thought, he was getting a touch overweight. He said, "What do you think?"

Venn frowned. He went up to the nearest mirror and put his hands on it. It was black and solid. "We're so used to going through mirrors," he said, "that we've forgotten what they're really for." He stared into his own wintry eyes. "They show us what we think is real. But it isn't. Nothing is real."

He opened his fingers.

And to Wharton's astonishment the wall of black glass held the tiniest point of light, diamond bright. As he watched, it grew, as if it zoomed toward them, became a circle, then a square, then filled the mirror and was a window down onto some peculiar street, narrow, sun-slanted and cobbled.

As they watched, it closed again.

"Was that real?" Wharton said, fascinated.

Venn had stepped back, every sense alert.

"Possibly. In some other time. Or it might be a trap set for us by Summer, because I'm beginning to think she knows we're here."

Wharton didn't like the sound of that. "There's nowhere to go."

"Maybe." Venn turned suddenly to Gideon. "You. Tell me. Why did you bring Sarah here?"

Gideon's green gaze flickered. "She begged me. I . . ."

"Felt sorry for her?" Venn advanced on him. "I don't think so."

Gideon stared back, fierce. "We made a deal. She told me that she would help me."

"How can . . ."

"She said that in her time *there were no Shee*."

The words seemed to spill like a whispered wonder into the room. Gideon clenched his fists, hugged himself, as if he had said something terrible, something fascinating, that should never have been spoken.

Venn too, Wharton saw, was both astonished and intrigued. He stepped forward and lifted a hand, but as Wharton jerked forward in alarm, Venn's fingers stopped inches from Gideon's white glare. "No more," he breathed. "Don't talk of that here. Summer will hear."

He paced, restless, furiously watching his own reflections pace with him. All, Wharton noticed with a sudden chill, except one.

Because there was one mirror that held no Venn, that held nothing but darkness.

Wharton looked at it. Sidled closer.

Venn turned. "I'll smash every panel in this place if I have to. There must be a way out!"

Wharton reached out. The mirror was black, but not glass. It was a door painted dark as midnight, and there was a tiny handle recessed into it, and he reached out and turned it, and it opened.

Gideon yelled, "No!"

Venn turned and lunged at the door.

But Wharton was gone. All he saw was his own face in the mocking glass.

22

Progress report: ALICIA HARCOURT SYMMES

Subject observed continually. Seems to meet co-conspirators only at alleged séances. Information likely to be passed here.

Subject may be aware of surveillance. Yesterday she left the house and winked at this officer.

ALLENBY Covert Operations

THE ROOM WAS set up as a crude laboratory. Alembics stood on the bench; a rack of bizarre glass retorts bubbled and spat. A skull watched them with empty eyes.

David crossed quickly to a small cupboard in the wall and unlocked it. He took out a tiny vial. "This is it."

He brought it over. "I've been trying to isolate an antibiotic. It's crude, unrefined. But it might work, Jake, it might save a few lives."

The vial was filled with a grainy substance, amber as honey.

A noise somewhere in the building startled them. They froze, listened to footsteps running up the stair outside. The baby made a small snuggling motion against Rebecca's warmth. The footsteps came close, passed the door. Then they pattered on up and died into the distance.

Jake breathed out. "Right." He undid the bracelet from his own arm and slid it onto Rebecca's wrist, clicking it shut.

"What?" She stared in alarm. "But we're all going together, aren't we?"

"Of course we are. But this is just in case."

For a moment she stared at him in dread, the possibilities of being lost in the endlessness of time reeling out before her. Then he turned her to the mirror.

"What do you use to operate this, Dad? There are no controls . . ."

"I've learned a few things about the mirror." David came toward the silver frame. "All that electrical input, you don't even need it. These letters here, these words. They're enough if you know how to use them. You put your hands here. And here. Sometimes I think it reads your DNA. But"—he shook his head, stepping away in dismay—"for God's sake Jake, every time I've tried I've gone further back! What if we all end up in some prehistoric swamp? What if . . ."

"We won't." Before his father could object, he moved, grabbing Becky and pulling her close. "Do as he says."

She touched the silver frame.

Under her fingers she felt it tremble, felt it sense the

bracelet she wore, the terror she felt. She felt it waken and become interested in her.

"Jake."

Jake grabbed David. "Now us, Dad."

The mirror hummed. It shuddered. The air in the room gathered itself up.

But what burst open, with an abrupt, shocking crash, was the door. The guards leaped inside, halberds at the ready. Behind, striding tall in his robe of damask, the condottiere of the palazzo entered and stared.

The mirror throbbed.

It opened like a sudden vacancy in the world and took Rebecca and Lorenzo into a sudden roaring gust of emptiness.

The guards fell to their knees, speechless with terror. A halberd clattered. All the retorts on the bench shattered; Jake was flung sideways, and in the seconds it took him to stumble up and get his breath back, the signore had a knife at his throat and one strong arm tight strangling around his neck.

He saw his father stop in midstride, fling up his arms, yell, "Signore! *No!*"

Jake gasped for air. His hands clutched at the warlord's arm, but it was firm as steel, and the man's voice was contorted with anger and fear.

"What sort of filthy devilry have you brought into my house, dottore?"

The very last ghost I ever saw was in January 1941.

I really should have given up by then, but even though I was an old woman, I could not stop hoping. My father had been so sure they would come—David or his son Jake, or their mysterious and rather thrilling-sounding friend Mr. Oberon Venn.

I had taken to keeping the mirror covered, and all those years it had been a silent presence in my room. It had never shown me anyone again but for my own sadly ageing face. Perhaps I had begun to wonder if David had ever existed. My father died, the world changed, another world war loomed over us. Food was rationed, London cowered under the Blitz.

And then, on a cold spring morning when the daffodils in the square were splitting their papery yellow buds, Janus came back.

I had long since ceased to be able to afford a maid. I had become a dusty old woman, gray and lined, but still my spirit was high. I was happy with my séances, which had become strangely popular, and my tea parties and my dear friends from the Psychic Society.

So when I entered the study that morning, the

fire was unlit and the blackout curtains drawn. I opened them myself, letting them rattle in their great rings, and was gazing sleepily out into the street when he said behind me, "Hello again, Alicia."

I turned, my heart thumping.

He had not changed by even the growth of a hair. Small and uniformed, his hair lank, his glasses blue discs, he stood on my hearthrug and smiled that twisted smile that had no warmth.

"You!" I gasped. Not my most original retort, I admit, but I was so shocked to see him out of the mirror. It leaned behind him. One of my china dogs lay smashed on the tiles of the grate.

"I hope you don't mind me appropriating your parlor." He waved a small hand. "I intend to meet someone here."

I stared, astonished.

"In fact, they should be here any moment now."

"Is it David?" I confess my voice quavered.

He smiled. "Ah yes. You have wasted all your life waiting for David. How pitiful a thing that is."

Now, I take pity from no one. I rose, drew myself to my full height, and said, "My dear sir, I have waited for anyone who would come from the Other Side. My father and I spent many years contemplating our next visitor. And be assured, we did not waste our time."

And with what I hope was a suitably grandiloquent gesture, I put my hand up and tugged at the lever hidden discreetly behind the curtains.

The concertinaed cage crashed down from the ceiling.

Electric wiring crackled on.

Janus stood startled and unmoving in the trap that for years had been awaiting him.

To say I felt satisfied would be too inadequate a word. I really felt rather gleeful. I turned, sat demurely upon my sofa, folded my hands, and contemplated my handiwork. A tyrant from the end of time was my prisoner. It was really rather gratifying.

Janus said nothing. He reached out curiously as if to touch the steel bars but I said quickly, "I would not wish you to harm yourself. There is a charge of twenty-five volts throbbing through that metal as we speak, enough to give you quite a nasty shock. My dear papa designed the whole apparatus."

"Did he now." Janus nodded, folding his arms. He looked at the mirror, safely beyond his reach. "My dear lady, I congratulate you. I really do."

"I'm only sorry you have no chair in there. I have no wish to make you uncomfortable."

He gazed out at me. The blue lenses of his glasses hid his eyes, and that made him so difficult to read. But with dismay I became aware that he was not as devastated as I had hoped.

So I said, "I am quite aware that you are using my séances as a cover for some fiendish device to trap me. Your men are continually watching my house. Really, it's ridiculous."

He looked amused. "My men? You really don't understand anything, do you?"

I looked smug. "I have hidden all the evidence about my father's device in a safe place. You will never find it."

He shook his head. Then he said in a voice as silky as poison, "Alicia, you are perhaps the most foolish old woman I have ever met."

I bristled. "Well, I'm not the one in the cage," I snapped.

"Ah yes. The cage. So may I ask what you intend to do with me?" he asked softly.

In truth, I had no idea. We had expected David, or Jake. We had expected to be able to demand the bracelet in exchange for their release. But I merely shrugged. "I have my plans," I said, deadpan.

His smile was fixed. "Indeed. Well, so do I, madam. And here they come."

The mirror hummed. I leaped to my feet and stood well back, hastily grabbing the remaining china dog and hugging it to my bosom.

The whole room seemed to collapse. A terrifying vacuum opened deep in the heart of the mirror.

My hair was torn from its pins, my skirts snatched and whirled, my very soul enticed. And I saw, for one appalling second, the blackness that lies at the heart of the universe.

Maskelyne turned the pages of Sarah's diary with his long fingers, reading silently. Behind him, Piers fidgeted impatiently against the table. "So you see? She's been in contact with Janus all this time! And it says *children*. What children? Those replicants?"

"Almost certainly."

"Well, we know what to do about that." Piers fished a great bunch of keys out of his striped waistcoat and hurried to a small wall safe. Opening it, he brought out a cellophane-covered package and carried it carefully back. Maskelyne, hearing the rustle of the plastic being unwrapped, looked up.

Piers was holding the glass gun that could kill replicants.

"That's mine," Maskelyne said at once. He put the

book down and took the weapon firmly from the little man's nervous grip. "Don't handle it unless you need to. It's a very dangerous thing."

Piers made an odd grimace. "Don't want to. It makes my skin itch." He sidled closer, watching Maskelyne check the weapon, slide open a panel in it, adjust a small glowing dial in there. "Is it still working?"

"Yes."

Piers shivered. "Good. Because something tells me we're going to need it."

Outside, the crack and slither of earth seemed to shudder through the damp walls.

Maskelyne placed the gun carefully on the table. "Listen to me, Piers. From what Sarah writes here, these replicants have appeared to Jake. Been targeting Jake, I would say. Janus has been implanting prophecies in his ear—only too easy to do, if you come from the far future."

Piers crowded closer. "What prophesies?"

"The *Black Fox will release you* was the first. That came true. Then *The Man with the Eyes of a Crow.*" He frowned. "Given the dates on the mirror, I have an idea what that may be. But what is this *Box of Red Brocade?* It contains something vital, that's clear. Something Janus wants and can't get, so he needs Sarah to get it for him. Therefore something she desires." He looked up.

Piers stared back, eyes wide. "The Zeus coin! Yes, but Janus can reach anywhere in time. If he knows where it is, why not get it himself and . . ."

Maskelyne began pacing, a lean, dark figure in the gloomy lab, lifting a hand. "Stop talking, and just think about it. The coin—if reassembled—will destroy the mirror. Janus doesn't want that, so he needs to keep the two pieces safe and apart. Who knows, maybe he's got the left side himself. The box must hold the right half of the coin, the piece Sarah gave to Summer. That must mean it's in the only place, the only dimension Janus cannot access. *And it needs to stay there.*"

They looked at each other across the malachite labyrinth.

"The Summerland," Piers said gloomy.

"The Summerland." Maskelyne stood in front of the mirror, gazing at its blackness. "That's where it is. That's where it's safe. If Sarah brings it out . . . that's exactly what Janus wants."

For a moment they were silent. Then Piers said, "What about you. You don't want that either."

"No. I don't." Maskelyne put the gun on the table and they stared at each other over it.

"Venn needs to know," he said.

→⊱⊰←

Sarah turned and saw Wharton slide through the door and shut it with a gasp. He smiled at her.

"Sarah! Thank heavens!"

She stared. "George? What on earth are you doing here?"

"Good question! Venn came after you and I came because . . . well, I was worried about you." He turned and stared at the smooth white wall behind him. "What happened to the door? What is this place? What the hell is going on?"

"I wouldn't trust him," the bird breathed softly in her pocket. "Ask him a question only he knows the answer to."

Sarah sat on a cushioned sofa. "We seem to be trapped in Summer's house of mysteries. When you met me at the British Museum, George, what sandwiches did you buy me?"

He stared at her as if she had gone out of her head. "Good Lord, Sarah, how am I expected to remember that? And what on earth does it . . ."

"Just try."

Annoyed, he blew out his cheeks. "Egg? Definitely egg. Egg and cucumber."

She smiled.

"Was that some sort of password?" He came forward, light on his feet. "Sarah, we have to get out of here, we have to find Venn and Gideon. Why on earth did you come here anyway? What are you looking for?"

"Don't say." The bird's words were less than a breath on the air, but Wharton tipped his head instantly. "What was that? Did you hear something?"

"No. So you want to know why I'm here? Why not make Gideon tell you?"

"Gideon?" he gazed around, baffled. "I left him with Venn. What . . . ?"

"No wonder you're puzzled." Sarah stood, wandering along the row of sumptuous sculptures, her feet sinking into the deep carpet. "You don't know what would make me come so deep into the Shee country, do you? What could be so important. That's what worries you. That's what's tormenting you. Because you're not Wharton at all, are you. You're Summer."

George Wharton giggled.

Then he began unraveling before her, his arms becoming slim and white, his boots shriveling to bare feet, his coat blanching to a turquoise-and-purple feathery dress with panels of lace. For a moment he was a patchwork being, part man, part woman, inhuman, un-Shee. Then he was Summer, and she was throwing herself full length on the sofa and giggling with glee.

"Oh your face, Sarah! And I thought I was doing so well! Such fun! Tell me, what did I get wrong?"

Sarah felt only a weary irritation. "If you must know, it was the cucumber."

"Really! Your mortal food is all very confusing, I really don't know why you bother about it at all." Summer stretched bare toes and pointed them. "So, do you like my house, Sarah?"

"It's beautiful."

"Sometimes it is. Sometimes it's a cobwebby, dark, damp hovel. Sometimes a cave under the sea or a temple on a hot green island. It can be anything I want it to be."

Sarah kept her hand on the box in her pocket. "It must be boring. Always changing, always staying the same."

For a moment she was scared; a sliver of venom crossed Summer's face. She said, "Oh I'm never bored, Sarah. Now. You have something of mine. I want it back." She held out her hand.

Sarah was calm. She had rarely felt so alert, her mind sparking with plots and lies. It was like the day they had broken through all the wire fences and electrified corridors into Janus's lab and entered the mirror, not caring if they were caught; the sheer audaciousness of it exhilarated her. She took the box and held it out to Summer. "I came for this. The prophecies told Jake about it, and I came to find it, because I thought it would help me defeat Janus. But I can't reach what's inside it."

Summer raised a perfect eyebrow. She snatched the

box and opened it and the bird unfurled itself, preened a green feather, and uttered a burst of tuneful song. Summer laughed. "You! I had forgotten all about you!" She extended a white finger and the bird hopped from its perch and gripped on, a tiny thing of string and feathers.

Summer glanced in at the bottomless abyss of stars and treasure. "Is everything in there? All my lovely things? Nothing missing?"

The bird slid a sidelong look at Sarah. She held her breath.

It would betray her. Surely. The Shee could never be trusted.

It said, "Gold and gems. Diamonds and dewdrops. Rubies and robins. Marcasites and the moon. Everything is here that should be here."

Summer looked into the depths of the box. She gazed a long moment, as if she could see all that it contained, and in that instant Sarah's heart almost failed her, because the powers of the faery queen must be immeasurable. But the bird winked at her and she tried to hold hope like a bright flame in her mind.

"Well." With a flick of her fingers, Summer snatched the bird, tossed it in, and snapped down the lid. "My box won't help you against Janus. And trespassers in my house need to be punished." She lifted her head and pointed a fine fingernail. "As you see."

And Sarah saw Wharton.

He was frozen, mid-step, in a cell of glass. It slid and protruded into the room like a great ice cube. His face was hard, caught in panic.

"What have you done to him!" She ran to touch him, but her hands slid only on a flat cold surface.

"I've stopped him." Summer came and stood by her, gazing critically. "How very ugly some of these mortals are, Sarah. Such ungainly animals. Wrinkled and heavy and weighed down by the world. Not Venn, of course. Venn is a sleek white leopard. Fierce and adorable."

"Let him go." Sarah's voice was a growl. Wharton's face, caught in this rictus of ridiculous surprise, annoyed and upset her. She felt humiliated for him. "I'm the one you should be punishing."

Summer smiled. "Well, yes. That's true."

She did nothing, but the glass suddenly slithered down and became four silver-haired Shee in white satin coats who hauled Wharton by the arms and legs into the room. He came alive like a fury, struggling and swearing terrible army oaths as they threw him down before Summer.

He landed on hands and knees.

Then he saw Sarah.

His astonished relief made her smile. But as their eyes met, she knew he had realized what she was here for, and his relief became wary and cold, and she felt a sudden, unexpected pang.

Of something that might have been shame.

Don't betray me! she thought.

Don't.

23

Once—before he met his wife—I asked Venn
what he loved best in the world.

"Freedom," he said.

After Katra Simba, after he was married, I asked
him again.

He looked away into the distance. "Leave me
alone, Jean," he said. "You know the answer now."

Jean Lamartine, The Strange Life of Oberon Venn

"DON'T HURT HIM. He's my son."

Jake felt il signore's surprise jerk the knife tighter.
He tried not to breathe.

"Your son, dottore?"

"Yes. Come from England, as he says."

"I do not believe the lies of devils. I saw the girl
vanish. Through that black portal of hell." The warlord backed, dragging Jake away from the mirror. It
leaned like a slant of darkness in the hot room. Flies
buzzed in the window.

"Listen to me." David took a step forward. "You know
me. I've served you now for four years. I delivered your
children. I bound your wound after the battle with the

Sienese and nursed you through the fever it brought. *I saved your life.*"

No answer. The grip just as tight. Jake made himself hold still. Sweat soaked his forehead. He tried not even to swallow.

"If that's not enough, I have something to give in exchange," David said. "Something of great power. Only you should know of it."

In the silence a cry rose from far off in the city. A woman's scream of grief. It rang in the sweltering, shuttered streets. In the pitiless blue sky.

"Do you hear that?" David said softly. "Signore, that is the city crying out to you. That is the cry of death itself."

For a second, nothing. Then the warlord turned his hawk profile on the guards. "You men. Outside! Allow no one in unless I call."

They obeyed him without question, though one glanced back, catching Jake's eye with a murderous glare. The door latch clattered behind them.

"Speak." Il signore turned the knife against Jake's neck. "And be quick."

David said, "Give me my son and let us both go in safety. We're no threat to you. In return I will give you this." He took the vial from the folds of his robe and held it up. The amber substance it held gleamed in the slant of sunlight.

"Some sorcery."

"Not sorcery. This is medicine. It may cure the plague. There is enough in this flask for you and your family, should you need it. No more exists, not in the whole of this world."

In the obsidian mirror Jake watched the warlord's face. Perhaps the dark glass magnified emotion, revealed its intensity, because he was sure he saw the man's eyes narrow with greed.

Jake tried to pull away. The knife blade, sharp as a razor, jabbed into his skin.

"How can I believe this?" Il signore's voice was a rasp of doubt.

"You have no choice."

"No? I could have your son thrown into a pest-pit. Infected with the plague. To see if you can cure him."

"Take him and I smash the vial to pieces. Shall I do that now?" David held it high. "Because hear this, signore. I am no demon, but a man who has scryed into the future of the world, and I know about this pestilence. You think it's bad now. It hasn't even begun. It will sweep Europe like a black rain. Men will die in the fields, at the table, men will drop dead in the counting-house and the church. Their bodies will lie unburied, heaped in the streets, and even the rats won't touch them. Two out of every three will die, kings and princes and dukes as well as peasants. Your citizens will be decimated, your army reduced to a clatter of empty armor. Trust me, signore. This is horror. This is the truth."

His urgency hung in the air like the murmured echo of his words in the high ceiling.

Sweat ran in Jake's eyes.

Il signore did not move. Jake felt the heat of the man's body in the strangling arm as he said, "Go where?"

"Into the mirror. Back to the place we came from."

"To England? Or to hell?"

"This is hell. Seeing our children die is hell. Unless we help each other. I'm not offering you damnation, Piero. I'm offering you life."

The vial caught the sunlight. It gleamed red now, red as blood, a warm comfort in the dim room.

The warlord moved, in sudden, powerful, decision. He forced Jake forward. "Very well. Put the flask on the floor and step back from it."

"No." David held the man with a steady gaze. "First you must release Jake."

They faced each other. Pinned between them Jake felt the struggle of their mutual defiance. He dared not move now, because the knife was a razor's edge between life and a sudden, slashing death. He kept his eyes on his father. His belief was fierce and blind.

Suddenly he was shoved forward, a violent release

that sent him sprawling against David. With the lithe speed of a snake, il signore snatched the vial and thrust it deep in his own robes and without even pausing lifted the knife and stabbed.

"Demon!" he snarled.

Caught in astonishment, David froze. The blade whistled; Jake hauled him aside with a great yell and grabbed the warlord's arm.

He was flung away like a rag. Something red and scorching ripped down his shoulder, his side, then David had hold of him and they were falling backward, back and back, into the exploding, enfolding embrace of the mirror, and the last thing he saw before darkness was the warlord on his hands and knees, staring dumbfounded at the opening in the wall of his world.

Rebecca burst out of the dark tunnel of the mirror with a scream of terror, straight into a mass of malachite-green webbing.

Crushed against her ribs, the baby screamed too.

The webbing caught her like a fly in a trap. Its mass of sticky threads bounced with the shock.

She picked herself out of it, breathless and confused. She felt as if she had been torn apart and reassembled and that all the pieces were in the wrong places.

"Maskelyne? Piers?"

The laboratory was empty. Strangely dark. Small lights winked on the monitors. Her breath smoked in the damp air. "Where are you?"

The chill silence unnerved her. She stood, turned, gasped in a deep breath. The mirror reflected her bedraggled anxiety. And where was Jake? Why hadn't he followed?

The baby cried again. She unwrapped the small heavy bundle and uncovered a white face that contorted itself in misery.

"Sshh," she breathed.

The Abbey seemed more silent than she had ever known it, and the lab darker. There was something else wrong, a new stench of damp and decay.

Something slithered and fell.

She turned in terror, her heart thudding.

The far wall, a dark patched surface of medieval brick, was bowing, swelling outward into the room. As she watched, a brick cracked, a patch of plaster fell off, as if some great unstoppable force was building up behind there, the whole weight of the hillside forcing its way in.

She stepped back.

Then deep in the house she heard an enormous crash.

As if a chimney had fallen.

Or a bomb.

→*→←

Venn prowled the mirrored hall with tormented anxiety. "Something's happening. Can you feel it? Something's changing."

Gideon, his face and hands pressed to one of the identical glass surfaces, gazed into his own green eyes. He too could sense it. A subtle distortion of space, a contraction. A breathing in.

He said, "The room's getting smaller."

"Smaller?"

"It's closing in on us. Collapsing." He could hear it now, the soft, creaking shrinkage of the chamber.

Venn turned with sudden purpose to the mirrors. "Then we smash our way out." He tore at the carved frames, but the gilded wood fell away as if it was rotten, desiccating in his fingers.

"Try this!"

Gideon found a chair, picked it up and crashed it down. Frail wood splintered. They each snatched a chair-leg, and attacked the walls. Already the room was half the size it had been, the floor and ceiling slanting at impossible angles.

Venn smashed the nearest mirror; it starred into jagged fractures. For a moment Gideon was reminded of the crevasses out in the ice field; he leaped back as the pieces fell in great slabs at his feet.

But there was no opening. Behind the first, another

identical mirror showed them their own despair.

Furious, Venn smashed that too, and found only another.

Gideon dragged him back. "That's no use. Think! You must have some power here. The Venns are half Shee, everyone says. Summon it! Use it!"

Venn's cold stare chilled him.

"No."

"But—"

"If I do . . . if I start that, where will it end?" He stared at the collapsing room. "That's what she wants, for me to give in to her, to enter the unhuman world. And it would be easy. So easy." He took a deep breath. "You above all know that. You've heard their music. You went with them."

Gideon nodded, but panic was growing in him. "I know. But if you don't, we die here."

"Summer would never . . ."

Gideon faced him. *"Summer would kill us like flies,"* he breathed.

Venn was silent. As if he made himself face the truth of that.

Gideon watched the man's struggle with a cold compassion. "You have to," he hissed. "The Shee all whisper about it. Ever since Oisin Venn your family have had the choice. The power is there, if you want it.

Do it, Venn. Destroy her with her own gift." His voice was fierce, he knew. His desire for vengeance on her shocked even himself.

Venn threw down the piece of wood and stood still.

Gideon waited, breathless. The room was so small now that he could reach out and touch both sides of it, as if the very cube of the world was dwindling to a point as minute as infinity.

Venn looked up.

The ceiling was a glass plane, still out of reach. He seemed to focus on it with a bitter, controlled fury. Gideon waited, fighting down panic. Glass walls nudged his arm. His own reflection pushed against him. He was replicated, hand to hand, face to face, an eternity of Gideons crowded together with his stifling terror. He would be suffocated, crushed against his own face, his hands clawing hopelessly against their glassy copies.

He tried to turn, but there was no space.

Venn shivered. He seemed thinner, paler. His fingers a little longer. His eyes bird-blue.

He had lost something of himself.

He crouched. "On my shoulders. Quickly!"

Gideon climbed, light and fleet; Venn stood, heaving him up. "Push. Push hard!"

He strained. His palms forced against the glass roof, but it was solid, hard as ice, impenetrable. For a second he understood the whole horror of being sealed in, the fear of the baby in the womb, the chick in the egg.

"Push!" Venn yelled.

The walls crushed against them.

Then, with a crack that sent Gideon's heart leaping, the world shattered.

Water roared down. Into his yell of terror. Into his mouth and eyes.

Sarah said quietly, "Are you all right?"

"I'm fine." Wharton was a little startled. For a moment he was not quite sure where he was. He looked around curiously at the sumptuous room, then at Summer, who smiled sweetly.

Sarah held his eye. "Good. Be careful. *Please.*"

She dared not say more. But if he guessed she was here for the half coin, surely he would know not to risk mentioning it. She felt the tiny half-moon of gold move against her skin, under her clothes. Now all she had to do was get it—and them—out of here.

"But where's Venn?" Wharton turned, astonished. "And Gideon?"

"Oh, I think it only fair they have a little difficulty, don't you?" Summer stretched her small feet languorously. She fixed Sarah with a sudden sly glance. "Because Gideon was supposed to be bringing me one of those lovely magic bracelets, and he has failed me. Again. How very disappointing."

She sat up. "And you see, Sarah, something else is all wrong." She stood and crossed lightly to the red box and picked it up. Wharton stared at it.

"I don't believe you came for this. I think you came for something else." Summer pouted. "Now, I wonder what that could be? Something so powerful you would even dare to come to my house for it?"

Sarah dared not move. She sensed Wharton edge closer.

Summer opened the box. "You, in there!"

The bird popped up and chirruped brightly.

"Stop that." Summer extended a finger. "Listen, I know she's taken something. What is it? Tell me at once or I'll turn you into a cockroach and you can crawl in dung for a thousand years."

The bird was silent. Then it looked at Sarah, a bold flicker of its beady eyes, and before it spoke, she knew that this time it would betray her.

"What do I get if I tell you?"

"Freedom. You get to fly in the greenwood."

"And change my shape back?"

Summer shrugged. "Maybe. Maybe I could let you be a real bird."

"A starling? And fly with the Host again?"

"Why not."

The wooden bird considered. Then said, "A half coin of gold. On a chain around her neck."

Sarah grabbed at the chain and leaped back. Wharton stepped between her and Summer.

Summer laughed. "That trinket! So the emperor's face does have power. I rather thought so when I asked you for it. But it must be far, far more powerful than I thought."

She came toward them and Wharton braced himself to stop her. But to his astonishment his body refused to move. His arms remained at his sides. Furious and terrified, he tried to yell. Nothing came out but the faintest of gasps.

Summer came up to him and stood on tiptoes to stare into his eyes. "Sorry, George," she whispered. "It won't last, I promise."

He tried to squirm as she passed behind him.

Summer came to Sarah and said quietly, "When a gift is given, it should never be taken back." She reached out lightly and took the chain from around Sarah's neck, her touch light and cold as a spider's.

Furious, unable to move or even access her invisibility, Sarah saw the glittering broken coin held before her eyes, the key to the mirror's destruction dangled like a taunting toy before a child.

A terrible, wrenching anger surged in her; she cried out in her mind, a great cry of despair that seemed to well up and burst into abrupt sound as if her ears had popped. Summer stepped back, astonished, and in that single instant the tiny bird flew; it snatched the half coin from Summer's fingers and fled with it, up and up, into the high white ceiling of the room, into the curtains, through the opened window out into the mothy night.

Sarah collapsed. Wharton gasped.

Summer screamed a shrill screech of fury and with a flurry of feathers became instantly a black hawk with yellow eyes; she flew and the room flew with her, the sofa transforming into a fallen log, the deep carpet a pile of leaves, the ceiling the crowded trees of the Wood.

And above, in the starry darkness of the sky, the tiny bird flew up and up and up, until it was lost to sight in the frosty galaxies, the endless black eternity of space.

24

Come with us! Join us, all you men and women who
have courage in your hearts. For what is life without
freedom?

Illegal ZEUS transmission

MASKELYNE HURRIED PIERS through the corridors of Wintercombe.

The crashing from outside was enormous, as if all the trees of the Wood were marching down on them. At the front door Piers hung back. "Why me? Why me? I can't . . ."

"You will. You must." Maskelyne grabbed the little man and turned him, pulling the white lab coat off him quickly. "Piers, we're all depending on you."

Piers laughed, a horribly nervous cackle. His red waistcoat darkened to brown, his clothes faded to the drabbest of tweeds. "Got to blend in, then. Camouflage." He pulled a coat from the rack and huddled into it.

"Now listen to me." Maskelyne already had both hands on the door bolts. "Get out there and find Venn. You have to tell him what Sarah is up to. You have to protect the Zeus coin. If Summer gets her claws on it . . ." He shook his head, anxious, the scar livid against his dark hair. "You're the hero now, Piers. Not the servant anymore. You're the warrior, the lonely defender against the dark. If you do this, Venn will never be able to thank you enough."

"You think so? Really?" The little man swelled a little. "Well . . . right."

"Ready?"

"No . . . Look. I don't . . ."

Maskelyne hauled the bolts back. The door crashed open. The gale hurtled horizontal rain across the hall.

Piers's objections were snatched away. He took a great breath, clutched the coat around him and was gone, as if he were a small brown leaf the wind had sucked up and blown far away.

Maskelyne instantly slammed and locked the door. Leaning his back on it, he stood there a moment like a shadow in the hall, his eyes on the rain patterns, the damp tiled floor, the stairs going up into the deserted corridors and attics of the Abbey.

Finally he allowed himself a small weary smile.

Because now, at last, he was alone. With the mirror.

Ignoring the darkness he ran swiftly along the Long Gallery and into the Monk's Walk. Down through the ancient arches the river foamed in its ravine below; the air was saturated with water, the walls running with damp.

The mirror called to him. He could hear its voice, that strange toneless whine that was always somewhere deep in his mind, modulating and searching, tormenting him with its anxiety, as if somewhere it had lost the language it had once spoken and yearned only to find it again.

"Hush," he whispered. "Hush now. I'm coming."

The lab was silent. He came in and stood there, listening. Then he approached down the tunnel of the malachite webbing.

The mirror waited in its silver frame. He knew those words; he knew their meanings. He reached out to touch them, and his fingers caressed the archaic spell that he had seen forged and placed here centuries before.

He said, "I'm back. I'm here. It's only us now. Forget the others, forget Venn. They're lost. Only we exist." He reached out for the new controls. "And now they never need come back."

His fingers closed on the switch.

Then, behind him in the darkness, a sound made him freeze. The most peculiar mew, a gurgle. *A message from a mind before speech, without language.*

He turned in terror.

"So don't I exist?" A girl's voice, hard with bitterness. "Or am I forgotten too?" She came forward out of the shadows, wrapped in some dirty robe, and his breath choked him because for a moment he had thought she came from a past so distant that he had buried all traces of it.

"Rebecca? When did you . . ." He stopped, staring.

The baby moved in her arms. He came and looked down at it, the round grizzling face, the tiny clenched waving fists. *"What happened back there?"*

Her face was scorched with contempt. "Not what you think. This is David's son. His mother died of the plague . . ."

Maskelyne licked dry lips. "Look, Rebecca . . ."

"What were you going to do?" She came forward, her head on one side. "Leave them there? Venn, Jake, David? Close the mirror against them? You know how to do that, don't you."

He did not speak, but she had her answer.

She felt the baby squirm against her. She said, "There is no way in the world I will ever let you do that. I thought I knew you, Maskelyne. I thought I loved you. But maybe I haven't a clue about who you are. Who you really are."

⤜⤛

This time I was a little more prepared. When the mirror opened, I held my skirts down and stared boldly into the black vortex. How shall I describe it? Like seeing for a second into the very depths of space, into the terrible emptiness beyond the remotest galaxy and the final ashes of the last star.

And when it ended, my room felt tiny and crowded.

A boy stood there, a tall thin lad in a dark suit. I saw at once that he was bleeding from a cut in the shoulder; he all but collapsed onto my hearthrug. And behind him, dropping a strange bird-face mask and hurrying to his side, was— at last!—David.

"Jake?" He looked up. "Venn! Get some . . ."

His voice stopped. He looked around. At Janus, standing calmly in the bars of my father's cage.

"What . . . ?" His eyes took in the details of my room rapidly.

"A little detour, I'm afraid," Janus said. His smile was a mockery.

I poured out some wine from the decanter and hurried over to hold it to the boy's lips. Instead he took it from me and drank a sip. He stared at me with dawning astonishment.

David stood slowly. "Alicia?"

"That's right, dear." I became very business-like. "How wonderful that you've finally made it! Now, this must be Jake, I presume, and really, what a nasty gash he has. Come and sit down, child."

They were amazed. David said, "Why here?" and Jake replied in a murmur, "I don't know." Neither of them could take their eyes from Janus.

"You mustn't worry about that wicked man from the future." I fussed Jake into a chair. "My father and I were quite prepared. As you see, he can never get out of that cage."

They looked at me as if I was a child. Jake—quite a handsome boy really—said, "Don't you understand? He's a replicant. He can walk through that anytime."

"Nonsense. Only a ghost could." I stood upright and looked at Janus. "Can you?"

He smiled. "My dear lady, I would never be so impolite."

It was then I truly understood the evil that was in him, as if for a second something dark and cruel flickered in my shabby room. I turned quickly. "He wants your bracelet. Go! Hurry!"

Janus was quicker. He reached out and pushed me aside so that I stumbled over the foot-stool and fell rather awkwardly on the rug. Jake leaped up.

"Move!"

Catching hold of his father's hand, he stepped back against the mirror.

I flinched from the terrible implosion.

But nothing happened!

Janus seemed as surprised as the rest of us. The he laughed; a short, amused laugh. "Well. That is surprising. It seems you've been betrayed."

"Betrayed?" David was frantically adjusting the silver ring.

"By Venn perhaps. Or by the scarred man." Janus frowned, as if at an irritating memory. I gathered my skirts around me and stayed on the mat. I was rather shaken, but David's anxiety was acute.

The mirror remained black, and solid.

Jake snarled, "You'll never get the bracelet. We'll throw it in the fire first."

"Then you will have done what I want." The tyrant had a flat, unpleasant smirk. It became annoying really quickly.

There was silence. But in the stillness I realized that the traffic in the street seemed to have stopped. There was distant shouting, a running of feet on the pavement outside.

I saw Jake's eyes fix in what I can only say was utter alarm.

He was staring at my calendar; a sweet thing, free with the Daily Mirror, decorated

*with pictures of kittens and puppies. It was
open on the date, 14th January 1941.*

*"Oh my God," he breathed. He looked at
me, hard, as if seeing for the first time my gray
hair, my sadly advanced age.*

Then he turned on his father. "It's now!"

"What is?"

*"The raid . . . the bombing raid! This is the
date I came here. The day she dies. It's today.
It's now!"*

*As if to answer him, up from the depths of
the city rose a sound they started at, but which I
had grown only too used to. The wail of the sirens,
the eerie early warning of the coming waves of
planes.*

*And far off, with the soft thudding of rain
on a roof, the first bombs burst open on the East
End, like murderous red flowers.*

❧❦

"Don't do this." Rebecca came toward him. "They need
you. Venn and Jake and Sarah. You made an agreement
with them."

"That girl will destroy the mirror! I can't let that
happen. Without them . . ."

"You can't leave Jake to die in some plague-ridden
past. I won't let you."

Maskelyne stood like a shadow between her and the

obsidian glass. As ever, it showed no image of him, as if he had never existed, as if he were only the product of her dreams, unseen by anyone else. Sometimes she felt she had invented him, created him, but now she realized that he was some mystery beyond anything she could make.

He smiled his dragging smile. "Don't hate me, Becky."

"Then don't make me. You can help them, work with them. You can wait. The threat to the mirror comes first. From Summer. And from Janus." She stepped forward, almost touching him. "Because who can save us from Janus if not you? I don't know who you are, but I know you're more powerful than any of us, maybe even than Summer herself. And I trust you."

A gurgle behind them. She turned and saw the marmoset, Horatio, and the baby face-to-face, staring at each other in mutual fascination.

When she turned back, Maskelyne was watching her, his eyes dark as the glass.

"I think only you keep me human, Becky," he murmured.

Sarah and Wharton scrambled through the Wood, torn by thorns.

"Can you see it?" she screamed.

He couldn't. The bird was lost in the misty cloud

that hung low over the treetops. And the Shee were coming now, swooping down from the rain, a dark birdfall onto the gnarled and lichened branches.

"Be careful!"

Her yell warned him just in time. The Wood fell away at his feet into a deep ravine; in its depths the river roared over stones hurtling toward the gray shimmer of the Abbey through the trees.

He skidded to a stop, sending soil and pebbles rattling down. Ancient gravestones rose from the saturated soil; leaning crosses and a languid angel with folded wings.

"Where is this?" he gasped.

"The green chapel. Some ancient part of the Abbey." Sarah stared up hopelessly at the gray sky. The bird had fled, but Summer would surely find it, fall on it, tear it to bits with her fierce beak and talons.

And take the coin.

She wanted to howl with fury and despair. Instead she said icily, "I suppose you're pleased."

Wharton backed from the crumbling edge. He said, "Of course not. Not if Summer knows the power of the coin. What a weapon against Venn."

They looked at each other, while the Shee fluttered down around them in a glittering flock. As each starling alighted, the trees were weighed with wings, rows of bright eyes, beaks pecking and squawking and fighting each other.

"And now you know it too," he said. "Who told you? That changeling?"

"You did, George. I . . . overheard you and Jake talking."

He grimaced. "Oh great."

The soil slid. She turned, to cover her odd feeling of shame, then stared. "The whole hillside is moving."

The graveyard shuddered. It slipped down toward the Abbey as if the weighted trees would crush the building, as if it would scatter stones and bones into the raging river.

Sarah gave a yell of fear. With a flicker of green coattails Gideon had risen up from the water and was being hurtled along down there, slammed against boulders and snagged timbers, then up again, gasping.

"We have to get to him!" A tiny trail running with rainwater led over the edge; without hesitation she was slithering down, grabbing brambles and gorse, ignoring the stings and scratches.

"Wait! Sarah!" Wharton scrambled after her, desperate at being so clumsy and breathless. As his feet slipped he looked up. *And saw Venn.* The man's blond hair was slicked by the current; he was swimming strongly. As Sarah reached the shore and raced along it, leaping flood debris, he slid under the brown waters and dived for Gideon.

For a moment there was nothing but foam.

Wharton crashed down beside her. "Where are they?"

"I don't know. Can't see . . . There!"

Venn surfaced and he had Gideon with him. In a tangle of limbs they hit a half-drowned tree and hung on. In moments Sarah was there; she grabbed Gideon and hauled at him and he scrambled quickly out, collapsing on hands and knees on the bank, spitting water.

Sarah turned back to Venn. Their hands gripped, his eyes, blue as ice, met hers. But he was heavy, the current dragging at him, and she knew as his hand slid from hers she didn't have the strength to hold him. She screamed.

Instantly Wharton was there, pushing her aside, solid as a rock in the water; Venn grabbed him and Wharton dragged, and through the terrible suck of the water hauled him out, sleek and soaked as an otter, and quite abruptly she knew he was safe, and sat down, weak with relief.

Beside her came a bitter, soft laughter. Gideon was pushing his long hair from his face.

"What?" she whispered.

"Did he think They would let me die? No chance."

"Maybe for a moment she forgot about you," Sarah snapped. "Maybe other things are more important."

She watched Venn and Wharton climbing up the rocks. All at once her failure came and crushed her; all her energy seemed gone, all her hopes lost.

Gideon stared at her. "What's wrong?"

Her voice was numb. "I didn't get the coin. And Summer knows. It's all over." The words seemed too weak for the weight of her despair; judging by his silence, Gideon was appalled too.

"At least you still have your dreams," he muttered.

Before she could say any more Venn was there, water dripping from his hands and clothes. She saw at once that something had changed in him. His skin was pale, his hair held a strange new silvery shimmer.

He stood and turned and yelled in an explosion of fury that shook the Wood. "Go! All of you! Leave my house alone!"

The starlings screeched. They rose in a mighty flock, so many of them, thousands upon thousands, that they darkened the sky, and Sarah felt the relief of the trees, the weight lifted from them, the slow, sliding arrest of their descent.

❧❦❧

Janus watched as plaster crashed from my ceiling. Then, as if deliberately enjoying my obvious terror, he walked straight through the bars of the cage!!

He stood face-to-face with David.

"Give me the bracelet," he said calmly. "Only I can save you now."

"Dad! No!" Through the ache of the stab wound, Jake watched his father anxiously.

David stared Janus down. But I saw he was quite defeated. He said, "We have no choice, son. None at all."

His fingers unclicked the silver snake.

But in that second the mirror pulsed, and out of it stepped a stranger, a dark scarred man. He too wore a bracelet, and carried a most peculiar weapon, made of glass. He leveled it straight at Janus.

"Yes you do," he said quietly.

All down the street, the bombs began to fall, one by one. And now I knew that under one of them, I would die.

25

... And since that day, in every generation, the
eldest male of the Venn family has faced the fearsome
choice. Some have died in strange circumstances,
others have fled the land, others have marched
recklessly to war and been killed in the front line.
As if each had a terror of what awaited him in
Wintercombe Wood.

But one day, a Venn will re-enter that dark forest
forever.

And its Queen will be waiting.

Chronicle of Wintercombe

PIERS RAN INTO them as they straggled back to
the house; Venn striding ahead, Gideon at his heels,
Wharton trailing behind with Sarah.

"Oh Excellency!" Breathless, he clasped his hands
to his hips, doubled up. "So glad I've found you . . .
message . . . Sarah . . . she's after the coin . . . knows
about it."

"Message from who?" Venn stared at him. "Piers,
who the hell have you left looking after the mirror?"

"The cats. And Maskelyne."

"Are you insane!"

Piers looked uneasy. Venn swung on Sarah. "You

promised to help me," he said quietly. "Instead you went after the one thing that will destroy me. How can I ever trust you now, Sarah? If my own family betray me, how can I trust anyone?"

She was silent. She wanted to say something to ease his pain, but no words came.

"So where is the broken coin?" His voice was bleak. "Did you get it back? Did you let Summer know the one thing she should never know?"

She was all at once too tired and dismayed to care what he thought. "I tried to get it and failed. Summer kept it in a red box that seemed to hold the whole universe. And though I didn't tell her what it could do, I think she's beginning to guess."

Venn snorted, looking straight ahead through the trees. "My greatest enemy owns half of the device that can destroy everything I've worked for. And *you* gave it to her."

Sarah was silent. She felt Wharton's hand squeeze hers, a reassuring warmth. He said, "Look, hadn't we better get to the Abbey? If Maskelyne takes the mirror . . ."

Venn was already running. They raced after him, through the tangled undergrowth of the bare wood, along paths muddy with rain, leaping fallen branches. Ducking out onto the overgrown lawns, Venn stopped, amazed.

The hillside at the back of the house had moved.

Now the wooded cliff and its overgrown graves hung at a new angle, the ancient chapel up there broken in strange formation, on the edge of the ravine.

He seemed struck by it; he whispered, "An avalanche of earth," and Gideon raised an eyebrow at Sarah.

She said, "Like on Katra Simba?"

Venn turned his winter stare on her. "What do you know about that?"

"Nothing. Except that you survived, and the others didn't."

He nodded. "And how I wept for them, Sarah. Deep below the ground, buried in that terror of whiteness, digging my way out with my own hands, how I cried out for them. But the mountain was inexorable. The mountain spat me out and ordered me away. There was nothing I could do."

He looked away, then said, "The rain has stopped."

She nodded. Far away, up beyond the gray lid of cloud, the sky was lightening.

As they hurried through the cloister, she felt as if something around them, something in him, was dissolving, cracking, opening wide. It scared her.

At the Monk's Walk all seven cats were sitting outside the lab.

"What's this?" Piers ran among them in dismay; he opened the door of the lab and tumbled in.

Rebecca turned. "Thank God!" she said.

Venn hauled her roughly back from the mirror. *"What on earth has he done to it?"*

For the mirror was not black. It was clear as ice, and through it they saw Jake.

And David.

And Janus.

Janus gazed at the weapon. The he raised the blue discs of his spectacles to Maskelyne. "I am beginning to suspect you made that especially to kill me over and over. Because of course I am just a replicant. A copy of myself."

Maskelyne nodded. "For now. But one day I'll find my way back to you. You took my mirror and used it for such evil."

"We." Janus's blue glasses caught the light. "We used it. You yourself experimented with darkness, my friend. You taught me everything I know. You were Blaize to my Merlin. I am simply the pupil who surpasses the master."

Maskelyne's aim did not flicker.

"Fire!" Jake growled.

"No need." The scarred man jerked the weapon toward the mirror. "Leave now. Leave us alone. There's nothing for you here."

Janus shrugged, a piqued distaste in his face. He bowed sarcastically to Alicia, who drew herself up stiff with dislike.

"Are you just going to let this man go?" she demanded.

"He's nothing." Maskelyne stepped aside. "The original is a thing far in the future. Ask Sarah."

Janus turned to David. "Tell Venn he will never succeed. Time is too much for any mortal. It will destroy him."

He turned to the mirror, and to his astonishment, Jake saw that it was a window now, completely transparent, and that they were all in there, Piers, Sarah, Wharton, Venn. And Rebecca, her gaze on Maskelyne, dark and troubled.

Venn came close to the silver frame. "No, it won't."

"Oh, you think you're so different, Venn." Janus nodded. "And maybe you are. Maybe you can evade time. But that will have its price. And one day soon, you'll really have to choose. Between being human, or being something other. Between bone or bramble, flesh or feather, love or liberty." He smiled, coming close to the mirror. "Who knows. Maybe you'll forget your beloved Leah. Maybe you're forgetting her even now."

Venn's eyes narrowed. But before he could snap out an answer, Janus was gone, walking into the clarity of the mirror. For Jake it was if the man strode quickly down a long tunnel of square rooms, diminishing into the vanishing point like a figure in some optical illusion, but for Sarah, just behind Venn, it was as if Janus walked toward her, growing huger and huger, so that she wanted to step aside, out of his way, but he passed through her, through the room, widening over ceiling and walls, becoming a gray shadow, a cobweb, a smudge.

And, following at his heels, three small shadows of himself, three small grubby schoolboys, who grinned at Jake as they passed, the last one swinging a yo-yo like a pendulum from his outstretched finger.

"Bye, Jake."

"See you, Jake."

"Soon, Jake."

Until they too walked into the shadows and were gone.

Jake's face was set with that brittle, angry look he often had.

But Venn stayed staring into the mirror. He said, "David?"

Sarah saw Jake's father. He looked exhausted, his eyes red-rimmed, his face dirty and ill-shaven. He said, "Yes its me, O. I'm coming back to you. It's just . . ." He looked up quickly at something she couldn't see. "There might be a tiny delay, that's all. Is Lorenzo safe?"

"Who?"

"Yes," Rebecca said, behind him. "We're both safe."

"What do you mean? What delay?" Venn gripped the silver frame. "David?"

Somewhere a deep boom sent a ripple through the mirror.

"What's that? David! *What's happening there?*"

Jake looked up, anxious. "We're under . . ."

An explosion. It sent an enormous shockwave of red-hot air across the lab. Glassware shattered. The mirror went black. Venn was blown backward, Wharton sent staggering into Piers, all the cats' fur flattened. The baby screamed, and even as she crashed against the bench, Sarah turned to stare at it in astonishment.

Piers picked himself up from the ruins of the work-bench. "What was that?"

Wharton looked at Venn. "It sounded like a bomb," he whispered.

→→←←

The ceiling imploded, plaster smashing down. Glass from the windows sliced in like shards of light, one catching Jake on the cheek with a splinter of blood. Maskelyne ducked, muttered something and grabbed him. "Come, Jake. We have to go."

"No!" He squirmed away. "Dad! Listen to me. We can't leave Alicia here. She'll die." His mind was weary with fear and pain; he struggled to make sense of it. "When I come . . . when I arrive, in a few minutes, I speak to her, but then . . . later . . . nothing. I thought she was dead. But what if . . . what if she goes with you."

Alicia, crouching by the broken sofa, looked up at him. For a moment their eyes met. She said, "You mean for me to *journey? Through time*? Oh, how absolutely marvelous!"

David caught her hand. "All right. But go! We'll be right behind you."

Maskelyne grabbed Jake. He looked at David and said, "First, listen to me now. We found Dee's manuscript. What it says is important. He says *Time is defeated only by love.* You must remember that! And the snake's eye on the bracelet. It opens. Use what you find inside."

"I will. But go!"

Alicia looked flustered. "Wait! Jake, I have to give you the ticket to the left luggage office. Now, where did I put that? Ah yes, the tea caddy."

Pressure in the air.

Jake gasped. He felt the scream of the bomb as it fell. He felt it hurtle down through smoke and tiles and rafters. Maskelyne was a darkness pulling him. The touch of the silver bracelet was spilled blood on his arm, the throbbing opening of the mirror his death. Terrible desolation fell on him. "No! Wait!" he yelled. *"Wait!"*

Too late.

He was dead, in the darkness, in the mirror.

It opened for him, he crossed the invisible threshold and fell out into Wharton's arms.

"Dad!" he screamed.

But George held him too tight and there was no going back.

Hours later it might have been, he heard Sarah creep into his room.

He lay with his face to the wall, and she sat on the end of the bed for a long moment before he spoke. "He hasn't come, has he?"

She said softly, "No. But . . ."

"They must have got away." He didn't turn; she wondered if it was her he was trying to convince or himself. "When I spoke to Alicia first in the rubble, she was still alive. They never found her body." He rolled over and his eyes were wet and furious. "They must have *journeyed*, Sarah, mustn't they? They must have got out?"

She had never seen him like this. "They had every chance."

"But where? And it was my fault, that he stayed with her! I needn't have told him. We could just have gone together."

"You did the right thing, Jake. You saved her life. And . . . your father . . . he wasn't . . . he's not the sort of man to abandon anyone in trouble. You knew that."

"You think he's dead."

She sat without looking at him, her bleak gaze on the scuffed carpet. At last she said, "I don't know what I think, Jake, not anymore."

"I found him, Sarah. Just for a few minutes . . . an

hour. He was there, with me. And now he's gone again."

There was nothing she could say. How could she say that she knew that loss? Because for a few moments the golden crescent of the Zeus coin had been in her hands, and now it was gone, and maybe her parents' lives and all hope of saving them were gone with it.

Maybe he guessed. He said, "You did what you thought was right. But Venn won't forgive you."

"I'm not asking him to."

"We have to be able to trust you."

Sidelong, she glanced at him, her blue eyes as cool as Venn's. "Do you know who the enemy is here, Jake? Not me, not Summer. Not even Janus. *The mirror is the enemy.* The mirror, and what it offers. It has us all in its power; we already all but worship it."

He was silent. Then, to her surprise he said, "We need to work together, you and me. Promise me we will. No more secrets."

She laughed. Then she nodded.

Deep in the house a gong rang. Piers's yell came up the stairs. "Supper!"

Jake rolled off the bed.

"I'm surprised you can eat," she said.

"I'm not giving up." He grimaced, feeling the strapping Wharton had put on the knife slash. "Not on my father. I know him. He'll be back. Anytime."

He went out and ran down the stairs. She wondered

if the glint in his eyes had been tears, or sheer determination; either way, she envied him. Instead of following, she crossed to the window and opened it, leaning her elbows on the sill.

The night was calm. Over the dark branches of the Wood the moon was a thin crescent.

Below her the kitchen light spilled out across the lawns; she could see the shadow of Piers and then maybe Wharton cross the window.

She stood still, listening, as if the evening called her.

It was the last night of April.

And it was strangely warm.

Small yellow flowers were opening in the aisles of the wood. Cow-parsley stood ghostly, its white umbels wide. She could smell the may, and even as she watched, the undergrowth seemed to ripple into the soft greenery of spring, as if Summer had forgotten her anger, lost interest in her revenge.

Smoke from the Abbey chimneys rose straight in the calm evening air.

A bird chirruped, high above.

Sarah breathed in the sweetness, and despised herself. Jake had failed. She had failed too.

Whatever he said, it was over. Unless . . .

A cheep called her, a last lonely whistle in the twilight.

She looked up, alert.

It fell from high in the blue-and-purple sky. It

dropped like a small crystal raindrop, a solitary snow-flake, so small she could barely see it at first. And then it was a tiny blue-and-gold bird of wood and feathers, giddying down to land on the windowsill with a broken gold coin in its beak.

Sarah stared in disbelief.

The bird put the coin down carefully on the stone sill. "There."

It had lost all its tail feathers. One eye had been pecked away. But the other, beady and black, fixed on her. "Of course, there's no going back now. I'll have to live in the Dwelling. You'll have to swear to protect me till she forgets."

Sarah reached out for the coin, her fingers trembling. She touched the face of Zeus and turned it around, the ancient god with his hooked nose and bold eye, gazing at her through the night.

The bird fluttered past her into the room. "I can stay anywhere. A cuckoo clock. Jewelry box. Anything like that, as long as They don't find me. And if I were you, I'd hide the coin under a stream of running water, because Summer won't be able to get it there." It perched on Jake's wardrobe.

Sarah held the gold piece tight.

"How did you get away?" she breathed.

The bird gave a puzzled whistle, and tilted its head on one side. "Not quite sure, really. She was on me, caught me, had me gripped in her talons, all ready to tear my head off. Then she just dropped me. As if something else caught her eye."

→⊷←

Wharton gulped a spoonful of the hot garlic and tomato soup with relish. "Totally fabulous, Piers. One of your best. Home-baked bread?"

"Of course." Piers wore a chef's hat at a jaunty angle and new checkered trousers. Happy, he surveyed Horatio chewing a banana, the seven cats licking from identical named bowls, Rebecca and Wharton eating, Jake picking at his bread. "Lovely old food," he said. "Nothing like it for cheering everyone up."

Jake flashed a look at Gideon. The changeling sat in the inglenook bench, hugging his knees, brooding into the fire, his patchwork clothes steaming dry.

"What will you do?" Jake asked.

Gideon shrugged. "Stay here. Refugee from the Wood." He was pale, as if the thought of Summer's fury chilled him. "At least until she gets back in here."

"Have some soup." Wharton pushed a bowl across the table.

"I don't need to eat."

"Then maybe you should start. This is not the Summerland, after all. Maybe if you eat, you'll feel more like a mortal and less like one of those unpleasant creatures."

Gideon uncurled and came over. Curious, he looked down at the hot liquid, smelled the savory aroma cautiously. "It won't bite you," Wharton said. "Actually, you bite *it*."

Gideon glared. He took the spoon, dipped it in, and tasted a tiny mouthful. His eyes widened. His whole body seemed to jerk.

Wharton grinned. "Well?"

"It tastes!"

"Tastes?"

"Of . . . things." Gideon shook his head. How could he explain to them that he hadn't known until now that everything in the Summerland was tasteless. That their food was like leaves and ashes. He sat and filled another spoonful, hastily, intent. Over his head Wharton raised both eyebrows at Piers.

Jake got up and wandered over to the fire. The cradle had been set up at a safe distance; the baby, changed and washed and full of warm milk, lay gurgling there in comfort, one chubby fist clutching the soft pink blanket.

Jake crouched. Quietly, so Wharton and the others couldn't hear, he whispered, "Don't worry. He'll be back. Your dad. Mine. We'll get him back, I swear."

He touched the baby's warm fingers.

His brother clutched him, tight.

→·←

In the lab, Maskelyne said, "You were right to rebuke me."

"What did Janus mean? About you teaching him things? That you worked with him?"

He touched the green webbing. "One day I'll tell you everything, Becky, I promise. About how I came to . . . find the mirror . . . and . . ."

"Find?" She came closer, a tall red-haired girl in jeans, so familiar to him, though sometimes it seemed only seconds since she had been a tiny child crying in the night. "I don't think you found it. I think you created it."

"Becky . . ."

She held his eye. "I think you were Mortimer Dee, and maybe many other people too, down the centuries. I think you and the mirror have been together a very long time."

He put his finger lightly to her lips.

"Then keep my secret, Becky."

They were silent a long moment. Until she said, "For now."

→✸←

Alone in his high tower room, Venn heard the spring arrive.

He heard the flowers open on the hawthorn bushes, the bees wake, the small furled buds of oak and ash and rowan rustle and uncurl. He felt the wind change and the breeze shiver, hedgehogs crisp through banks of leaves, tadpoles in the lake open their eyes and grow tails and swarm in the deep green water. Folding his arms, he watched the moon rise and the moths flutter.

He felt light and strange. As if the long dig out of the avalanche on Katra Simba had only ended now, and it was here that he burst out into the fierce blue air and breathed again.

He knew he had taken some step away from being human.

He waited until the hawk flew out of the night and landed on the head of a gargoyle on the sill.

Her bright yellow eye, black-slitted, unblinking, fixed on him.

Her talons gripped the stone.

Venn nodded. "Even you can only delay the spring. What is it you want from me, Summer? What's your price for our survival?"

But he knew her answer, even as she turned and flew off, high into the purple twilight, and as he watched her, he allowed his eyes to widen to the hard blue of sapphire, let his glance shift, let his face become beaked, alert, fierce as a predator, let his whole body cast off the weight of the earth and the pain of loss.

And fly.

So when Piers slammed the door open moments later with the tea tray and said "Thought you might like some soup," the room was empty, the window open, only a scatter of dark feathers drifting down on the sill.

Piers put the tray on the bed, came over, and leaned out into the twilight.

Two hawks were soaring high up over the trees. Far off, in the Wood, the strange rhythmic music of the Shee came to him, and he remembered that this night was Beltane, the eve of May Day, one of the magical cusps of the year, and that bonfires would be burning on the moor.

He closed the window and turned, looking up at the portrait of Leah.

Her face, pale in the moonlight, laughed down at him.

"He needs you," he whispered. "He needs you now or he's lost forever."

But she was silent and he knew she could not hear him.

End of Book 2

TURN THE PAGE FOR A GLIMPSE AT THE
FINAL BOOK IN THE TRILOGY

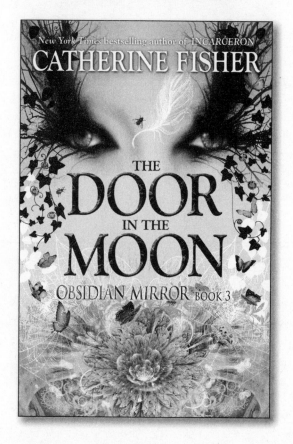

1

On summer nights? On sweet summer nights
Wintercombe is a house of shadows!

Nothing moves in its hundred rooms but a drift of
curtain at a window, and halfway along the Gallery,
the gilt hand of the grandfather clock.

The cloister gate, always hung with a row of
rusting iron implements, creaks very softly in the
sultry stirring of the air.

And, oh my dear, the night smells wonderfully of
roses!

Letter of Lady Mary Venn to her sister.

WAS IT THE moon that woke him?

Because as he opened his eyes, a low slant of light lay
across them like a silver blindfold, making him turn
his head aside in annoyance on the hot pillow.

Jake lay sprawled among the sticky web of his dream.

He had dreamed of a hot, dirty room.

*His father had been standing in it, struggling to take off
a mask—the sinister crow-beaked mask of the plague doctor.
"For God's sake, Jake, help me with this, will you? I can't
breathe."*

*Jake had reached out. But the mask would not come away
from his father's face. It was stuck. And then its eyes came*

alight, yellow as gold. Strange garbled words emerged from its opening beak, and his father was gone; the bird-faced creature had become someone else, and the language it spoke was a garble of clicks and warbles, some Shee-tongue of the Wood, a speech of trees and grubs and scurrying insects.

Jake snatched his hand away, cried out "Dad!"

And that one word had wiped everything away.

He was awake and the dream was lost.

It left only moonlight, and the dusty canopy of the bed above his head; he lay still, staring upward, empty and crooked, the single bedsheet all tangled around his knees and chest. He was breathing fast and listening hard, sheened with sweat, because his father was still lost, still out there, somewhere in some other time, suffering.

Worry became anger; he slipped into the familiar tormenting whirlwind of rage. It was taking them so long to control the mirror! And Venn's neglect infuriated him.

He made himself breathe out, trying to let the fear go, pushing his hair from his eyes. Then he rolled over, edged a book aside and saw the small green letters of the bedside clock.

Three fifty a.m.

A curtain drifted in the open window.

A floorboard creaked.

He whispered, "Horatio? Is that you?"

No answering chatter. That wasn't unusual. The marmoset had taken to sleeping wherever it felt like in the vast dim house; sometimes curled up cozily in the kitchen with the seven cats, sometimes swinging on the dusty chandeliers of the empty bed chambers. After all, it had plenty of choice.

From the next room came the deep growl of Wharton's snoring. Jake grinned, lay back, turned over.

Into an ice-cold circle of metal.

His heart leaped. The pistol was steady, it was deadly, it was held against his forehead by a black-gloved hand. Behind it a shadow in the darkness said softly, "Make no sound, Jake Wilde. Not even the very slightest murmur. Or I promise you I will blow your handsome little head right off."

He wanted it to be another dream, but he knew it wasn't. He was tinglingly awake, every nerve alert, every pore of his skin prickling with the exhilaration of danger.

How many of them were there? One?

A movement to the left, in the corner of his eye, flickered across the stripe of moonlight.

Two.

Had they come in through the window? Climbed the ivy-smothered wall? His mind flicked through the options. Had Janus sent them? Were they Shee? Hardly—not with a gun.

Mortal, then.

Thieves.

To steal what?

The mirror.

He opened his mouth to yell. A great slab of sticky adhesive was slapped across it. His arms were grabbed and yanked behind him. He felt the tight cords scorch his wrists.

He moaned a savage curse into the pillow.

Too late.

Sarah was lying suspended in the green depths of some crystalline ocean, a dark dreamless place of infinite silence, when a voice spoke in her ear.

It was a tiny piping voice and it sounded worried. It said, "Mortal, listen, I really think you ought to wake up."

"Why?" she muttered.

"Because something very strange is happening."

Fish swam in and out of the words. She wondered why she dreamed of underwater, because she had never dared set foot near the sea. In her future world at the end of time, it was a poisoned, venomous place. Nothing lived there. The coral reefs were dull with dead plankton. Janus's dark tyranny had killed the world.

Her thought turned into a silver-and-blue jellyfish and pulsed rhythmically away through her brain.

She said, *"Strange?"*

The word woke her; she sat up.

The attic room was dark and hot. Through the window, wide-open, drifted the eternal whisper of the trees of Wintercombe Wood, and the distant hoot of an owl somewhere far down the valley.

"What sort of strange?" she whispered. "The baby?"

Lorenzo's wails erupted at all hours of the night.

"No. Not quite sure who." The wooden bird sounded apologetic. For a moment she couldn't even see it; then the moon came out and the silver light showed her its tiny form, stuck with false feathers. It was perched on the wardrobe, its single beady eye turned to her. "Only that whoever they are, they don't seem to be properly mortal and they're already inside the house."

Alarmed, she said, "The Shee?"

"Oh no. I'd certainly know if they were Shee. "

Sarah was already out of bed. She grabbed jeans and a top and flung them on. "Where in the house? Why haven't the alarms gone off?"

"Don't ask me." The faery bird tipped its head to one side.

"The coin!" Fear flickered through Sarah like lightning on the dark moor. "Do you think they could be after the coin?" But then, no, no, they couldn't be, could they, because no one else here even knew she had it, the half of the broken Zeus stater, the only object in

the universe that could destroy the mirror. She forced herself to be calm, pulled on her shoes, stood up.

Don't panic.

The coin was safe. Hidden in a very secret place. Hidden until she could find the other half and bring them both together, and cancel the future—Janus's terrible future—before it ever even happened.

"I'm going out to take a look," she said. "Stay here. Don't let anyone see you."

"Don't worry." The bird shuddered delicately. "I won't. Even the spiders on the cobwebs won't see me. They're usually Summer's spies, did you know that?"

Sarah had already moved to the door. Before she opened it, she took a breath and pushed her cropped blond hair behind an ear.

Then she stepped out into the corridor.

It was mid-June and the weather had been hot for weeks. The ancient house smelled of wax-polish and lavender and roses—of sweet mingled midsummer scents, phlox and honeysuckle. All its windows were wide, as if it struggled to breathe, as if down here in its deep combe beside the rushing river it was slowly being suffocated by the heat and pollen and the leaf-heavy branches of the trees.

The attic corridor stretched, white-painted, into the dark. She didn't put a light on, but walked softly along it to the top of the servants' stairs and stood listening, straining to pin down every tiny sound in the sleeping house.

A creak.

A murmur that might have been a voice.

She frowned. The mirror was down in the medieval part of the building, the Monk's Walk, safe behind Piers's defenses of alarms and lasers. Surely no one could get at it there. And there had been no alarm from the gates, so no vehicle could have even tried to come up the drive.

She listened again.

Tiredness came out of the night and washed over her. Briefly the green ocean slid back into her memory, beckoning and cool. The Shee bird was surely wrong—or playing some mischief.

She'd strangle the manky little thing.

Then, as she turned away, a sound came from up the spiral stairwell, the ghost of an echo. Immediately Sarah was flitting down, silent and quick, avoiding the boards that creaked, slipping through the arch at the bottom, ducking behind a great vase on its pedestal.

She peered around it.

Before her the Long Gallery, a corridor wider than a room, stretched the whole length of the house, its white ceiling frosted like a cake with patterns of pargetting, its walls lined with ancient bookcases, great vases, statues of Greek philosophers and Roman senators.

The main bedrooms were along here, Jake's, Wharton's . . . and Piers's, though she wondered if that odd creature ever had to sleep. Right down the far end was Venn's room, but she knew all too well that it would be empty, because he was rarely in the house these nights.

As she frowned with anger about that, she saw Jake's door slowly open. A sliver of light widened.

She was relieved, went to step out and say "Did something wake you too?"

Until she saw him shoved into the hallway, the shadow behind him. And the gun.

→→·←←

They had let him dress and pull his boots on, and Jake was glad of that because behind his fear his fury was intense, and when it came to kicking someone, he could do a lot more damage this way. He wasn't blindfolded, but the two men—he was sure now there were two of them—kept behind him, and they each had smeared their faces with dark camouflage. They wore hoods and black coats. One was bigger than the other—the tall one did the talking. They smelled oddly of oil and some vaguely familiar sweet scent.

When he was a kid, just after his mother left, he'd had a phase of sleeping fully dressed with all sorts of daft kids' weapons stuffed under his pillow. Maybe it had been from films or stuff he'd been reading then, or because of all the disturbance in his life. He'd had a constant fear that something would happen in the night and that he had to be ready for it. It never had.

Until now.

As the tall man shoved him forward his eye caught a flicker of movement in the darkness at the end of the gallery. For a moment he was sure someone was there, but as he stared he saw nothing but shadow.

"Remember, Jake. Not a sound." The muzzle of the gun caressed his cheek, the gentlest of reminders. "Now walk."

They followed him along the corridor. He tried to step on as many creaky boards as he could, but Wintercombe Abbey had its own secret vocabulary of creaks and squeaks, and they rarely woke anyone used to the breathing and stirring of the ancient house.

But as he passed a windowsill a dark mass uncoiled and sat up.

The tall stranger hissed; the gun swiveled.

Jake made a squirm of alarm through his taped mouth. For a second he thought it was Horatio; then a pair of green eyes opened and stared at him intently.

"Leave it." The smaller shadow spoke sharply. "Can't you see it's just a cat?"

"Bloody thing."

"Hold your nerve. Look. That's the door."

They had stopped at the door to the Monk's Walk.

They obviously knew their way around the house. Jake slid a look back; the cat was watching, its fur bristling.

The taller man crouched, his long coat sweeping the dusty floor. He drew out a small tool, made a few deft arrangements to the ancient lock. It clicked, and the door swung open.

Jake swore silently. He was sure now they were after the mirror, the black obsidian glass that was the precious doorway to time. They must have a way to deal with all of Piers's security.

But the cat had seen them, and the cats—all seven—talked to Piers. With any luck, this one might be slinking along the skirting board to wake him right now. Anxiety tingled in Jake. He had to play for time. Not let this happen.

"You first." The tall man caught his arm and thrust him through the door. Deliberately Jake stumbled into the dim interior, fell on the cold stones, and rolled away fast into the darkest corner, tugging the bonds on his wrists with furious energy.

The man swore. "Where are you? Get up! Or I'll blow you to bloody smithereens."

And wake the whole house? Jake thought. I don't think so. One thumb was almost free. Ignoring the scorch of rope on skin, he fought to separate his hands.

Then a cold blade point was touched lightly to his cheek.

"Naughty, Jake." A whisper at his ear, clear and quiet. He looked up, straight into the smaller thief's eyes. They were bright and mischievous, and he knew all at once that this was the more dangerous of the two.

"Seems to me you're getting some silly ideas, Jake. About bolting. About raising the hue and cry on us. Do you think we don't carry a few silent weapons too, Jake?"

The blade of the knife, sharp as a pin, pierced the skin under his right eye. Jake kept utterly still.

"That's better. Because, believe me, your throat would be cut, and we'd be through that mirror, before your friends got their dainty little toes in their furry little slippers. No point in being dead, eh Jake? Not with your father still to find."

Astonishment shot through him. What the hell did they know about his father? Before he could breathe, he was hauled up between them and dragged along the stone arcade of the Monk's Walk, stumbling through the gothic fingers of moonlight that stabbed down through the broken tracery.

Far below in its deep ravine, the Wintercombe rushed over its rocks, but the sound was no longer the dreadful thunder of the spring floods. It was a murmur, a song, a pleasant liquid ripple and splash.

It hummed under his feet.

⇢·⇠

Sarah had made herself invisible with the terrible ease Janus's gift had given her. It was an ability she loathed, but as soon as she had seen the two dark figures behind Jake, and the moonlight glinting on the pistol muzzle, she'd used it without hesitation.

They passed within touching distance of her. Flattened against the paneling, head sideways, she dared not breathe. They opened the door and shoved Jake through.

A creak followed, on the hessian matting.

The cat.

Those Replicant creatures could see her, she knew, so she whispered, "Get Piers! Hurry! Tell him I'm going after them," and slid into the Monk's Walk, breathing more easily because there were no creaky boards down here, just cold stone.

Far ahead, shadows flitted through moonlight.

She slipped after them, thinking fast. Surely the lasers around the mirror would stop them. And Maskelyne would hear—the scarred man slept down here now, in some monkish cell piled with books and circuitry, close to the mirror that infatuated him. She raced through slots of moonlight, through the terror of not being able to see her own arms and legs, of being nothing but a wisp of spirit and snatched breath. Into the labyrinth.

It was a funnel of malachite mesh, a tangle of wiring and computer monitors, and in its heart, dark as a great venomous spider, lurked the obsidian mirror.

She stopped dead.

Seeing it here in this darkness, tied down in its tangle of cables, it seemed a sinister vacancy, a moonlit door to nowhere, to non-places outside the very universe itself.

It had always made her afraid. Now as she crept on, breath held, it seemed to reflect the terror inside her.

Keep calm, Jake told himself. They couldn't have stolen the bracelet because Venn kept it on his wrist and never took it off, and without a bracelet, they wouldn't dare use the mirror.

The thought was a relief, but he was trying not to panic. They had hauled him, struggling hard, through the green mesh and he had seen with disbelief that no lasers had triggered and no alarms howled.

Whoever they were, they were experts.

He tried to yell, fought so hard a flask toppled from a bench and smashed, a star of glass shards.

"Hold him! Hold him still!" The small man walked up to the mirror and pushed back one dark sleeve of his coat.

Around his wrist curled a silver snake bracelet with a stone of amber.

Jake swore, kicked free, turned to flee, but the tall

man gripped him with wrathful ease. Already the mirror had opened into a throbbing emptiness, the wide black doorway into time. Jake yelled, *"No. No! You can't do this!"*

"Just watch us, Jake. "

They grabbed him, one on each arm, and before them was nothing but darkness, and they forced him forward and leaped into it. But just as Jake felt the throbbing terror of the mirror envelop him, his eyes widened in astonishment.

A small hand, cold and invisible as a glass glove, had slipped into his.

And *journeyed* with him.

The cat waited until the black vacancy had collapsed, until the room had stopped shaking, until the mirror stood silent and solid. Its own fur and whiskers were flattened with the terror of the implosion, its green eyes wide.

Then it padded to a secret infra-red beam that crossed the floor, and very deliberately, put a paw on it.

Every alarm in the house exploded into noise.

New York Times bestselling author
and queen of fantasy Catherine Fisher's
OBSIDIAN MIRROR trilogy!

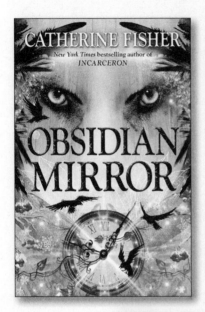

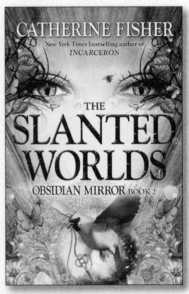

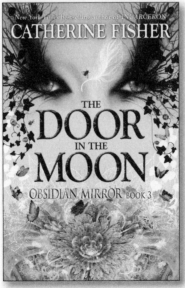

Read more from bestselling author
Catherine Fisher!